I0607393

Polyandrion:

Becoming the King of Hell

Sandor Desmond

Sandor Desmond

Polyandrion: Becoming the King of Hell

Copyright © 2024 Sandor Desmond Haas-Neill

Second Edition October 2024

All rights reserved. No part of this book may be reproduced in any form or by any electronic or mechanical means, including information storage and retrieval systems, without permission in writing from the publisher and author, except by reviewers, who may quote brief passages in a review.

ISBN 978-1-7778434-0-3 (ebook)
ISBN 978-1-7778434-1-0 (paperback)
ISBN 978-1-7778434-3-4 (hardcover)

Published by: Sandor Desmond
YouTube: https://www.youtube.com/c/TheForgottenGrove
LinkTree: https://linktr.ee/SandorDesmond
Email: theforgottengrove@gmail.com

All characters and events in this book are fictitious. Any similarity to real persons, living or dead, is coincidental and not intended by the author.

Sandor Desmond

Table of Contents

Sandor Desmond

The Planelands - 1

"Can anyone tell me who the Katharnians were?" Mrs. Barrister asked, leaning against a pavilion and lighting a smoke. The go-getter at the front of the pack of students fluttered her hand in the air excitedly. Mrs. Barrister rolled her eyes and took a long drag of her cig. "Thank you, Darneice, but I'd like to hear from someone new. Dunstan, how about you?"

Dunstan flushed beet red; he had been trying so hard to avoid eye contact. "I'm sorry Mrs. Barrister but I don't know," he replied sheepishly.

Mrs. Barrister released an exasperated moan. "Alright, Darneice, who were the Katharnians - "

"The Katharnians were an ancient civilization of people who created our calendar!" Darneice piped up.

"That's right, thank you, Da -"

"- In the year one a great man, 'Sulomar,' discovered a powerful energy source that brought the warring tribes to heel. Sulomar was the first King of Katharnia, and for centuries the civilization he created enjoyed prosperity and decadence."

"That's right; thank you, Darneice."

Dunstan's eyes drifted up from the archeological dig site

they were visiting today. Dark, billowing clouds swept over the murky mud field and kissed the roof of the museum.

"- it was the Katharnians, they had technology far more advanced than ours today. It was they who first discovered the cosmology of our world – knowledge which has been passed down through the historical record." Mrs. Barrister's voice popped the bubble around Dunstan's daydreams.

"As you may have learned from your parents, there are two hells below us. If you are a good person in this life you go to 'the Squalor' when you die. If you are evil, you go to 'the Spoil.'"

"Mrs. Barrister, how do you go to heaven?" Little Darneice's voice squealed over the chatter of the group.

"There is no heaven," the teacher explained coldly.

"But doesn't God decide if you go to heaven?"

"There is no god."

"But, I can go to heaven if I'm really, really good!" the child bargained.

"... yeah, sure, Darneice."

Another girl raised her hand and Mrs. Barrister excitedly called on her to speak.

"What happened to the Katharnians? If their technology

was so advanced, why did their civilization die?"

"That's a great question, Erica," Mrs. Barrister reinforced. "The last King of Katharnia, King Breowakoe, was a very weak man who was uninterested in ruling. Without leadership, the infrastructure of the Kingdom started to fall apart allowing a terrorist organization to take power. In the year 1406 they seized control of a bioweapon called 'the Gloom' and deployed it over the Kingdom, turning the majority of its citizens into hideous mutants." Dunstan again found himself drifting off, imagining the dying moments of the civilization, staring into the dirt under which it now lay.

"Mrs. Barrister, what's it like in the Spoil?" Darneice couldn't let it go.

"No one knows the answer to that," Mrs. Barrister explained matter-of-factly. "But I'm sure you'll learn one day..." an underhanded utterance trailed off.

"Mrs. Barrister, what's it like in the Squalor? -"

"- Darneice, go wait on the bus!" Mrs. Barrister's short fuse had expired. The little girl moped as she made her way over the hill and out of view. "The rest of you, thirty more minutes in the museum and then we will all meet Darneice on the bus!" Mrs. Barrister called. "I recommend the corpusapien artefacts exhibit; when you touch them they transfer 'body-knowledge' to you, and you'll feel something you can't quite describe!"

"My mom said corpusapien artefacts aren't safe to touch because they can give your body powers you can't control!"

"That's true, Jessica, but this is a curated collection of lesser artefacts. Don't worry, these ones will just give you interesting feelings without transferring any powers," the teacher reassured.

The artefacts in the museum were of little interest to nine-year-old Dunstan. He instead ventured out further into the lot of picked-through, ancient dirt, indulging in the feeling of dread that crept over his heart. The rain finally started and the dirt became slicker. Dunstan's shoe slipped from under him and he fell onto a strange piece of metal in the ground that caught the skin of his knee, tearing it from his bone. An odd cacophony of perceptions flooded into his mind but in the next instant vanished before he could process them. Shock turned to horror as the boy stared down at his exposed patella, blood gushing from the wound. His face scrunched up as he tried not to cry, and he limped back to the bus.

He made no fuss as the other students clambered in

around him, and on the ride home he was able to distract himself from the pain by watching the downpour lash at the flooded flatland.

In general, Dunstan didn't like drawing attention to himself. His mother always told him he wouldn't get anywhere acting needy. Other kids watched TV and played games together, but Dunstan had never figured out how to make friends. Playing in the muck of his fenced off yard was one of his favourite pastimes. His teacher tolerated him, his parents seldom seemed to notice him, and apart from those adults he lived his life like a ghost. He tried not to feel sorry for himself but sometimes a hollow feeling crept into his heart.

The bus bounced as it made its way along the gravel road into the Shallaway, the small mining town in the Planelands that Dunstan called home. He could see his house on the left, a small shack encompassed by black pools of soot-filled water. The bus passed it and made its way up the muddy hill to the school. The final bell rang as the boy limped out and fiddled with the lock on his bike.

A heavy rain pissed down on the Shallaway and Dunstan walked his bike along the stygian ponds. He was anxious to get home and have his knee looked at but it wasn't safe to ride in this weather. It had been a while and he worked up the courage to look down at his knee, a loose flap of skin was swinging from it and finally Dunstan began to sob. Squinting through the water, he could just make out the fenced-off mud lot to the side of his house. Dunstan lifted the latch by reaching over the wooden gate and stashed his bike against the inside of the fence. He approached the side door of his house, slid the screen open, and entered.

"Mo-o-o-om!" he yelled, hoping for some help in dealing with his wound.

He heard no response but could see the back of one of her elbows in a red sweater. He walked through the living room towards her.

"Mom! I slipped in the mud and -"

Dunstan's mother whirled around, and upon seeing his muddy shoes on the family room carpet became livid.

"Dunstan Briar! Get off the carpet, now!" she screamed, taking three long, angry strides toward him.

He did as she demanded, moving over to the hardwood. Patiently, he waited for her to see his knee and the tear marks on his cheeks, hoping she would understand that this time, his transgression was exceptional.

"Goddamnit, Dunstan - how many goddamn times have I told you to take off your shoes before you come in the house!" She picked him up and dragged him over to the front hallway. "Now wash your feet, get a rag from the linen closet, and scrub that out before your father gets home!"

"But Mommy," Dunstan pleaded, upset now that she didn't care - or hadn't even noticed - that his patella was exposed.

"I don't want to hear it, Dunstan! GO DO IT NOW!" his mother huffed back to the kitchen.

Dunstan obeyed, first washing his feet off in the bathtub, then scrubbing out the mess he had made. He threw the rag into the laundry pile at the bottom of the stairs and propped himself up on one of the chairs at the kitchen table. He looked over at his mother who was standing over the stove. She was looking out the window with a stern brow and pursed lips. Jittery, she moved her head from side-to-side in short turns of her neck like a nervous bird.

The pain in his knee had started to die down. Dunstan took another look at it; he could push the flap of skin around without much pain. He alternated between playing with the skin flap and biting his fingernails.

"Oop - look at that, your father's home from the mines," Dunstan's mother said, tensing up even more.

Moments later, the front door burst open and Mark walked in. He took off his hat, trench coat, and boots to walk silently past his wife, running his fingers through his hair.

As his father approached the kitchen table, Dunstan turned to the right in his chair to better expose his knee, hoping now that his father would notice. "Hi Daddy!" he said, trying to sound cheerful.

His tall father looked down at him with the intensity of a crow as he walked past, giving a terse nod of acknowledgement, followed by a double-take. He stopped in the middle of the room, and an angry expression appeared on his face.

"Donna, why is our son's knee busted open like a goddamn pinata?"

"What?" she snapped, always ready for confrontation from all sides. Her husband pointed to Dunstan's knee and Donna's eyes traced the invisible line.

"What the hell? Mark, I swear, I've never seen that before! Dunstan, how long have you had that? Why the hell didn't you tell me?"

"GODDAMNIT, DONNA!" Mark roared, "Why the hell have you let our son walk around like this all day?"

"I DIDN'T SEE IT TILL NOW YOU UGLY, OLD BASTARD! He could have got it just now for all we know, he's been clumsy since Mary-Jane bopped him on the head!" Mark went silent at the mention of his estranged mother and grimaced behind his closed lips. "- By the way, guess what, Mark? Our lights went out today!" Donna said accusingly, as Mark rolled his eyes. "Yep, YEP!" she asserted. "The lights went out today, Mark, because YOU forgot to pay the hydro bill!"

"OH FOR THE LOVE OF GOD, DONNA, WOULD YOU KEEP A LID ON IT IN FRONT OF OUR SON!?"

"I've been on the phone ALL DAY trying to get it sorted out -"

Dunstan plugged his ears. He was accustomed to the content of these arguments, but the cilia in his young ears had not yet adjusted to their volume. He watched the muffled yelling on the stretched faces of his angry parents' for a moment, then escaped through the living room side door and into the rain.

It was brighter out than it had been, with higher clouds.

He gazed over the small plot of mud before him. It looked different every day, thick and turbulent and interesting. He thought it best not to play in it, today, however, given his wound. Instead, he just sat there, enjoying the sounds. Like the shape of mud, the sound of the rain moment-to-moment, second-to-second, was always and never the same. In the distance he could hear a dog barking.

"WHY CAN'T YOU EVER...." the sound of his parents once again spiked and trailed off, suffocated by the enduring rain.

The dog's bark became stronger. There was a jingling noise, perhaps the dog was coming closer. Dunstan cocked his head to the right, peering over the short gate and expecting the dog to run past. He could hear panting, and suddenly, an animal leapt the gate! It was a brown, shabby-looking dog. Dunstan couldn't tell if its fur was naturally brown or just caked with dirt. With confidence, the dog bounded toward him, bombarding him with affection.

"Whoa! Whoa, boy!" Dunstan said with a laugh. He petted the happy dog and it rolled over to expose its belly. It righted itself to leap up and over the thick mud. The dog buried its nose in the ground near the fence and dug up a half-rotten stick, bark flaking off it. It placed the stick at Dunstan's feet and wagged its tail excitedly.

"You want me to throw this, boy?" Dunstan picked up the stick and the dog perked up. "Go get it! Go get it, boy!" He tossed the stick through the yard; mud flew as the dog excitedly chased the makeshift toy. The dog retrieved the stick and the two repeated the game a few times before the happy critter tuckered himself out. He left the stick in the mud and plopped himself down next to the seated Dunstan.

It seemed almost surreal. A creature so pure that wanted nothing but to be in his company; it gazed up at him lovingly as it panted, its warm little body making him feel a little less alone. Dunstan's eyes started to water as he leaned in to hug the musky creature.

"You're amazing! Mr. Doggy," he sniffled. Mr. Doggy returned the affection, leaning in and giving him healing kisses on his wounded knee. At first it stung, then Dunstan giggled.

"Stop that, Mr. Doggy! That tickles!" The dog continued to lick and the boy laughed and laughed.

"Dunstan! Get your ass inside; it's dinner time!" his mother angrily called from the kitchen.

Dunstan pried himself away from his oblivious companion, fearing his parents' ire. "I'm sorry Mr. Doggy, but

I have to go now. I have to eat my supper to make me strong and healthy!"

The dog whimpered. Dunstan didn't want to leave its side. Trudging into the heavy atmosphere of his home, he still thought about Mr. Doggy. Although the food was out on the table, his parents were still in the thick of the same argument.

"I BUST MY ASS DIGGING EVERY DAY AND I COME HOME TO THIS, DONNA? DON'T YOU HAVE ANY APPRECIATION FOR WHAT I DO?" His father's raged on.

Dunstan slid into his chair, and quietly began to eat his food.

"YOU KNOW WHAT? YOU'RE WELCOME NOT TO COME HOME, AT ALL; I'M SICK OF THIS TOO. DRIVE OFF AND DIE, FOR ALL I CARE!" There was a pause as Mark registered these comments shortly before he lost all control.

He darted toward Donna, slinging his massive hand and striking her face. He clasped her throat tightly with both hands, bending her backwards over the counter. She thrashed violently – disoriented from the initial blow – knocking pots, vases, plates, and glasses shattering onto the floor. She gasped out something incomprehensible, slapping helplessly at her husband's wrists and face. He released her, smashing her into the fridge. Donna let out a terrifying series of gasps. Mark was now clasping his own face, sitting in the corner of the room with his knees up to his chest shrieking and crying, sputtering. Dunstan chewed with his eyes closed. He thought about Mr. Doggy.

"He told Buckly to fire me before waddling his fat ass back to his comfortable office. Buckly had no choice - I've got no job. The part that pisses me off the most is that spoiled asshole, Edgar Mullen, never worked a day in his life. He just shits on people because he can..." There was defeat in his father's tone.

Dunstan got up to put his plate in the sink. His mother said nothing, but cried silently to herself, arms still lifted over her face defensively. The boy crept back toward the living room where he could see that his new friend was still outside, its brown tail wagging in the gloam. Stealthily, Dunstan snatched a cooling, buttered potato from his father's plate and carried it outside. He knew that his Dad wouldn't eat, now.

"Hey, Mr. Doggy, thanks for waiting. I brought you something!" A very delighted Mr. Doggy gobbled up the potato vigorously, licking Dunstan's fingers and face after swallowing the last morsel. Dunstan sat on the side porch enjoying the sounds and melodies of the rain with his best friend in the world. Up the street a voice called from a car that was sloshing down the muddy pavement.

"Bruiser! DAMN IT, BRUISER, YOU NEED TO STOP RUNNING AWAY!"

Mr. Doggy's ears perked up when he heard the voice; he whimpered and barked, rising off his rump to all fours.

"Hey, I think I heard him down there!" a passer-by called from the sidewalk. The car rolled up and its driver sprung out.

"Come here, you little mutt!" the man said, glaring over the gate at Mr. Doggy.

Mr. Doggy barked and growled back at the man, who took steps toward him. Dunstan sat passively, worried for his own safety as well as his friend's, as now Mr. Doggy tried to take shelter behind him. The man paused.

"Who the fuck are you? That's my dog. Give him to me and we won't have a problem."

Dunstan was shocked and disappointed to find that Mr. Doggy had an owner, but it made sense - he had noticed the collar. He withdrew from his initial instinct to be protective; he had to let the doggy go. The man reached around Dunstan to grasp Mr. Doggy, but the little dog turned and nipped him.

"OW! FUCK YOU, YA LITTLE SHIT!" The man snapped his hand back and kicked the 20-pound dog, sending him into the side of Dunstan's house. Mr. Doggy yelped as four of his ribs cracked, and continued to whimper in pain as his master hoisted him up by his chest.

This display was more than Dunstan could bear. "MR. DOGGY! NO!" he screamed in a shrill voice, at the top of his lungs. He rose to his feet and tried his best to hit the man where he knew he had a chance to do harm, his testicles.

The man whirled around and observed the tiny boy who had struck him. A weak but effective second hit landed "OW! What the hell?!"
Mr. Doggy's owner drew one leg up to block his groin with his knee, looking angrily at the upset child's face. With all his hostility he booted Dunstan's bad knee, causing the joint to snap and bend backwards.

It took a moment of shock, face down on the ground, for Dunstan to actualize an amount of pain that his little body must not have thought possible. A high-pitched scream of some intensity left his mouth as he realized his thin leg had folded grotesquely beneath him. Another involuntary scream followed. Mr. Doggy's owner had already made his way out the gate, cringing over his battered testicles, but now found himself even more enraged by Dunstan's screams.

"You've gotta be kidding me... SHUT UP, YOU ANNOYING LITTLE FAGGOT!"

The man withdrew a pistol from his belt, pointed it at Dunstan and pulled the trigger. The bullet went through Dunstan's head with a soft popping noise, and his blood frothed and shot out into the mud with a splash. Mr. Doggy was delirious with pain; he didn't understand what was going on as he was tossed into the back seat.

Dunstan's parents rushed outside, their great haste accompanied by the sound of tires screeching away. The confusion of the ordeal was cleared away in an instant by the wasted corpse of their nine-year-old son, face down in the mud.

The Squalor – 2

The body of a nine-year-old boy fell out of the darkness and landed with a splat upon the grave heap. Nameless, stripped of memory and identity, he joined the sea of human shapes in this garbage disposal of biological waste. Their tiny, silent windows of consciousness, each pried open into a half-dream, were forced by some remnant of hatred to perceive terrible things in this fetid, odious reality. For ten years in this solecism of existence - punished for nothing more than still somehow existing, smothered deeper and deeper into the pile of rotting tissue - the once-boy grew.

-

For the first time in the Squalor, a man opened his eyes to survey the ominous dark. A half-decayed head lay immediately before him, its jaw detached and hanging loose. The head's eyes were wide open and moving rapidly, glazed, preserved by a blood fog, eyelids missing. It appeared to be dreaming, trapped in an endless nightmare with a horrified look on what remained of its face.

The man was terrified, it was hard to breathe in the thick, putrid atmosphere. He tried to flee but could barely move. He found that through conscious effort he could budge his arms from where they had lain since he was still a boy. As his body came to life, he couldn't remember who or where he was, and yet he knew this was knowledge he should have. A sense of dread gripped him as he craned his neck every which way, assaying the corpus matrix of which he was a part. He was pinned under a great many decaying bodies still, smothered in their rancid tissue. Their rotten humours spilled over his face and into his eyes. But wherever he was, he could feel gravity and he knew the way to the top of the pile. The man curled and contracted himself, sliding headfirst through the opening between one body and another, all congealed together.

The bodies were less densely packed the higher he climbed until at last he reached the top. He reached under a corpse's arm and dragged himself up onto its back. The blood fog was ripe in the air but peering through it he could see that he was in a column, about one kilometre square - a great polyandrion glutted with the dead. There was no light, but somehow he could see. Something was dancing overhead: pure, visible energy, swirling into eddies that formed portals to the world of the living. Fresh corpses poured out of them like beautiful blood rain in the blackness to land with a heavy splat on the pile, breaking the silence of the near-airless chamber. Weary organs, so tired and spent, spilled much of their remaining moisture upon impact.

Desperately, the man searched for an escape - some opening - but there was none. Its zenith extended to infinity. He jumped out of the way a little too late as a woman landed heavily on his leg, her eyes already glazed and jittering. She had fallen from maybe a kilometre up and snapped his shin. The man's screams reverberated off the walls. It was too dangerous to remain up here. He slithered between the bodies, deeper into the safety of the pile. If 'up' didn't work, he would have to try 'down.' Why did it seem that he was the only one who was awake? Why did it seem that he was the only one who wasn't rotting? He could not know that they were all still trapped in the endless loop of nightmares he had broken out of. The man pushed through his claustrophobia. He pushed through his panic and stayed focused on digging.

The matrix-foam of humanity became thicker as he continued to descend further and further, kilometres upon kilometres down. The appearance of the husks changed as he made his way backward through the history of his species. The bodies seemed to become smaller as they packed tighter together under increasing pressure. Facing straight down and wriggling through the openings still available, he followed his only guide - the force of gravity - the only thing he felt certain was not an illusion in the murk of madness.

-

Three months passed. At the depth he had reached, the individual human corpses were now indistinguishable from one another but for an odd, glazed pair of eyes in the bloody heap of rot – revealing, as a window into their minds, their fantastical suffering dreams. Without a hole to slip through, he had trained his hands to dig through the mass. Forcing his fingers into a squelching abdominal cavity, elbowing the ribs to break them, prying them to the side, removing the organs and bursting out the back after a solid booting. This was incredibly time consuming, and on a few occasions he had cut his own chest or back on a spine while climbing down through someone's gaping torso.

It was beginning to get impossibly stuffy and he could

barely breathe with the blood fog so thick, yet he realized he should have died of thirst and hunger months ago if dying were possible, so he pushed through the discomfort. With the realization of his apparent immortality, the man's corpse-digging strategy evolved. He could take the time to carefully dig through the carrion in a vertical line, climb the shaft of the tunnel he had created, and jump down, using the gravity of the chamber to accelerate him like a bullet through the flesh.

A few times, he had been injured while employing this strategy: breaking an ankle or - on one horrendous occasion - getting caught by a rib through his throat. But he found that he healed quickly from these incidents. Blood mist would emerge from the cavernous darkness to repair his physical form, that his mind might suffer longer. For some reason, this didn't apply to the other corporeal forms around him. The blood mist would repair their tissue damage, but at a much slower rate. After another month - the man had dug a straight column through fifty metres of macabre meatloaf and climbed back to the top of the pit. He stood over the chasm and marvelled at how quickly the darkness hid its vast depth.

He had carved out enough around the opening to stand, legs parted over it. There was no sense in his fearing the drop, as he was already in hell. The man jumped up with a spin to add more penetrating power to his feet. Blood mist peppered his grinding teeth as he fell faster and faster through the bodies, losing feeling in his gut, ready for the pain. His feet sank into the mound. There was so much indiscriminate gore whizzing by that he lost his sense of distance. One of his toes caught on something and was promptly ripped off. A hail of bone cuts covered his body. He strained to keep his legs tense, but they were going numb. Suddenly, for a moment, all feeling stopped and there was nothing but darkness.

He struck the bottom – a solid mat of what looked like flesh but with no evidence of human features. His legs instantly crumpled, breaking in several places under him and a bone snapped under his rib cage, puncturing his left lung. He gasped for air, too shocked to feel pain, yet overjoyed to have reached the bottom. He lifted himself as well as he could to survey this lower plane, knowing that his legs and lungs would heal.

The lower plane of the Squalor was a funnel that focused the square walls into one circular centre. Gazing upward, the man realized that, mysteriously, the bottom of the grave heap was about ten metres over his head, as though the massive pile of humans sat atop an invisible floor that somehow he had broken through. Now on the true, sloped floor, he marvelled at the beautiful spider-web canopy of putrefying humans above him. What was keeping these bodies suspended in the air? His eyes shifted down to the centre of the cone.

He noticed that he was not healing as he once would have and imagined that the force responsible for maintaining this post-mortem prison was now able to distinguish him from the others. He imagined that it perceived him as a threat. Determined to understand, he crawled down toward the centre of the cone on his arms, dragging his shattered legs behind him.

Upon arriving at the center of the funnel, he peered over the lip of the bottleneck opening. A colossal, bloodshot, yellow eye filled the circular space in the spout of the funnel; it must have been two metres wide. It flicked over to glare at him. The man gasped, shocked, and even afraid. He retreated from the opening to try to catch his wheezing breath. His one good lung fluttered; he waited for his death to come. It didn't. He peered once more over the edge. The eye violently flashed over to him again, its pupil dilating and then fixing upon him where he trembled, as though its loathing for him was the only reason it existed, as though it longed to obliterate him but lacked the means.

The moment the man met the gaze of the eye, he felt that he understood it. He could feel its hatred for humans, and that it was the keeper of this Squalor. The longer he stared, the more sure he felt that he could destroy it and the more compelled he felt to do so. He quickly pushed off with his hands and launched himself to land with a wet thud atop the open eye, bouncing and slipping off the sclera to the side where the eye met the cylindrical wall. The protruding cornea followed him over and compressed his fractured legs into the flesh wall. The pain was intense, but the man was focused.

He straightened and flexed his fingers, shoving them downward as hard as he could, piercing the cornea of the eye and taking advantage of the leverage to work his thumb in, as well. The eye's disembodied bellows rumbled throughout the Squalor. Using his shoulder strength, the man ripped a gelatinous chunk from the cornea and tossed it out of the pit. He thrust his fingers in once more, continuing to dig deeper into the creature until its aqueous humour escaped. The putrid liquid stung as it washed over the man's bloodied legs and he plunged himself into the pool, one hand propping him up on the edge of the yellow iris and one on the lens. The horrible bellowing screams continued to flood and resonate within the chamber of the Squalor. The lidless eye thrashed about violently, now, trying to shake him off. Without functional legs, the man paddled frantically, trying to stay afloat in the inner eye's liquid. He couldn't help but inhale some into his good lung. His tendons were raw from prying the firm corneal tissue away from its host, and searing pain shot through his right wrist. He reckoned that his hands would be unable to grip any more.

Working his numb fingers under the yellow iris and pulling in the opposite direction with great difficulty, he peeled it back to expose the lens. The eye had stopped moving, perhaps it was playing dead, or perhaps it was accepting its fate. The man balled his hand into a fist and pounded on the lens. It was a dull pearl about a foot in diameter and felt like a boulder. He needed something to hack it with. Looking down at the sharp bone poking out halfway up his shin, he had found the solution.

With a torsional force, he grasped and snapped his shin from where it connected to his ankle. The man screamed in agony. The pain was spectacular and his blood dispersed in the ocular fluid beneath him.

With the sharpened bone firmly in hand, he now hacked into the lens with the mightiest hews he could muster. The disembodied bellowing picked up again as dents became holes in the collagen. His heart was pounding and adrenaline was flowing as he made it to the center. The hollow eye fell silent and the man collapsed backwards into the fluid pooled within it. With violent instinct subsiding, he allowed his remaining lung to fill with fluid as his wasted body sank down over the retina.

The thick, invulnerable optic nerve that protruded from the dry ground of the Spoil and extended up into the floor of the Squalor began to buckle. It tumbled upon itself like a long coiling rope as the husk of the great eye fell from where it had nested. A nineteen-and-a-half-year-old man lay cradled in its vitreous humour, cushioned by the sclera, as its final catastrophic flop into the desert hell of the Spoil delivered a vicious but pleasing crunch. The spectacle was seen by none, as the eye had landed far upstream in the arid wastes, shrouded in sandstorm and by the haze of distance.

Goliah of the Spoil - 3

Far upstream in the desert, a pair of human eyes opened. Crystal grains of sand spilled delicately over the lip of the cracked eggshell eye he lay in. He felt stiff but his joints appeared functional. The man sat up violently and hacked up the dust that had collected in his lungs. Dehydrated and disoriented, he rose to his feet to look around. A gentle, steady breeze carried his mind with the dust and sand to a brief instant of peace. As he looked back at the remnants of the eye he had climbed out of - almost entirely covered in sand – some memories slowly returned. He traced the optic nerve that roped along the ground to a fixed point nearby. "What was that place I escaped from," he wondered, "... and where am I now?" The man looked down at himself to see his clothes tattered and limbs intact. He dropped to the sand to get a closer look at his wrist and the shin that he had previously torn from his body. They looked fine; there was no sign of swelling. He took a deep breath and could feel the dry air filling both lungs. He had healed completely.

"How long have I been out?" he asked himself. He stood up again and looked to each horizon for something other than sand, desolate-looking shrubs, and animal carcasses; but in the

33

absence of anything substantial, he trusted his instinct and headed into the wind.

When the breeze ceased, he knew he had made the right choice. A monolithic city rose from the sand of the distant desert, obsidian towers erupting from its centre. At first, it was difficult to discern what he was looking at. The enormous city was surrounded by a structure that made it look small by comparison - giant walls of dirt and stone. The entire city, in fact the entire world, appeared to be within a massive, rectangular, underground tunnel about ten kilometres high and twenty kilometres wide. In the indiscriminate distance, casting an orange light between the city's black spires, a monstrous, feral star hung ominously in the center of the tunnel. Violent flares licked at the atmosphere around it expelling waves of heat he could feel subtly even so far away. A flash of existential dread took him briefly before his exhaustion managed to disarm it, and he again wondered where and who he was. It seemed safe to assume that in this city he would find the answer to one of these questions.

The low sun and the buildings cast long, cool shadows over the desert as he shuffled up to a destitute suburb on the outskirts of the city. The low shanties were cobbled together with thin scraps of wood half buried in sand. The rooves were made of sheet metal poorly fastened to the walls and in some cases hanging off or displaced and propped up against cheap siding.

Empty shells of semi-conscious people shuffled about, even their movements seeming sedentary. A blank-faced couple sat on the porch of the house closest to him, overlooking the vast desert. Their skin was baked, but somehow grey. It sat on their bodies looking almost detached from the muscle beneath like a leather body-bag that always surrounded them. The skin on their lower lips and eyelids hung off in loose pouches that collected dust and revealed yellow crooked teeth and swollen bloodshot eyes. The man on the porch had his feet in a rusted bucket while the woman sitting beside him knit. The two of them cast vacant glares at the man as he crossed through their purview, passing between the shanties.

Moving among the shelters, the man's eyes darted from the bleak architecture to the departed expressions. He noted a bizarre sign above a shack that read, "Upstream Goliah Meats." Was this a business operating among this dread, and if so, was the city called Goliah?

He was startled when, seemingly from nowhere, an old hag in a black hooded cloak bumped into him. She looked up with intense, glazed-over eyes and he sputtered in shock, taking a step back. Before he could create a comfortable distance, she reached out, grasped his shoulder firmly, and calmly uttered, "Come this way, boy."

She turned and slowly made her way to a particularly small hut. The man looked around expecting thugs to drag him away, but he was not being coerced. He traced her footsteps with his eyes and realized after a moment that he had a desire to follow her. He doubted her ability to harm him, and she might be willing to answer his questions.

He entered the shack after her and noted its interior for being larger than its outside appearance would suggest. It also achieved a state of comfortable, cool humidity as most of the walls were decorated with decaying plant matter. The woman gestured to him to take a seat on a cushion across from her at a low, round, wooden table bearing a teapot and two cups. He obliged, making his way across from her and plunking down. The crone removed her hood, revealing a long mess of curly, grey hair.

"Tea, my boy?" she asked, lifting the kettle.

"Yes please, thank you..."

She poured and handed it to him and he gulped it down hot without bothering to taste it. The beverage was calming. He brought his attention to the old woman before him. Bathed in green candlelight reflected off plant matter, she began.

"You are the one they will come to call 'Breowakoe, the false god'."

As the words left her lips, his head pounded and his vision fragmented as though some piece of his mind had just shut down, or turned on.

"Where am I?" he drowsily mumbled.

The old woman sat back with a smirk, the corner of her eye ablaze, "You might as well ask who you are, boy. You are a fraction of this place. Having shattered the subjugated hell, you now find yourself at home in the dominant: 'Ervalui' in the Satrian tongue; 'The Spoil' in yours."

A feeble noise escaped Breowakoe's lips as a thick haze of memories drifted just behind his consciousness. He knew he had heard of this place before but could not remember where. His breathing became rapid and his eyes flicked about.

"Relax, boy. The most fearsome creature down here is you."

"What do you mean? And what do you mean, I am a fraction of the Spoil?"

"Not *a* fraction..." Her smirk grew deeper and she raised an eyebrow. "Two of the fragments of this place have taken root within you."

"What does that mean? How many fractions are there in total? What does it mean to be a fraction of the Spoil? What do the fractions do?" He asked, annoyed.

The woman held her finger to her lips to silence him and then lifted all eight of the digits she had. "The fragments offer their holder influence over the thrae – thripsis, the energy of hell. Each fragment is a specific aspect of the Spoil and each can be held by only one person at a time.

The holder of the aspect of control can use thripsis for fine detail and a mastery over that which lies in their immediate vicinity.

The aspect of apathy can be used to still the thripsis in the mind of its holder, rendering them calm and the unable to feel pain.

The aspect of hatred allows an infinite amount of thripsis to flow through its holder; they will never tire.

The aspect of power increases the volume of thripsis one

may use at once.

The aspect of cunning grants cleverness and also allows the holder to manipulate thriptic flow through the minds of others, planting ideas in their heads.

The aspect of cruelty intensifies the thriptic flow around its holder, their thripsis may be used more... obscenely.

The aspect of creation is rival to them all; it is equal to the sum of all the others – Verivoluae, the great star that burns at the end of the infinite tunnel – the embryo that became the Spoil."

The hag turned her head to the long shafts of light poking through the thatched wall. Breowakoe followed with his eyes but remained lost in thought. He turned to look at her with brow furrowed, still unsatisfied.

"Which of those two do I hold? Also, that's only seven. What is the eighth aspect of the Spoil?"

"It is not my place to give you every answer, nor to tell you how to navigate this strange land. Despite what you may feel, Breowakoe does not need guidance. He needs only to be reminded of suffering and to let that pain be his raft on the waters of his rage."

Breowakoe felt frustrated.

"Go now, go contend with the world!" the woman scowled, rising to her feet and hitting him with a stick.

Breowakoe rose to defend himself and backed out of the tent. He tried to think of a question or comment that might manipulate more information from her, but no words came.

"That's it boy, on your way. As you blacken creation you become the Spoil."

He stared at her blankly, deeply unsatisfied as the door of the hut slammed in his face.

Stumbling into the street, Breowakoe struggled for consciousness, unaware that his tea had been drugged. The heavy, humid air vibrated around his ears and eyes to the beat of his heart and suddenly, he found that his gaze was being pulled up toward the roof of a nearby crumbling house. There, on its roof, sat a large owl. Its eyes were sunken and its grey feathers seemed to suck the rotten light from the sky. It looked strange, out of place, like it didn't belong there. The owl cocked its head to look at him, and Breowakoe found himself mirroring it. His eyelids would barely stay open, but in another moment the owl stretched out its four-foot wingspan and flew over his head. He was too disoriented to follow its path, and he was already distracted by yet another oddity.

A rickety wooden carriage bumped around to his left, kicking up dust. Giant, jet-black stag beetles were towing it. The haze over Breowakoe's eyes and ears thickened, and a white buzzing flooded his senses as a man and woman emerged from the carriage into the fog. He felt their hands grip his numb shoulders and guide him into the shade. Echoes of voices reverberated in his head, but Breowakoe couldn't tell if they were sound or memory. He put his trust in the ever growing numbness, and fell unconscious.

Kaimaradan - 4

Sunbeams perforated yellowed blinds and set the dust world ablaze. Breowakoe opened his eyes in someone's musty living room - in physical agony from head to foot. Rusted barbed chains pierced his wrists and ankles; he had been stripped naked, was covered with scabs and dry blood, shackled to the wall. It was obvious that he had been used as some sick person's plaything. He noticed the stale taste of his own vomit under his tongue and looking down, he saw a series of organized razor blade cuts along his torso.

Shock overtook him. He bellowed out, "H-E-E-E-E-LP!," twitching and digging a wrist barb dangerously close to an artery; but in a state of advanced dehydration, he had no voice beyond a dry mewl. Adrenaline coursed through his body, as he was hyperventilating. Rigid shuffling, then slow footsteps rattled the thin plywood floor, muffled somewhat by a thick, red, shag carpet that extended from the room he was in to somewhere around the corner. All the furniture seemed old and woolly with a sort of burgundy hue. A skeletal-looking woman poked her head around the corner with a crooked smile. Craning her wiry neck, she looked back into the other room. Breowakoe recognized her from the back porch of the shanty he had seen overlooking the desert when he entered Goliah. He regretted making eye contact with that couple but was at least able to infer where he was.

"He's awake, dear!" she crooned in a gentle but raspy tone.

She turned back to Breowakoe with a grin and stepped out from behind the wall. Her limbs were as thin as her neck, and from the crown of her head jutted a dry, straggled ponytail. She approached him, stroking the fingers of her left hand with her right, scratching a scab. Breowakoe's heart pounded but he dared not move again, as the pain in his wrist was already nearly unbearable. A ghoulish man glided silently around the corner.

"Well, well. You were right, my love. Rise and shine, my little bird!" He spoke with an overabundance of glee.

Breowakoe was deaf to the tone. He wanted to let his eyes roll back in his head and free him from consciousness until the moment they chose to kill him, hopefully soon.

"O-h-h goodness, our little birdy's shaking!" the woman falsely pouted, running her fingers over the wounds in Breowakoe's chest and looking back at her husband. "Honey, should we give Parrot some water?" She now spoke over her shoulder while surveying Breowakoe's thin-but-chiseled body. The man paused for a moment, looking Breowakoe in the eye and smiling before heading back into the kitchen.

The woman took the goblet from her man's hands and poured a bit onto a damp face-cloth. Breowakoe's breathing became more rapid as he anticipated a multitude of horrors.

"Relax, Parrot." She put the cloth on his forehead tilting it back and raised the goblet to his lips. "Coo for me, little Parrot," she said softly.

Breowakoe was unsure of the meaning of the statement, whether it was rhetorical or a command, but he had come to understand that these people called him 'Parrot.'

"I SAID, COO, PARROT!"

The man dashed for a blood-crusted scalpel that sat on a bench against the wall.

"Coo," Breowakoe said, almost questioningly but with an appropriate whimper. The man approached him with violence in his eyes. "Coo, coo, coo, coo, COO, COO, COO, COO, COO!"

Breowakoe grew increasingly desperate until his 'coos' were less a fragile bird and more an uncontrolled scream. The man pressed the blade to him and sliced a six-centimetre cut down the side of his chest. Breowakoe kept 'cooing' as the pain set in, helplessly hoping for its end.

"When we tell you to do something, you DO IT, Parrot..."

"Yes, sir, I understand!"   A strike to the side of his head left his inner ear in ruin.

"YOU SAY, 'SQUAWK-SQUAWK,' WHEN YOU ADDRESS ME, PARROT!" The man trailed off.

-

Breowakoe awoke to a dull ache; he looked at his strung-up hands to see that his left ring and middle fingers and his right thumb, index, and ring fingers were missing. He wondered how long that had been the case.

His body was so accustomed to shock, however, that he felt no horror or repulsion. There was an IV in his arm connected to a drip bag containing a yellowish liquid, possibly dirty water.

Breowakoe could hear activity outside - the purring of heavy engines and machines rolling past. He could make out darkened shapes through broken spots in the blinds mere metres away from him on the other side of the thin wall. He heard one of them speak.

"Yeah, there's been a spike in thriptic density in this area for over a week. Tiricora's gonna kill us if we come back empty-handed."

Hope filled Breowakoe's heart. "H-E-E-E-E-LP; H-E-E-E-E-E-LP!" he tried to scream, but as before his throat yielded nothing but pitiful, dry squeals. The room was spinning, he was reeling, and gurgling he slipped back under the waters of unconsciousness.

-

When Breowakoe came to, he was standing in a nine-foot-tall cast-iron boiler that had been converted to some sort of cylindrical coffin. His hands were tied over his head with rope and looped through a pair of slats in the roof. Looking out of the open door of the coffin, he realized he was in a concrete room. To his right was the underside of a splintered wooden staircase with no back on its rungs. He must have been in the couple's basement. The room was cluttered with shelves containing various oddities, the heads of animals in jars and dried vegetation hung from lines of twine. It smelled of mold and preservatives.

There was thumping over Breowakoe's head, he could see two pairs of feet coming down the stairs. The woman stopped at the bottom to peek at him between the rungs, grinning as the man continued into the small cellar. He approached Breowakoe with a half-scowl, half-smile.

"You're going to learn the consequences today, Parrot..." he started vengefully.

Breowakoe remained silent, still emerging from his concussed daze and looking soberly at the man's feet.

When the man stepped toward the coffin's entrance, Breowakoe chirped up with a "Squawk, squawk!"

The man came to rest again as glass baubles clacked behind him. Smiling, he took two steps back to allow his wife the space she needed. She carried with her a massive jar, about two feet tall. Coiled up inside it was a giant centipede. A black-shelled body with razor sharp legs had two red stripes running down either side of its back, branching off to each of its legs. It must have been at least a metre long and four-to-five inches wide. Breowakoe re-learned repulsion. He shifted back, imagining the ways his torturers were planning to use this unprecedented horror.

"O-o-oh, honey, look! I think Parrot is excited!" the woman squealed in delight.

"No! No please, no."

"Squawk for us, Parrot!" the man commanded. The woman carried the jar over to Breowakoe and bent down.

"No, please – I don't even know what I did! Why are you doing this?!"

The woman only grinned as she fiddled with the jar's lid. The coiled centipede began to stir in anticipation. Breowakoe was struck in the face by a heavy blow.

"YOU DON'T TALK BACK TO US, PARROT! THIS JUST GOES TO SHOW YOU NEED THIS PUNISHMENT!"

"No, I seriously don't! Squawk, squawk! Please I'll never talk back again! I don't even know what's going on!" The man struck his face again. There was no bargaining to be done.

"Centi-centi-centipede!" the woman gleefully chanted as she finally unscrewed the lid and pressed the lip of the glass jar over Breowakoe's pubic bone. Breowakoe couldn't help but watch. He knew he should look away and remain still and just try to brace himself but the centipede was too spectacular to ignore, uncoiling itself with its powerful muscles and lifting its head out of the jar to survey Breowakoe's soft belly.

"Please, take it away..." he mumbled, with an undertone of resignation.

"It? This is a sh-e-e-e!" the woman sang without taking her eyes off the beautiful, glistening insect. "She's a pretty, pretty cen-ti-pede!"

The dexterity of the creature was unnerving, but not as unnerving as its apparent intelligence. It gently placed its monstrous pincers on Breowakoe's skin, then halted itself and gazed up into his eyes. Breowakoe stared deeply into the beady, black eyes of the creature. The couple was silent, watching the two interact. Breowakoe's heartbeat was visible through his chest, but he felt oddly that he was connecting with the creature. Perhaps it saw his suffering - perhaps it was gentle and would not harm him.

The centipede snapped its head down and inserted its pincers under the skin of Breowakoe's belly, then reared up like a bull. The woman's shrill laugh resounded off the thin walls.

With preposterous strength it tore the skin off the patch of abdominal muscle beneath. Breowakoe could no longer hold back his screams as the centipede wore the skin of his belly like a hood. The creature's powerful legs kicked into action, latching onto him and forcing its head - which now veered off to the left under his skin - deeper into the wound. Shearing and flaying as it went, the centipede bore a tunnel between skin and muscle around Breowakoe's lower back, up around his solar plexus and upper back to finally place its head over his heart. The couple cheered as the centipede found its way in, but Breowakoe's own screams were all he could hear.

His voice finally silenced by damage to his vocal cords, Breowakoe still tried to scream as the centipede maliciously wriggled its legs under his skin. The couple pulled up small chairs to watch, bellowing with laughter. After a harrowing span of time, Breowakoe had become numb to this new level of pain, but the creature had stopped writhing. Suspended in a kind of euphoria, he could barely react as the couple rose from their chairs and approached him. "Can you get it out of me, now?" he thought, but couldn't get the words out.

They said nothing, and offered him only calm smiles as the man slowly closed the heavy door of the coffin over him. Dread mounted in Breowakoe's heart. It was pitch black and he could hear his captors locking a bolt on the outside of the coffin, the stairs creaking, and a door closing. He accepted that he would die, as the centipede's uncomfortable outline stretched the skin of his torso. He was entirely at its mercy and supposed it would devour him from the inside. Despite his worry, Breowakoe's thoughts escaped him, and he fell unconscious.

-

"*Artrie! Wake up!*"

Breowakoe awoke in blackness. Panicking, he looked about for the couple but remembered that he was still inside the boiler in their basement.

"*What is your name, boy...*"

A voice spoke so clearly that Breowakoe snapped to check behind him. It seemed to speak right into his ear. The centipede inside him writhed and Breowakoe let out a yelp. The centipede stopped.

"*Wake them up if you like... I will not stop you.*"

As the echo of Breowakoe's own voice faded, he was dismayed to realize that the centipede was speaking.

"What? Please don't do that with your legs again; what do you want?" Breowakoe panted.

"*Your name, boy... And you need not speak. I hear your thoughts as you hear mine...*" The centipede's patience was tried.

"B-Breowakoe." It took him a minute to think of it.

"*I see... My name is Kaimaradan. I am the last of the Satrian people.*"

Breowakoe was too desperate to inquire about anything beyond his own immediate situation.

"So, you *are* intelligent. I don't understand - why are you doing this to me? You were strong enough; you could have gotten out of that jar easily!"

"*I am strong because, like you, I hold one of the fractions of the Spoil. I have held the aspect of cruelty since the moment Verivoluae created Ervalui, and I have lived as one of the four demon lords. Many wish to see me dead. I sat in that jar awaiting either the end of time or a stimulating way to pass it, whichever came sooner. And now you have arrived. You are not like other Nethriel, you have intrigued me, boy.*"

Breowakoe perked up, recognizing the aspect of cruelty as being one of the seven aspects the old witch had told him about; yet he hated this centipede creature. "Intrigued you? All you did was torture me, you filth," he said, gritting his teeth in anger.

"*Your suffering to me is... sublime.*" The wicked centipede let out an angsty, breathy laugh. Breowakoe could feel that in her heart she delighted in the suffering of others, she wasn't kidding.

"You're sick..."

He gritted his teeth harder. Kaimaradan stilled herself before speaking again.

"*There is no use hating me, child. You are my pet, my plaything while I reside under your skin. Test my words and you will see the bone child.*"

Kaimaradan shuddered and Breowakoe felt the tines ready to ravage his flesh once again. He hated her in silence, not knowing what the bone child was but knowing a threat when he heard one.

"*Do you want to kill them, boy? Do you wish to be free?*"

Breowakoe was puzzled at first, then realized she meant the wicked couple, likely sleeping upstairs.

"What do you want in return? Why would you help me?" Breowakoe carefully considered her motives, wondering if this could be yet another set up.

"You have nothing to offer me outside of your life, but here you are, still living. If you trust nothing else, trust this herrili, youngling: if you should ever interest me less than the power I would gain by killing you, I will not hesitate to do so."

Breowakoc felt a jolt of excitement and fear, as deep down, he believed her. This mysterious power - aspects of the Spoil - the old woman had mentioned could apparently be transferred from one to another through killing. Breowakoe's brow furrowed as again doubt crept into his mind.

"Are you not loyal to these people who have sheltered you for years?"

"These 'people' are worms. They are no different to any of the other millions of degenerates living in this foul city. I have no loyalty to the weak and the wretched." Kaimaradan seethed.

"Ok. What do we have to do to get out of here?" Breowakoe resigned himself to whatever fate followed this decision, with a renewed sense of optimism.

A deep, prickling energy emanated from the demon centipede wound tightly around his core, pumping static into the iron coffin and making Breowakoe's hair stand on end. He could feel the rope around his wrists starting to slacken. He could see it in the dull glow of light pouring in through the slats at the top of the coffin: the rope was rotting and fraying, weathering before his eyes.

"*The chaotic nature of my aspect of cruelty causes my thripsis to shred wood, rope, even metal.*" Breowakoe was relieved as he pulled his hands free for the first time in a week.

"My fingers grew back. How did you do that?" he asked, pleasantly alarmed. Kaimaradan ignored his question.

"*I am going to feed my thripsis through your body now, and you will become strong. I have only so much so you will need to move quickly. Jump to the top of the boiler and pull yourself through those holes.*"

"Those tiny slats? There is no chance I am fitting through there…" Breowakoe felt helpless and irritated.

"*My silly child. Ere ghit – Everything fits.*"

The prickling thripsis in the air rerouted and began to flow through Breowakoe. Although it was uncomfortable, he felt light and strong despite a week of imprisonment. Focusing, he did as he was told, leaping effortlessly to the top of the coffin and pulling his head towards the slat next to his knuckles.

The atmosphere changed. Breowakoe could feel a

stranger thripsis emerge from his abdomen as Kaimaradan engaged the aspect of cruelty. The cast-iron, and even his own body seemed to become a bloated putty as this new terrible power flowed into them. It didn't feel as though he were in any reality that hc could have imagined; it felt as though the room bent to Kaimaradan's will. Breowakoe pulled his head through the four-by-one-inch gap, and still his putty arm had the strength to drag the remainder of his body out into the basement until it was the only thing that remained in the boiler. He could not justify it rationally, but his body moved on instinct until at last his fingers passed through the far side of the smooth, cold iron.

The terrible energy retreated into the creature dwelling under his skin. He leapt to the floor of the dark cellar and took a moment to touch his own face and neck. They felt normal.

"That was amazing…" he whispered.

"*Ehh… I have fit much larger things through much smaller people.*" Kaimaradan seemed to take pride in her morbid statement, as Breowakoe imagined the horrors she must have inflicted over her vast lifespan.

He took a moment in the dark to listen for the couple upstairs. There was only silence.

"*Well?*" Kaimaradan asked impatiently.

Breowakoe tepidly crept across the cold, concrete floor and then up the creaky, wooden steps. He was weak without Kaimaradan's thripsis and it was difficult to stay upright. He slowed his pace, trying to make as little noise as possible, but it was unavoidable. The door at the top of the stairs creaked loudly as it opened and the light of a new day strained his eyes even as the dilapidated blinds tried to conceal it. The couple was not on the couch.

"WHAT DO YOU THINK YOU'RE DOING, PARROT!?"

A metal pot wielded by the woman struck Breowakoe in the temple and he crashed backwards over the IV rack, falling to the spot where he had been chained up days ago. The man came out of nowhere and began kicking him in the gut, winding him when his boot caught a spot unshielded by Kaimaradan's body. Another boot to the mouth knocked his teeth into the back of his throat and Breowakoe choked on them, tasting his own blood. He was completely disoriented, unable to defend himself.

Kaimaradan burst forth from the skin of Breowakoe's chest. She fully emerged and leapt onto the man, crawling around the surface of his body. With a rapid series of cuts her sharp legs sliced off all his limbs. Now only a torso, the man screamed as the woman made a break for it, heading into the kitchen toward some other exit at the back of the shack. A soft felting noise accompanied the centipede charging after her. Breowakoe fought to come to his senses. This was his chance to escape; the front door was only a metre away, just to the left of the yellowed blinds. Still gasping for air, still so dreadfully broken from torture, he crawled away as the woman's piercing screams resounded. After an odd, wet sound, he heard only a hideous gurgling. He looked over his shoulder, but his view of the kitchen was blocked by the couch. He struggled to reach for the door's handle but his finger only grazed it. He needed to prop himself against the wall to get to the lock. A sharp pain penetrated his ankle and he looked back to see the centipede's pincers hooked through his bone.

"*You are mistaken, herilli. Our time together has only begun.*"

He could feel her amusement echoing in his head as his back burned on the foul shag carpet. She dragged him foot-first to lie next to the aged man. Breowakoe watched her mount the man's torso and gouge out his eyes with her front legs.

Kaimaradan tilted her head down and vomited up a fuming acid bile into the man's mouth, replicating the concert of sounds heard from the woman.

Breowakoe's breath returned to him, he clamoured back on all fours, beside himself with terror, almost pitying his captors. But relegated by the wall he had no natural retreat. Kaimaradan looked over at him with her beady black eyes and for a moment was still. Blood spewed from the almost-corpse with each withdrawal of a leg, and the centipede swiftly approached Breowakoe to re-enter her perch, forcing herself under his flapping skin, piercing his muscle and scraping his ribs, winding around to his musical screams.

At last, she arrived with her head snugly mounted over his heart. Breowakoe breathed heavily. He wanted to cry, but he could not. Reluctantly he got up, shuffled to the door and stumbled out into the street. Even though he now wore his prison, he felt an inkling of relief to be free of the couple. His mind somewhat eased, he stumbled into the dusk, finally collapsing in the sand.

The Vemanen District - 5

"*Wake up, boy...*"

Breowakoe awoke to find he was in an enclosed space. The tiny room was shaking and jumbling him around. It was the back of a truck.

"What happened? where are we going?" he thought, so Kaimaradan could hear.

"*The tallest tower in Goliah.*"

"What do you mean? Why?"

"*Not any idea of mine - some of Tiricora's thugs picked us up and threw us in here; they will be taking us to her.*"

"Who is Tiricora?"

"*Tiricora is the aspect of control and the Nethriel who runs the entire city of Goliah.*"

"You called *me* a Nethriel; what is a Nethriel?" Breowakoe interjected, frustrated with all these terms.

"*A human... naive little boy. As for what she wants: power, more aspects to claim. You have heard them rolling past when you were trapped in that house have you not? The patrols? No doubt Tiricora has been licking her lips at the massive thriptic presence she detects. The closer aspects are to one another, the better we sense each other. Can you feel her presence?"*

Breowakoe struggled to sense anything, straining and relaxing different parts of his body. "Which aspect do I possess? When I first got here a crazy old woman told me I had two of them -"

The truck's door flung open, and his eyes struggled with the light.

"Get out of the truck slowly and come with me," a man's voice said.

Breowakoe nervously did as he was told. He emerged into an underground warehouse to find himself surrounded by armed men pointing their guns at him.

"You're gonna need to put some clothes on before you can meet with Tiricora."

The man handed him jeans and a buttoned shirt. As he changed, the group stared wide-eyed at the outline of the giant centipede circumnavigating his torso.

"All right, let's head up," the man said to everyone.

Crammed into a tiny elevator, the ride up seemed impossibly long and Breowakoe's ears started popping.

"Do not trust Tiricora. She will not try to kill you if she believes you know how to use your power, but do not show her

how weak you are."

Breowakoe could feel that Kaimaradan was nervous. This Tiricora must really be formidable.

When the doors opened Breowakoe was standing in a single room. The men remained in the elevator and its doors closed, leaving him alone with a woman sitting behind a desk across the room; she had short blonde hair slicked back and a bizarre smile on her face.

"Ahh, come in, come in!" she called out, rising. Her posture was exceptional – her neck was long and she was tall. She walked on the balls of her feet around her desk. Her fingers flicked about, and her eyes moved rapidly, as though she were focusing on many things at once. She walked over to him, continuing to offer a broad smile while the look in her eyes was cutting. She clearly possessed a high level of intelligence. It seemed as though she were deciding whether or not she could kill him.

"Unbutton your shirt, please. I want to keep an eye on your friend – oh boy - look at you!" Tiricora crooned suggestively.

"This is bad. With the aspect of control, she can kill us both in one thriptic blast while my head is over your heart."

Kai began shuffling back as Breowakoe unbuttoned his shirt, trying not to show his pain.

"Where you are now is fine, Kaimaradan. No need to come out," Tiricora condescended.

"*Child, you must imagine the air and the energy around you. When you breathe, feel your body force the air to move as you wish it to, in and out. Then do the same with energy - the thripsis - pull it into then push it out of your body.*"

"What?" Breowakoe thought, alarmed. Kaimaradan seemed certain that Tiricora would attack.

"Are you two having a nice chat?" Tiricora asked with a smirk.

"Can she hear us!?" Breowakoe broke out in a cold sweat.

"*No. She knows we Satrians convert thoughts to corpusapien - body-knowledge - and that we speak through touch.*"

Breowakoe considered turning the centipede over to Tiricora but realized there was no way he would come out of that alive, either.

"Tell Kaimaradan she can relax. I want you to work for me, Breowakoe."

"How do you know my name?" he blurted.

"Oh, so sorry - you remind me of a King I once advised. His name was Breowakoe, too. Coincidence, I suppose..." Tiricora stared into his eyes curiously, deeply.

"What could I even do for you?" he asked bravely.

"Oh, just a bit of reconnaissance, and I will give you something you want in return." Tiricora smiled.

"Something I want? I don't know what I want... I woke up in this place not knowing who I was or how I got here."

Tiricora's eyes lit up.

"Well, wouldn't you like to know... child of the Planelands?"

A peculiar tingling crept up Breowakoe's spine and splashed up over his cranium. A part of him knew that the mention of 'the Planelands' had brought him closer to finding the truth. Tiricora walked around her desk and slid open a drawer; from it she drew a crystal capsule that sat comfortably in the palm of her hand, an extravagant, large pill.

"This is a capsule of essence. The air down here in the Spoil is battered daily by thripsis. All things down here are filthy, unclean, impure... but the air inside the capsule is from the Planelands. When I break it in front of your face and you breathe it in you will remember your time there, your past life."

Breowakoe stared wide-eyed, feeling hopeful.

"Na-ah-ah, you've got to earn it. These are exceptionally rare. They drip through and fall from the rock wall above this place every 100 years or so; it's not something I'd waste on even my best employees," Tiricora teased, slipping the gem back into her desk.

"So, what is this reconnaissance I have to do?"

"O-o-oh, I like that attitude." Tiricora strutted back over. "Well, you'd have to become better than my best employee, which means succeeding where all the others have failed. Discover the location of an aspect or capture it for me, but do not kill it yourself."

Breowakoe again considered turning over Kaimaradan.

"*Disrespectful, foolish little swine! Once I am dead she can easily kill you too, you will never see that capsule.*" the centipede hissed, tensing her legs, readying herself for combat.

"Where would I start to look for one?" Breowakoe queried, knowing Kaimaradan was right.

"Well, it just so happens that this crew that brought you here is leaving to check up on a lead we received just this morning." She checked a clock on the wall. "Now. Come with me."

Tiricora brushed past him at a brisk pace, making her way to the elevator.

"You'll be going to the Vemanen district. Goliah is a city of 100 million people, about 45% Nethriel, 5% Vemanen, and 50% Oxalthry. As you know, Breowakoe, we are Nethriel. Oxalthry are also Nethriel, but they believe they are a distinct race and that it is their religious duty to exterminate us. They currently wage war in the centre of my city downstream from here."

Breowakoe wondered how such a bizarre situation could have come about.

"The Vemanen are a quiet race of demons, although unlike your friend, there," Tiricora gestured to Kaimaradan, "they were genetically engineered by the Piccaros and are not native to the Spoil. They had established a settlement along the starboard wall of the city back when it was young; these days it's just a densely populated ghetto. With the war going on, they keep to themselves but likely won't appreciate intrusions into their district. They don't like the sunlight, either, preferring to hide from Verivoluae's gaze."

"What do they look like? How will I know when I see one?"

"Tall. Adults range from seven to eleven feet. Nethrieloid, but incredibly slender, their skin is grey and they move silently. I mean it: dead silent, despite powerful legs and extra joints that give them the ability to move at blistering speeds. You'll need to be vigilant. They have pointy ears that look relatively small on their heads, but I promise you they are very sensitive and can hear your heartbeat from 20 metres away. Their eyes appear a bio-luminescent yellow but are non-functional, and their nose cavity is filled in with more grey skin – they have no sense of smell. Most can speak, but they prefer not to; don't expect a lot of chatting."

The door of the elevator opened and Tiricora's legs exploded into the brisk pace once again. Breowakoe followed quickly after her back into the underground warehouse. The Nethriel men who minutes ago were holding him at gunpoint were now loading gear into an armoured truck. The leader looked concerned as he turned and saw the man he had just abducted following his boss.

"Ben, I know you've met but you haven't been properly introduced. This is Breowakoe, he will be accompanying you on this patrol. Do you have an extra vest he can throw on?"

"Uhh, yeah, he's a big guy, but I think I have something that will fit… Can I talk to you for a second?" Ben had a nervous twitch in his eye, trying to sub communicate something.

"There is nothing to worry about. Yes, Breowakoe is an aspect and you did excellent work finding him, but we have decided to cooperate. He will help you track down other aspects and he will be paid handsomely."

"Yes ma'am, but -"

"Not another word." Tiricora cut him off, eyeing the rest of the men one by one as they had all been eavesdropping. "I am choosing to trust Breowakoe, just as I have chosen to trust each of you!" she called sternly into all corners of the room. Tiricora turned to Ben once more.

"All right. I expect success gentleman! Good luck!" Her hand brushed Ben's shoulder delicately as she made her way back to the elevator.

"Understood ma'am."

"Oh, and Breowakoe! This is my best, most experienced squad; don't slow them down." The elevator doors closed and Tiricora was gone.

"Yes ma'am," Breowakoe gulped.

"Breowakoe, was it?" Ben started.

"Yes."

"Ok, Breo - your squad mates here are Logan, Shane, and Felix. As you already heard, my name is Ben - I'm squad leader. While we're on this mission my word is law, got it?"

"Got it."

"Good to go, boss," Logan said as the last trunk was placed in the back of the armoured truck.

"All right, get in back, Breo." Breowakoe waited for Logan and Felix to climb onto the steel benches in the back before he could get in. Shane was driving and Ben rode shotgun. The doors of the truck all slammed and the engine started up.

They rode in silence for 5 minutes. Sitting across from Breowakoe - Felix kept glaring at him and Logan was breathing heavily, staring off into space.

"Breo, do you know what we're doing?" Ben called from the front.

"We are going to the Vemanen district to look for an aspect?" Breowakoe confirmed.

"Yeah, more or less. This morning we got a tip that the

aspect of apathy is hiding somewhere far downstream in the Vemanen district."

"Downstream means towards the sun, right?" Breowakoe attempted to clarify.

The cabin was silent as Logan slowly broke a smile, thinking Breowakoe was joking, but as his eyes darted about it faded quickly.

"Oh my god," Felix sighed in annoyance.

"No shit, you better start taking this seriously." Logan now joined Felix in glaring at him.

"... anyways, we're gonna get in there, bust a few kneecaps, and find out where the aspect is. From there I'll decide whether or not we proceed with searching, capturing, or falling back to share intel with Tiricora. Next, arms, speaking of which you need to get strapped up."

Logan opened one of the trunks and took out a large automatic rifle. Breowakoe felt the truck's engine powering along as they accelerated very quickly.

"Ideally, you won't be using this, because it's a stealth mission. We don't need to go pissing off the Vemanen and starting another war," Ben continued.

Breowakoe held the weapon awkwardly in his arms,

unsure of how to use it or even to connect it to the back of his vest the way the rest had.

"Then, you've got this..." Logan drew a machete with an unusually large, cumbersome-looking handle and hilt. "You turn it on here and an electric current runs through." He flicked the switch and Breowakoe heard a soft buzz. "Well... the electricity doesn't actually run through until there's an impact, but it's armed now. This is what we'll use most."

Breowakoe placed the rifle in his lap to take the machete. A bassy rumble shook the truck. He perked up and looked around; there were tiny windows near the top of the truck's interior. Breowakoe could see the low-hanging sun through them and in the distance a pillar of smoke. More explosions erupted on the horizon, flattening little shanty houses. The people in the streets right beside him remained calm, keeping their heads down to trudge through the open sewers.

"What's going on?"

"That's the war, retard," Felix said, continuing to hate Breowakoe for no apparent reason.

The men sat quietly as the truck continued to move forward, swaying gently as the concussing air-blasts from explosions far away finally reached them.

"Oh, right, there's one more piece of equipment I need to show you." Logan took out a strange looking cube with a monitor on one of its faces, wires and antennae sticking out from it in every direction. "Tiricora developed this, it's sort of like radar for detecting the thriptic presence of aspects." He flicked it on.

"Just got to wait for it to calibrate..." The machine erupted in a spasm of sound and colour. "Whoa, what the fuck." Logan shut it off. Felix took it from him and began examining it.

"Is it busted? Try the spare," Ben called back.

Logan tried the spare and got the same result. "What the hell!?" he snorted before staring up at Breowakoe with a blank look.

"Oh right, Breo is an aspect..."

The cabin again fell silent.

"It's fine, we don't need it for this mission, do we? The aspect of apathy can cloak its thriptic presence anyway, right? That's what made it so hard to find in the first place," Shane said, joining the conversation.

"Well... so far yes, but when we get close it may be

invaluable, we simply don't know…" Ben answered and again, silence.

"Ok, I'm calling Tiricora..." He sighed.

"Hello?" Tiricora's voice sounded slightly awry.

"Sorry to bother you, ma'am. Our aspect radar is going haywire with Breo in the truck."

"Ah, yes. You'll have to isolate the frequency of his aspect of hatred and calibrate it to zero." Breowakoe's ears perked up.

"I don't understand, ma'am. When you demonstrated this using yourself, even at a closer range than this, it wasn't spazzing-out. What gives?" Logan shouted from the back.

"Well, Logan, he's got another one embedded right under his skin," she answered calmly. Logan remained silent, confused.

"Kaimaradan, the aspect of cruelty, is wrapped around his torso under his skin, Logan," she explained as Logan and Felix's faces opened in awe.

"Oh, so that's why you didn't kill-"

"That's enough, Logan." Tiricora snapped over the speakerphone. "He can't kill me, either. He hasn't figured out how to awaken the aspect yet, and even when he does he will lack the skill to harm me, so don't get any ideas, Breowakoe." Kaimaradan stirred, uneasy.

"How did she know your aspect had not awakened…"

Breowakoe's mind wasn't keeping up with the current conversation. He was more fixated on the information that his aspect was the aspect of hatred. He was trying to recall what the crone had said about that aspect. Logan fiddled with the machine trying to calibrate it.

"Will that be all, then?" Tiricora asked impatiently.

"Wait, sorry ma'am, which two frequencies are his?"

"Are you stupid, Logan? The two that are appearing right in front of your face! Not the little background ones," Tiricora snapped back.

"Sorry ma'am, but there are three appearing right in front of my face."

Silence struck the cabin once again. Breowakoe's head perked up, Ben looked back at Logan with a mean mug. The silence endured for a second, and a second, and a second, until count was lost.

"Tare all three of them, then," Tiricora said softly before swiftly hanging up.

-

Night fell as the patrol reached the starboard side of Goliah. The streets were empty when they rolled up to the maw of the Vemanen district. This was the closest Breowakoe had been to one of the great walls of the tunnel that was the Spoil. A large, dark mass of rock extended to the ceiling, it looked monstrous up-close. Breowakoe wondered if anyone had ever tried to climb it. Grey clay houses with small black openings for windows extended downstream as far as the eye could see. There were no lights on in the houses or in the streets. The entrance to the district was merely a break in the houses where the pavement stopped and a thin, gravel road began. The truck had difficulty fitting through the gap, but once it had, they were able to cruise downstream at a brisk clip. The only light was coming from their own headlights, the only sounds from the engine and the wheels crinkling against the gravel. Felix stood up and opened the skylight, poking his head up through it and resting his arms on the machine gun.

"So, we're heading all the way downstream, literally to the edge of the city where Goliah turns into the tar sands," Ben said, looking over at Shane, who nodded.

"Just a couple more hours, boys!" Ben chuckled.

Felix pulled his head back down and shut the skylight. Breowakoe dozed off and awoke to Felix and Logan playing cards. They put their game away as nervous chatter started up front.

"Word travels faster than we do, apparently..." Ben grumbled.

Felix and Logan moved up to peer out one of the small windows on the side.

"Oh, shit..." Logan said.

Breowakoe climbed up to one of the tiny windows beside him and peered out. Their headlights reflected off the road illuminating the street in an eerie, grey shimmer. He could barely see the outlines of the houses in the dim light. Windows appeared in the walls, sculpted out of the near blackness. Hundreds of yellow eyes peering out of them reflected whatever scraps of light they could.

"It's all up the street, too. Somehow they know..." Ben said, as Breowakoe moved up front.

"Somehow? They have really good hearing, right?"

"Yeah, they do, which is why it's weird that they chose to peek out only five minutes ago. You were asleep; there was none of this for the past two hours. Seriously, look at them all."

Breowakoe leaned in close to the windshield to see thousands of eyes peering out windows up and down the street, piercing through the grey mist and the black night. He shuddered.

"Ok, we're almost there, but we can't keep drawing this much attention: we're going to pull into an alley and continue this on foot," said Ben.

Logan and Felix started ripping open trunks and throwing on spongy-looking shoes; they donned weird helmets that silenced their breathing and speaking. Breowakoe did as they did. He noticed that his helmet had built-in radio communication. By the time Shane pulled into a tight alley and had turned off the truck, Ben was also ready.

There was no sound. Felix peered out the back windows, then looked back at Breowakoe who fiddled with his machete.

"Get your gun strapped up just in case everything goes to shit..." Felix commanded.

"I don't know how to use it," Breowakoe announced nervously.

"What the fuck -"

"Shut up, Felix. There's no time to teach him; if we need to use them, we're probably gonna end up dead, anyways." Ben spoke matter-of-factly. "You ready, Shane?"

"Just about," the now-masked Shane grunted as he pulled on his shoes.

"Ok, so Breo, make sure you lift your feet up between each step; the sponge soles will allow you to walk silently as long as you aren't dragging the gravel. If you have to fight, aim for the neck - it's soft and contains a lot of vital stuff, just like ours," Ben explained.

"Ready, boss." Shane rose to his feet.

"Let's do this!" Felix cheered, as he opened the doors and the five men stepped out into the cool night air.

The smell in the air was a peculiar sort of dank as they slowly made their way around the corner and onto the main road. Breowakoe looked behind him. The glow of eyes had vanished. The Vemanen would be well camouflaged in this environment. In the absence of light their eyes were the only way to identify them.

The group was barely around the corner when a whirring alarm went off in the alley where they had parked the truck.

"Shit, that's the car alarm," Shane's voice buzzed in

Breowakoe's ear.

They took brisk but careful steps back around the corner. Breowakoe heard the sound of glass cracking, but couldn't see the source.

"Three, maybe four of them... they look short... adolescents, I guess. Little vandalous shits..." Ben said.

"How do you know?" Breowakoe asked.

"Night vision switch is on the right side of the visor, new guy. You were walking in pitch black this whole time? What the fuck?"

"Shut up, Felix, just take them out," Ben commanded.

Now able to see, Breowakoe moved swiftly to cover the far side of the alley while the others made a beeline to the truck. He saw two of the creatures charge immediately toward Logan and Felix.

Tiricora hadn't been kidding; even when charging in to attack, the Vemanen made no noise. It was daunting to contemplate the dexterity of their sliver-thin bodies. Also daunting, these "adolescents" were about six feet tall. Ben and Felix caught hold of the two and overpowered them, bringing them to the ground and penetrating their necks with the blades of their machetes.

"Oh, shit!"

There was a Vemanen only two metres away from Breowakoe, moving blindingly fast. Without thinking, he swung his machete at its head as hard as he could. There was a hollow thunk as the skull cracked under the blade's pressure. The thin strip of metal cut smoothly on an angle down through the creature's forehead, coming to rest right over its left eye. Breowakoe attempted to retrieve the blade to strike again but it had become lodged in the skull. Screaming in an alien pitch, the Vemanen youth flailed like a marionette held by an amateur, electric current running through its brain. The adolescent clawed at Breowakoe, driving incredibly sharp barbs into his ribs between Kaimaradan's legs. A kick to his groin launched incredibly sharp toenails into and through his inner thighs. He yanked his blade down hard, as his mind shielded him from the pain. The Vemanen collapsed to the dust, still thrashing about. Breowakoe shoved the point of the blade into the ground to stabilize the head, then placed his foot on the adolescent's neck, jostling the blade back and forth to try to loosen it.

He lifted his boot and stomped down on its neck, crunching its windpipe until a red pulp spilled out. The

Vemanen youth stopped moving, and the blade came out easily.

"BREO! THIS IS YOUR LAST CALL; WE'RE GONNA LEAVE YOU BEHIND!"

Only now did it become apparent that Ben had been screaming at him for some time. Breowakoe looked up to face the main road. A wall of adult Vemanen towered, incredibly thin but monstrous in stature: glaring with their useless, yellow eyes.

He turned from the mass of grey flesh and sprinted to the truck where Logan and Felix were ready to close the doors at any moment. Breo dove in and Shane stepped on it.

"Doors closed? Good. cultivators up!" Ben commanded.

Shane flicked a switch and the front and back bumpers of the truck unfolded into a scaffold of rapidly spinning saw blades. Shane reversed hard into the wall of adult Vemanen. Most were ready and bent their long legs to jump onto the rooves of houses, but a few were shredded. Mammoth wipers arose to clear the blood off the back windshield. Shane switched gears, drifted the truck 180 degrees, and sped off down the gravel road. Adult Vemanen watched them from afar as they continued their journey downstream.

"FUCK. ME," Felix yelled. "How did we botch that so fast?"

Ben remained silent, focused, looking in the rear view as Shane drove.

"We aren't going back empty handed, Felix," he said softly. "Drive up another 5k, or so; then we'll blow a hole into the wall of houses and drive into the desert."

Felix and Logan perked up, confused. Shane remained focused on the road.

"Is that not Oxalthry territory?" Logan asked.

"No. The Vemanen district extends further downstream than the rest of Goliah by quite a stretch. We're outside the city."

"All right."

A sharp pain in his inner thigh inspired Breowakoe to hoist himself onto the metal bench. He and Logan looked down simultaneously to observe the damage. His blood-soaked pants were torn to shreds; blood dripping from them pooled on the floor.

"Shit, Felix - get the first aid," Logan said, leaning down to better survey the problem.

"That Vemanen kid slashed me the fuck up," Breowakoe

groaned, thinking that to be an appropriate way to communicate with these guys.

"Shut up. Get your pants off; we have to patch you up."

Breowakoe complied, and within moments he had been locally anaesthetized and Logan was stitching up his inner thighs.

"You're lucky you didn't get your nuts sliced off -"

"Now!" Ben said from the front. A loud whine erupted and two missiles curved from their vehicle into the row of clay houses on their left.

"Hang on tight!" Logan said, as he quickly closed the first aid kit and sat up on the bench beside Breowakoe, holding his arm across his collar bone to keep him in place.

The truck crashed into the rubble, violently jolting as it traversed it. And in an instant, they were on the other side, drifting through the desert sands.

"Ok... just the bandages now," Logan said as he continued patching up Breo.

At last, they reached the furthest downstream point of the Vemanen district; the row of clay houses turned toward the starboard wall of the Spoil, sealing the residences away from the tar sands but for the few dark windows that overlooked them. Shane parked the truck.

"How do you want to do this, boss?" he asked.

Ben sat quietly surveying the houses with a telescopic extension to his night vision. "The tip said, 'third house from the corner,'" he mumbled.

"That looks about right…" Felix confirmed on the aspect radar.

"Get ready to go; we're gonna break in and interrogate," Ben snapped out of his stupor to say.

He ached when he walked, but in a few moments Breowakoe had joined the men standing outside the tall back door of the third clay house from the corner. Shane wedged the blade of his machete between the door and its frame and a soft buzz sounded in the air as it cut through the lock. With night-vision on, Breowakoe followed the men and stormed the dark house.

There was shrieking in the kitchen and Felix was yelling something in a language Breowakoe did not understand. Breowakoe could not see far enough down the hallway to know what was going on. Ben crept into the living room through a doorway to the side keeping his eye on the display of the aspect radar. The noise in the kitchen stopped.

"They weren't going to tell us anything," Logan's voice came on the radio.

"That's fine," Ben answered, "Bring the construction lights in here, Shane; there's a kid here in the living room."

As Breowakoe turned the corner he felt something peculiar. The child Ben spoke of sat alone on a wood chair, facing the kitchen where his parents had just been murdered.

"He's been touched by the aspect of apathy," Ben said, as Logan and Felix entered the room.

"Let's just do the test to make sure," Logan started.

"Turn night vision off; lights are coming on everyone," Shane warned.

A moment later, they were staring at the boy with their masks off. Ben was drawing a blood sample from the five-foot-long creature's arm as its dead, yellow eyes stared blankly straight ahead.

"Yeah, the cells are damaged; he's been exposed to intense levels of thripsis. Do you speak our language, boy?" Ben asked calmly, placing two fingers on the child's head to turn its face toward him.

The thin, grey lips of the child offered a knowing grin but it refused to look at Ben. Felix sighed and opened a trunk, removing a convoluted armband fixed with thin wires and a pump. He slipped it over the Vemanen child's thin, pale arm and looked up, eyebrows raised at Ben who raised a finger back at him.

"We know you've had contact with the aspect of apathy. All we seek is information. Who is this aspect? Where did you meet it? Where can we find it? Tell us, and we'll leave. Ignore or lie to us, and we'll hurt you."

The child gave a weak smile as he stared blankly into the kitchen, listening intently to the flow of blood trickling out of his parents. Then, his pointy ears twitched. Ben nodded at Felix, who carefully poked the four wires into arteries and veins in the child's arm.

"All right. You go ahead and tell us whenever you're ready to talk."

Ben nodded at Felix once more to signal him to begin. Felix pumped air into the device and Breowakoe witnessed the dark grey, steel fibres forge upstream, ripping through the blood vessel walls and tearing into the flesh beyond. Breowakoe looked away as the experience, even second hand, made him cringe with ghost pains. The child, however, did not scream. A comfortable smirk rested on its face as he swayed his head from side to side in time with the pumping wires.

"What's going on? Why isn't it working?" Felix masked his fear with frustration.

Ben said nothing and stared down at the child's smiling face. The child halted its swaying and perked up. Its pointy ears twitched mechanically again, as though acting independently. Felix stopped pumping. The child slowly turned his head and with his vacant eyes stared past Ben. The smirk broke into a disturbed smile once again.

"They're here!" the Vemanen child crooned.

Ben's eyes peeled wide and the heads of the men spun wildly to reassess their surroundings. A cragged wall of grey had amassed outside the small windows in the front and back of the house. The poisonous gaze of hundreds of yellow eyes peered at them through the openings, but the Vemanen stood perfectly still.

"Breo, get in the corner with that child; we aren't done with him yet!"

Felix, Logan, Shane, and Ben all simultaneously scrambled for the rifles on their backs and positioned themselves strategically around the room.

"Back door's still wide open!" Logan called out, backing

into a corner of the kitchen.

"Is the front locked?" Felix yelled.

"No time to check; guess we'll just have to find out! BREO! MOVE NOW!" Ben growled, as he worked himself into a divot in the wall between the kitchen and living room.

Felix took the side opposite Ben, and Shane pressed his back to the wall near the corner where Breowakoe now shuffled, dragging with him the Vemanen child strapped to a chair.

A deafening shriek sounded in the air before Breowakoe could settle himself, and the sensation of falling took hold of his heart.

"What is that!?" he asked but soon realized no one could hear him.

Grey, spindly arms erupted from the window. Shane sidestepped quickly to avoid being pierced by the sickle-like fingers. Felix was first to start shooting, aiming his gun at a spot behind the wall that Breowakoe couldn't see; the look on Felix's face suggested a terrifying presence. Logan was next to start shooting as the front door burst open with a loud crack. Breowakoe could see the massive, limber creatures pouring in like a fluid – their speed inhibited somewhat by the mechanics of their group movements in close quarters. Piles of bodies began building in the doorways, spilling out into the living room and kitchen as the fury of the living Vemanen drove forward, slicing through their deceased comrades to reach their enemies.

Logan and Felix needed to reload simultaneously. The onslaught did not waver and Shane found himself shooting across the room to cover Logan, Ben to cover Felix. Shane had perfect aim, instantly shooting each Vemanen in the head as it approached Logan.

Vemanen pressing through the back door, first targeted Felix but soon realized they needed to stop Shane and Ben. As hissing Vemanen broke free of the stream and charged towards Ben, he was unable to cover the other side of the room. One Vemanen dove across the room with fingers extended to slice Shane's arm off at the elbow, as though it were cutting through a ripe fruit. Felix, having just reloaded, drew his rifle and shot the creature down instantly. Shane looked panicked as he reached for the gun lying on the ground in front of him, the hand of his disconnected arm still lightly gripping it. With his left hand he raised the gun to see that across the room Logan had reloaded and was holding his own. Shane hit the deck and crawled under the stream of Felix's fire to join Logan in the other room. Breowakoe, feeling helpless, shuffled to try to get even deeper into the corner with the child.

The assault continued and a heap of corpses on the ground became increasingly more amorphous. Atomized blood coated the walls like spray paint and the razor-sharp appendages of the living Vemanen thrashed the corpses to a pulp in the stampede. The ooze spread to coat the floor under Breowakoe's feet.

"I'm almost out of ammo!" Felix called out as the screeching finally stopped, leaving only the sounds of gunfire, falling bodies, and sloppy gore.

"I think we all are!" Ben called back. "BUT WE WILL SUSTAIN WITH MACHETES!"

Ben dropped his rifle to the floor and in one swift motion took and armed his machete, brought the blade up, and lunged at an approaching Vemanen's chest. The creature, who had been unprepared, squealed in pain as the blade went through.

"Breo, get over here and help! We've got to keep them in the choke point," Felix yelled as he ran up to the doorway with Ben who looked ready to lunge at another Vemanen.

To Breowakoe's horror, the Vemanen raised its arm lazily and thrust its long claw at Ben's face. It made contact before Ben was even close to it, piercing both his eyes and continuing to push to the back of the skull.

Ben's bellowing was high in pitch and rough.

A narrow little grin started on the Vemanen's face. Felix lunged in to stab it through the chest. In shock, the Vemanen lurched its arm back, dragging Ben's head with it. Ben's roars ripped through the air and his arms moved about as if searching on their own for an end to his suffering. Felix stabbed the Vemanen again, unintentionally causing it to bring its wrist down hard – slicing down through Ben's brain and all the bones of his face with its impossibly sharp fingers. The flesh around Ben's chin tore away from the bone and flapped back down over it as his body collapsed to the floor.

The shooting on the other side of the room had stopped, as well, but while close to the door Breowakoe didn't dare to look. A Vemanen was approaching them fast. It lunged and took a swing at Felix who quickly pivoted, cutting off its arm, then sliced it up from its belly to its throat. Felix looked over at Breowakoe and held a finger to his lips with wide eyes. It was then that Breowakoe remembered the creatures' blindness and realized that his panicked, heavy breathing was making him easier to detect. He shut up. In the silence, Breowakoe and Felix stood in the doorway stealthily slicing away at hostile Vemanen. Logan screamed from the kitchen, Breowakoe whirled around to see him cornered, the blades of a Vemanen's fingertips in his gut. Another two Vemanen joined in the fun, shoving their fingers through Logan's gut and lifting him into the air. Blood spilled from Logan's mouth; he stared down at his predicament in disbelief. The Vemanen smiled. They lifted Logan straight above their heads, pushing him through the ceiling and letting his soft internal organs slide down over their hands.

"BREO!" Felix screamed, diving to cut off the hand of a Vemanen that was only a few feet away.

Breowakoe stabbed the Vemanen in the neck and chest realizing he had foolishly stopped paying attention. Cleverly, however, Felix took two steps back so the Vemanen entering the room lunged pre-emptively forward to meet the air, then his blade. Breowakoe felt his arm beginning to tire, but he dared not quit. A figure caught his peripheral vision to the left and he swerved to look at it.

"Has Shane fallen? No..."

Shane had moved back to the living room entrance as the next natural choke point on his retreat. A guttural blubbering sounded. Three massive talons had gone straight through Felix's throat from the side Breowakoe should have been guarding. Blood splashed onto his face and Breowakoe backed away in shock. This was it. In moments he would die a violent death at the hands of these horrible creatures he'd learned of only earlier that day. He would die in the company of comrades he barely knew but whose company he had grown to appreciate and skill he had come to respect.

The Vemanen slowed their pace. The herd was thinner as they entered the house but there was still a small army waiting outside. They smelled the air and flicked their ears, searching for him with their arms extended. They would find him in a matter of seconds; he had backed himself into the corner and hid behind the child who sat still in his wooden chair. Looking out from behind it, he could see Shane battling Vemanen in the doorway to the living room and that Shane had not realized the living room was compromised. Vemanen poured through the doorway Breowakoe should have been defending, lunging toward Shane's unguarded back. Shane jumped back and sliced the lunging Vemanen's head clean off. He was the most skilled of this crew. He fought silently and with a nuanced physical coordination that meant none of his movements were wasted. He stood in the centre of the room combating assailants on all sides. Breowakoe's heart was pounding, he wanted to believe Shane could win, but he was too cowardly to help.

"Kaimaradan... please... give me your thripsis. We can still make it; I can beat these guys."

Kaimaradan said nothing. He could not feel fear from her and supposed that she was confident in her own ability to survive. This whole ordeal was likely nothing more than amusement for her.

Breowakoe rose to his feet in a moment of indecision. In his peripheral vision, Shane saw him rise but had thought himself the last Nethriel alive. Terrified that a Vemanen had made its way that far behind him, he whirled and thrust his knife towards Breowakoe's chest. As a reflex, Breowakoe brought his blade upward, slicing off Shane's hand. The two stared at one another in horror for a moment. The silent second passed and four Vemanen simultaneously pierced Shane's head, neck, and chest before ripping him apart in every direction.

"So, this really is the end."

Breowakoe trembled where he stood. Contemplating the magnitude of his failure and the injustice of his trial, he realized he had been helpless from the start. He wanted to give up, to just die violently - and this is what he felt he deserved. He hated Tiricora for tempting him, and all the monsters who in his short time in this place had used him for entertainment. But the hatred that burned deepest inside Breowakoe was hatred of himself: for his weakness, for allowing his comrades to die. He couldn't stop the immensity of it building in his chest. A violent death was too good for him. He trembled no longer from fear but from the intense, unquenchable desire to kill himself and everything around him, to destroy everything, to erase all the disgusting creatures that had so violently, sadistically murdered his friends.

Breowakoe stepped in front of the chair. His body shuddered and every tiny hair stood on end; he felt heavy, as though the weight of his hatred was physically crushing everything in the room. He swung his blade rapidly side-to-side as he dove towards the wicked creatures. The air in the room churned and became hot. He could feel a peculiar energy transmitting down the length of his arms and leaving his body.

With his blade still two feet from the nearest Vemanen, he felt a slight resistance and the creature's torso exploded. Its blood boiled and vaporized instantly as scorched shards of bone blasted backward and sideways into the oncoming Vemanen. The cinders combusted on their dry, grey skin, setting them aflame. As the blade tore through the air, thickening the blood-mist, the room's clay walls shook. Boiling blood seared the eyes of the Vemanen approaching the doorway and a hail of flaming bone fragments made a paste of those that breached the room.

The Vemanen picked up their pace and extended their arms fully to pierce him but they could not get near him, let alone make contact. There was a chorus of shrill screeching and within moments all had retreated. The inside of the house looked like a recreation of the lower Squalor with flesh and sinew and bone welded together into an inconsistent heap of corpse.

Breowakoe stood, panting and surveying the destruction. He was now aware of the aspect of hatred, and could feel its thripsis in the atmosphere - and under his skin. He could distinguish it from Kaimaradan's thripsis. The Vemanen child still strapped to the chair was gasping behind him, slowly dying in heat, drowning in the blood vapour. Breowakoe swept him to the back door and outside.

"Th-that feeling... that was the same... You're an aspect, too? Like Globramora?" the child asked, its bio-luminescent yellow eyes looking up at Breowakoe.

"Who is Globramora?" Breowakoe asked, repressing his surprise that after all that had happened, the mission would continue. The child looked down again and with a sombre voice continued.

"I was playing with my friends... last week, in the tar sands -"

"Where in the tar sands?" Breowakoe asked authoritatively.

The child looked downstream.

"Right here, at the edge. The winds picked up, and I could feel the same prickly feeling I felt in there just now. A cone formed in the ground and the sand under our feet became quicksand. Then, with a roar, Globramora, the sand demon, rose out of its centre and grabbed a hold of us. I was imbued with its thripsis but managed to get away. My friend, however, was consumed by the monster." The child spoke beyond his years and finished the story matter-of-factly. He was truly touched by apathy.

"Thank you," Breowakoe said after a pause. "You're free to go." He turned toward the truck to see it was still there but vandalized.

"Wait..." the child spoke up. Breowakoe turned again. "Please just kill me."

Breowakoe took a moment to register what he had heard, but did not question it for a moment. The child looked briefly surprised, and its ears twitched.

"Ah, there it is... the lyre... the bone child plays for me. May you find what you're seeking in this world, Nethriel." The blank stare on the creature's face remained as its head landed next to its feet. The clean stroke of the blade had made for a quick death.

Breowakoe walked to the truck, perplexed. Despite its ravaged aesthetics he found it to be functional. The night was calm as he drove back through the desert. In silence, he stewed in his thoughts through the rest of that long, haunting night.

-

At dawn, Breowakoe found himself standing before

Tiricora, his blood-soaked body dripping onto her carpet. She was silent as he recounted the events of the night. It was not difficult to tell he was being sincere, and she offered him a bunk on a lower floor of her tower.

"You did well. Sleep for the morning and prepare yourself. Tomorrow evening you'll join me on an elite patrol. Once I have the aspect of apathy, you will have your reward."

Breowakoe barely remembered that he had been doing all this for essence of the Planelands. He descended the elevator and located the room to which he had been given a key. He showered in the small, but clean bathroom. He lay down in the small, but comfortable bed. He snapped off the lights and remained in the dark, staring at the ceiling.

Ten minutes went by without a sound or any hope of sleep.

"*The great eye you slew, 'Raityuria - The Cultivator,' had been the aspect of hatred since Ervalui spawned. His optic nerve, that rushed up from the ground, is invincible. None could touch Raityuria, for his vulnerable eye existed in a dimension of his own creation, 'The Squalor,' wherein he shared his hatred with the inhabitants of the overworld.*"

Breowakoe stared deeper into the dark. He wanted to

scold Kaimaradan for leaving him for dead, but she was not his friend, and as she was offering him information, he thought it best not to interrupt her.

"*The aspect of hatred mobilizes all the thrae of Ervalui, summoning and commanding it with ease.*"

Kaimaradan sounded as though she were herself in awe.

"*I never imagined it would generate such intense, unquenchable heat or that it could compress thripsis into the extension of a blade. You are a fortunate child, indeed, to have awakened your aspect when you did.*"

She began to jab her legs into him. As a reflex, Breowakoe flexed the muscle he had only just learned to use. A steady stream of thripsis collected and circled the bed as he targeted the creature inside him. Kaimaradan flinched for a moment, then laughed.

"*You had me going for a second, my arrogant boy. But you still cannot control your aspect well enough to defy me!*"

A burst of thripsis from Kaimaradan dispelled what Breowakoe had summoned. She writhed for five minutes to punish him; he jolted and screamed as she struck nerves but held his own. The two were silent once his punishment had ended and a sleepless hour of silent resentment passed.

"What is the bone child, Kaimaradan? You mentioned it at that couple's shack." Breowakoe stared into the infinite distance. "The Vemanen child really did seem to be haunted by something he heard, or even saw, moments before his death."

Breowakoe could feel Kaimaradan sigh within him.

"The bone child is a glitch in the Spoil."

"A glitch..." he repeated.

"Yes. It is said that during the ten seconds before death in this place, one sees and hears the bone child, playing its lyre."

Breowakoe's blood went cold thinking about this mysterious entity.

"Did Shane see it?" he wondered. "He didn't seem surprised by it, if he did..."

"It appears for all, the bone child will have appeared to him, but in the commotion he may not have noticed it. All those countless Vemanen will have seen it, too."

Breowakoe again retreated into his own haunted thoughts.

"What if I see it, but then I change what I was going to do? By changing my actions, can I avoid dying?"

"This world holds many secrets that I may never know -

but I would guess that death is certain."

"I see."

He closed his dry eyes, and drifted off to sleep, uncomfortable in the desert heat, dreaming of the bone child.

The Indifference of Globramora - 6

Fully healed from the night's rest, Breowakoe investigated a loud knock on his door, which turned out to be Tiricora herself.

"Be in the underground lot in five minutes," she said crisply before whirling around and disappearing.

Breowakoe looked about the room. There was nothing there but a small cot and a crumpled sheet. He owned nothing in this world. His body was his only possession, and his claim to that was contested daily by the coiled creature inside him.

The warehouse doors cranked wide open and twelve armoured trucks rolled out into the street. People standing under Goliah's tallest tower stopped in their tracks as the patrol pushed past them.

Breowakoe imagined the spot where the tar sands met the edge of the Vemanen district. He wondered what Globramora, the aspect of apathy, looked like, and wondered if he could kill it himself.

"*Silly, arrogant boy. You think that because you released your thrae once you are Yoorkapala, the false god of death himself, do you?*"

"Well, that's not exactl -"

"Listen to me, Herilli... I will repeat once more what I told you last night. Make no mistake, the men who sit in this small cabin with you - indeed, every man, woman, and child in this city - are cattle, even before an unworthy, pampered, silly boy like you, spoiled by his happening upon an aspect right after leaving the wretched womb of life. But cross Tiricora, or me, or any aspect with a little experience in this world, and you shall die so fast the bone child will appear the night before."

Breowakoe stirred, wondering why Kaimaradan was so testy today.

"When one aspect kills another they possess two fractions of the Spoil. And yet, in all of time this has not occurred. So vulgar. Nothing good will come of this. It is a challenge to Verivoluae itself," Kaimaradan cautioned.

Breowakoe did think it distasteful the way Tiricora sought power, but his participation was necessary. He hoped the essence of the Planelands would guide him to some forgotten truth.

Their caravan of trucks, upon reaching the outer wall of the Vemanen district, turned left to continue downstream through the Nethriel suburb. This meant they would be travelling through a war zone, but Tiricora had now evidently realized the true danger of the Vemanen district - that it was not as it once was. It was a rough ride, but the active battleground had been cleverly avoided by travelling this far starboard. Several hours later they arrived at the place where the last few houses in the Vemanen district fed into the vast desert. Breowakoe peered out the window, looking for the body of the child he slew. It had disappeared. Tiricora's voice came over the radio.

"Is this the place, Breo?"

"Yes," he replied sullenly.

Three of the trucks pulled up to the edge of the tar sands. The truck ahead of Breowakoe's turned off to the left and his shortly followed, veering off into the desert, as well.

"Wait, where are we going?" Breowakoe called up to the faceless thug driving.

The thug in the front passenger seat responded. "She wants us guarding the outskirts in case anything comes out of the desert."

Breowakoe felt a twinge of anxiety.

"Why would anything come out of the desert?"

"Orders are orders, man - just calm down."

He reluctantly obeyed.

"She wants to keep 'Globramora' out of your reach lest you steal her prize."

"You know the aspect of apathy?" Breowakoe thought.

"He is an old rival. A King of another ancient race, the Blonaks. I once despised him, but now I empathize; he and I have much in common," Kaimaradan mused.

They came to a halt, and soldiers bled from every opening of the truck. Breowakoe casually followed, not having been ordered to do anything. The wind was slight and the heat, blistering. The five men spread out into positions on all sides of the vehicle – guns at the ready - and one climbed to the top of the truck to give himself more of a lookout. Breowakoe walked out a ways into the vast desert. Enough sand was being juggled up by the wind that he couldn't see the port wall, nor the ceiling, not even the starboard wall near to them. The fine grains stung his eyes and he turned back, looking now towards the tar sands where Tiricora walked alone, ahead of twenty armed men.

It was difficult to discern one face from another at this distance, but Breowakoe could tell Tiricora apart from the others by her thriptic presence. He took another moment to focus on the thripsis around him: he was still easily aware of his own, of Kaimaradan's, Tiricora's a little further away, and many great volumes that hung in the air from unknown sources. The greatest mass of all from Verivoluae, which by sand was also shielded from view. There was another decent-sized presence that he detected from upstream of port and another far away downstream that was nearly masked by Verivoluae. Breowakoe wondered if these were other aspects.

The energies changed rapidly as another massive presence suddenly revealed itself starboard. Breowakoe looked up, his heart rate elevated, but saw nothing. Tiricora had taken a fighting stance and Breowakoe could make out traces of muffled yelling. She must have felt it, too. This novel mass of thripsis was moving on Tiricora under the tar sands.

"He is confronting her directly? Has he gone mad?" Kaimaradan puzzled.

A large, dark circle was emerging a few metres away from Tiricora. The tar sands within the boundary appeared to be becoming wet and, slowly, a monstrous creature emerged. It looked like a heap of thick sludge three times the height of Tiricora and a diameter half its height.

Globramora roared to release a visible shockwave, and in moments a blast of hot wind seared Breowakoe's skin. The twenty men who had been standing behind Tiricora were screaming, steam coming out of their mouths and eyes. They had collapsed and were writhing on the ground. The men around Breowakoe were grunting in pain, as well, their skin starting to melt where uncovered. He stared on in awe, realizing that the aspect of the Spoil within him made him resistant to the thripsis of others. Breowakoe gazed back over to the battlefield, newly interested in how Tiricora was fairing.

She appeared completely unharmed, despite having tanked the blast at close range. Tiricora was striking the air with her index fingers pointed towards Globramora. Each thrust of her fingers focused her thripsis into a visible thread. The energy shot through Globramora like bullets, but he seemed unphased. His large, goopy arms swung heavily at Tiricora and she flipped gracefully high into the air over them. Globramora pounded the ground as she landed; Tiricora had trouble breaking her fall properly. Globramora tried to grab her, but with a fine thriptic wind she cut off his hand.

"Eyes to the desert! Something's coming!" the guy on the truck yelled.

Breowakoe felt his blood pressure rise as he wondered what had brought the war so far downstream. It was hard to take his eyes off the battle in front of him, but he turned to face the desert. He could still see only the blowing sand. He listened intently, but couldn't hear anything other than the battle behind him and the breeze. Oh - but there *was* something: he noticed a steady buzzing noise, it sounded like a swarm of insects.

"Grobut patrol incoming! Shoot to kill!" The man on the truck sounded panicked as he climbed into a prone position and readied his weapon.

"What? Grobut?" Breowakoe thought, realizing there were still unfamiliar threats in this place.

The sound of buzzing grew louder and louder, and the soldier in the front started firing his rifle as the man on the truck followed. Breowakoe squinted as dark figures began to emerge from the cloak of sand like spectral beings in a room of billowing curtains.

They were hideous beasts. Their dirty-grey bodies had the wings and eyes of a house fly; the horns of a bull; and wide mouths with large, human-type teeth. Rigid, black insect hairs protruded from bare and muscular humanoid chests, from their two sets of arms and hands – many of which were armed with hatchets - and from their legs that ended in hooves. From their behinds protruded something that looked like an elephant trunk or flattened insect abdomen; was it some sort of distended anus? Or was this their sex organ?

There was little time to wonder. Bullets tore through the flesh of a Grobut eye, and its wide mouth contorted unpleasantly as the beast collapsed to the ground. Breowakoe quickly counted that there were eleven more. The Grobut began to bellow a sort of war cry, and they flew faster towards the makeshift human outpost.

"Protect Tiricora at all costs!" the man on the truck screamed.

Bullets hurtled from all the guns, now, ripping three more Grobut apart. Breowakoe tried to take a fighting stance, readying himself for the unknown. A Grobut leading the charge held a hatchet between its legs, as the tip of its abdomen pushed through from behind to deposit some sort of milky liquid onto the blade. He hurled it at the Nethriel soldier crouching at the front of their formation. The axe made its way into the side of his head and he rolled onto his back, muscles twitching spastically. An axe flying from an unknown direction struck Breowakoe in the ribs, and he flinched in shock. To his luck, much of the force was absorbed by one of

Kaimaradan's armoured legs. The axe did not make it in deep, and instead fell to the sand. With adrenaline pumping, now, Breowakoe looked up to scan for additional incoming projectiles.

In the instant he had been distracted, carnage had become of his squad mates. The man behind him was coughing up blood, an axe buried in his gut. Three Grobut were pounding on the soldier to Breo's right, ripping the man's limbs off to the tune of guttural despair. An axe was buried in the head of the soldier on the truck. A Grobut knelt over the man, dragging the corpse's head into position by the axe handle and sliding its insectoid abdomen into the corpse's mouth. Similar horrors played out upon the soldiers at the front and on the left. A Grobut was going crazy with two hatchets, hacking a man to pieces.

Two Grobut were buzzing toward Breowakoe, devilish grins on their faces. He readied himself, breathing deeply, but to his surprise could not feel the flow of his own thripsis, or any thripsis, for that matter. He tried to summon the heat and the energy he had when dealing with the Vemanen, but it was lost. A feeling of dread came over him and he turned to flee.

"Ooo, do you feel that? This one is special. Bring him.

He stays alive!" a voice growled behind him.

Four hands grabbed his arms and he was lifted into the air. Again, he tried desperately to summon his thripsis, but it would not come. Breowakoe kicked off the sand, trying to free himself, but the bugs flew higher and he lost contact with the ground.

"That's enough struggling, Nethriel, don't make me cut your legs off," the deep voice growled again.

The horror of the sacked outpost came into view as Breowakoe was carried off into the sandstorm, the soldier on the truck looked sickeningly bloated, no doubt with that abdominal bile. His expression made it evident that he had been alive when it was forced into him. Breowakoe was deeply disturbed but could not look away. Somehow, it was the most horrific thing he had ever seen, topping the writhing husks of the Squalor and even witnessing a centipede make his body its home.

In the distance, the enormous body of Globramora collapsed. The light in the long hallway that was the Spoil turned blue. Breowakoe turned toward Verivoluae as the Grobut that carried him landed and did the same. It was as though all in this world dropped whatever they were doing to witness this rare cosmic event. Even through the sandstorm they could see that its light pulsed from its natural orange to blue. A deep horn sounded, blowing away the sandstorm in an instant. A physical wave could be seen travelling upstream along the sand and shaking the rock walls and ceiling of the Spoil itself. Far away, Tiricora was lifted into a small tornado of wind and sand and then was set back to the ground. The next instant, Verivoluae resumed its orange hue, and the Grobut lifted Breowakoe into the air again.

"*Well... she has done it, that crone. The aspect of apathy is hers,*" Kaimaradan whispered in disgust, unconcerned with Breowakoe's predicament.

Exhausted, he was carried further downstream than he had ever been before.

Bile Inoculum - 7

Breowakoe was carried to a camp of two large, burlap tents that bunked six Grobut each. The Grobut took him to a large boulder downstream from the tents and dropped him face-first onto the sand. His arms were completely asleep and he struggled to pick himself up. From the corner of his eye, he could see two Grobut fly off even deeper downstream.

"Get the chains," one of his captors snarled at another, who buzzed into a tent.

The Grobut lifted him up by the left arm and pinned him against the boulder. Breowakoe sized him up. Like the others, this disgusting fly creature was about a foot taller than he and looked heavy. Knowing he would not be able to take on a demon of this size without using thripsis, Breowakoe closed his eyes. The sensation of thripsis had returned to him, but his connection to it remained mysteriously weak. He could feel his own mass of thripsis and, strangely, a small mass of thripsis from within the Grobut grabbing him. He tried to avoid looking at the demon so as not to arouse suspicion. This Grobut behaved like a common foot soldier, but was he an aspect? No... after focusing more intently Breowakoe realized that each Grobut scuttling around the camp had a small mass of thripsis stored within it. It didn't matter, as he could feel that his own was the greater power.

Breowakoe planned to take his captor by surprise. He slowed his breathing, letting the thripsis amass inside himself. But a jarring blow to the face broke his nose as his head clashed with the boulder behind it. Breowakoe was concussed, his vision blurred. The Grobut had released his arm but now grasped the top of his head, forcing Breowakoe to look up toward the rock ceiling.

"Nice try, Nethriel, but we can sense thripsis, too."

Breowakoe's ears were ringing; it sounded as though he were listening from underwater. A wet putrid substance slapped across his face, stinging his eyes and flooding his mouth and nose. Breowakoe squinted to see his captor holding its own abdomen with one of its lower arms, forcing it toward Breowakoe's face. The same milky substance he had earlier seen the Grobut coat their axes with was dripping onto the sand beneath him. He collapsed forward, vomiting up some of the bile he had accidentally swallowed. He panted, unable to feel his thripsis anymore - he could not even feel Verivoluae.

"So, it's a poison that cuts me off from thripsis," Breowakoe realized.

The Grobut lifted him from the sand and pinned him face-first against the rock. Another joined him and fastened Breowakoe's chest to the boulder with chains. The Grobut leaned in behind him so that he could feel the demon's hot, stinking breath coating his ear in a film. The dry skin and prickly hairs of the beast's face brushed Breowakoe's cheek and neck.

"You Nethriel men never know your place," he chuckled into Breowakoe's ear, taking a twisted delight in his own moment of power.

Anxiety climbed as Breowakoe realized how vulnerable he was.

"I can tell you've never seen a Grobut before. But let me tell you, to the Grobut, you Nethriel are livestock. I never even thought to count how many Nethriel men I have eaten, just as you don't bother to count the plump little chickens you consume. Nothing would please me more than to rip off your head and pump my fallow eggs into your carcass."

The Grobut slapped and grabbed Breowakoe's rump. Breowakoe was trembling. He could not believe this was happening again, and so soon. It had been only a few days since he escaped the couple's living room in Goliah. He had learned to harness a great power inside him but here he was, right back in the same helpless position.

"Kaimaradan... please help me," he whispered in thought.

"Once, we were on a raid to a village in the starboard lands," the beast behind Breowakoe continued. "I thought I might have more fun if I veered away from the swarm and to a house at the back of the village. I kicked open the door and a Nethriel man charged me, carrying a pitchfork; he was about your size, actually. I kicked him at the knee and he fell, legs broken; you should have heard the screams, spectacular. He tried to hide his babes from me. He was like you. He also knew nothing of the Grobut. We can see heat, warm little bodies - even through the trap door where they cowered."

The Grobut slobbered on Breowakoe's shoulder as he laughed.

"Kaimaradan... Don't ignore me. Do not let this happen to me again. I won't forgive you if you let this happen."

"*It is hardly my concern, needy boy - leave me be.*"

"Why are you acting like you're busy? You're just sitting there? Why? Help me and we can make him suffer. Wouldn't that be more entertaining to you, anyway?"

"*I do enjoy suffering, but yours will suffice.*"
Kaimaradan chuckled.

"You bitch..." Breowakoe scowled, tears filling his eyes.

"I ripped the babes from their mother's arms. First I devoured the infant boy..." the Grobut behind him growled on. "In a bite, I took his head. It was bitter and I spat it to the floor, so daddy could get a closer look. I sucked the blood from the body but it was so small, I knew it couldn't satiate my hunger. Instead, I took his little girl, I could see in his eyes how much he loved her, how much she meant to him. I bit her hand off at the wrist and enjoyed its crunch; I did the same with her feet. Her mother tried to fight me, and I wrestled her to the ground. The Nethriel man, that cocky Nethriel man that thought to stand up to me, the noises he made as his wife imbibed my bile, sputtering. It was all so delectable. I returned to my meal, sitting on the floor in front of that broken Nethriel man. Bite by bite, like a bear I ate his daughter alive. He recognized the power of the Grobut, then. He begged me to give him death but I let him be. I knew he would finish the cleansing himself. But before I left him, I located his nest... do you know what that is?"

Breowakoe said nothing. He was barely even listening to

this filth.

"It is the part of your warm Nethriel bodies where our King likes to lay his eggs, and where his flylets grow."

The Grobut pulled down Breowakoe's pants. Breowakoe flinched and tensed, so dreading of what he knew was coming.

"Those of us who are not King, drones we're called. We are sterile, and even in the warmth of a Nethriel our eggs will not grow. But the bile we produce still has many subversive effects on your species, some of which you've already noted. Well, why don't I show you what I mean." He giggled.

Breowakoe now had stress tears streaming down his cheeks, and the hatred he had for this creature was cosmic.

"Kaimaradan, I swear on my life I will feed you to Tiricora if you let this happen to me! I DON'T care about my own life. I will offer us both to her. I will take great pleasure in watching her tear you from my chest and rip your legs off one by one. I hope she segments you and boils you alive, you disgusting, sick creature. I have nothing but contempt for you."

"*Idle threats, boy, enjoy your rape.*" Kaimaradan whispered coldly, as Breowakoe could feel the Grobut positioning behind him.

"You cowardly bitch, what do you even want? Where are

the rest of your people? You were their Queen, weren't you? Is this how you sat idly by as they died? Queen of the heap."

"Herilli, how dare you... HOW DARE YOU! Yours was the cowardice that created this mess."

Breowakoe could feel that he had really struck a chord; she truly felt angry.

"You have no notion of leadership. I will not be compared to you - you sicken ME, you pathetic, disgusting, weak man."

Kaimaradan was losing control of her emotions - he could feel it - the deep sadness and pain within her. She writhed inside him and he screamed, twisting his spine on the tight chains that held him. He could feel her shear deeper past the muscle tissue in his chest and could feel something scrape past his rib. Was she killing him, was this it? In panic, he remembered the bone child and looked up thinking he would see it.

Kaimaradan's tongue poked into the left ventricle of his heart, and from it a cold liquid was dispensed into his blood. Time seemed to freeze as Breowakoe went into shock. The Grobut behind him grabbed at his shoulders timidly, evidently never having seen a Satrian under a Nethriel man's skin. The tortuous substance quickly traveled throughout Breowakoe's body, chilling him and leaving a painful prickle. He could feel his thripsis again and released it immediately, shredding the chain that held him.

"Thank you," he thought, surprised that Kaimaradan had actually chosen to help him.

Breowakoe whirled around. The Grobut behind him looked alarmed, and Breowakoe noticed that the thriptic presence he had felt inside the beast before had now nearly disappeared. His former captor swung its many arms, but they landed like soft kisses. The monster flew into the air a metre and tried squirting its bile into Breowakoe's face again. The liquid landed, but it seemed whatever Kaimaradan had done was making him immune to the bile's effects. Breowakoe grabbed the hoof of the Grobut and dragged him back down, turned him around and ripped off his wings. Five other Grobut were running out of the tents, hurling axes in Breowakoe's direction. He calmed his breathing as Kaimaradan had taught him, then roared a shockwave of hot air, more focused than Globramora's had been, if less powerful. The axes were repelled, the blast expanded and struck the wings of three Grobut, lighting them aflame. They began screaming and rolling on the ground to put the fire out. Breowakoe grabbed the bulbous eyes of the howling Grobut who had tried to rape him and fed his thripsis into them. Their humours boiled, and the creature's eyes burst. The Grobut screamed in anguish.

"You should hear your screams - spectacular!" Breowakoe mocked, reaching inside the sockets to boil its brain.

It died more quickly than Breowakoe had hoped but now five more Grobut were closing on him, two in the sky and three on the ground. He practiced the measured breathing again; he could feel the aspect of hatred within him becoming aroused. He could feel the limitless energy it generated within him and he opened it fully to the hell that had created it.

Thripsis poured out of Breowakoe's body in every direction, the two Grobut in flight fell out of the sky into the fetal position on the ground. Breowakoe had become a massive source of ionizing radiation. The Grobut exoskeletons made them resistant to the heat, but this more violent energy could penetrate even deeper, to boil their guts. The three Grobut that had been charging him on the ground also doubled over. The range of this hot energy was about ten metres in all directions from its now formidable source. Breowakoe stopped channeling and pointed at the nearly dead Grobut before him, as it still tried to crawl away. The energy was more intense when channeled in a straight line. The carapaces of the Grobut caught fire and rolled back through the sand in the hot wind before taking root, lifeless, twenty-five metres away.

Breowakoe cut the flow of his thripsis and walked to peer into the first burlap tent, ensuring all were dead. There was nothing of interest inside, plain mattress bunks with metal trunks at their feet. He wondered if they had carried all these things by hand to this outpost, and from where?

The soft wind of a flying axe graced Breowakoe's neck as it narrowly missed him. In a panic he channeled thripsis and turned around. Behind him, and to the side of the rock he had been chained to, was a large carriage with prison bar windows. It was being driven by enormous stag beetles twice the size of a Grobut. Two more Grobut were buzzing toward him, the two that had initially flown off downstream when they first arrived.

Swiping his hand through the air, Breowakoe released a thread of energy that scorched the eyes of both Grobut, leaving them blind. Another axe was thrown in his direction but was wildly off target. One of the Grobut was descending, afraid to fly blind and Breowkaoe pointed a finger at it. This time

Breowakoe allowed the thripsis to build up in his finger *before* discharging it. The energy was so dense it was visible when finally released. It punched a hole straight through the torso of the Grobut. Breowakoe repeated this on the other Grobut, disintegrating its head.

The door of the caravan opened and Breowakoe pointed at it, charging up once again. A Grobut stepped out, but this one was different - he wore colourful robes and was clasping both pairs of his hands together. He looked as though he might have hailed from an academic or scholarly caste of the demons. Breowakoe held the thripsis at the tip of his finger but delayed its fire. A Nethriel woman then stepped out of the caravan. She was wearing a short dress and had a collar around her neck. From his brief encounter with the Grobut, Breowakoe immediately had a pretty good idea of the kind of life she lived.

"You must be the aspect of hatred," the scholarly Grobut started. "I am Turia – a forager Grobut, and this is Mischa. We are servants of Coabra Grona, King of Gol Paqua."

Breowakoe's finger remained pointed at the Grobut, as he half considered attempting to rescue the Nethriel woman.

"Be patient. Listen to what they have to say first, you

dense child..." Kaimaradan whispered.

"I want to apologize on behalf of King Grona for how our drones treated you. They are brutes, to be sure, without the ability to recognize excellence in a Nethriel. I am pleased you put them down. We would like to invite you to visit Gol Paqua to meet our beloved King, under his protection going forward, of course."

Breowakoe felt anxious, he didn't want to make this decision. He didn't want to make any decisions. He just wanted to return to Goliah and collect the capsule of essence from Tiricora.

"Why?" he asked plainly.

The Nethriel woman, Mischa, smiled. "He admires strength, being the aspect of power himself. He can offer you a good life, as he offers to all Nethriel who strive towards the glory of Gol Paqua."

"I'm already working for Tiricora in Goliah," Breowakoe retorted. "I have a bounty I need to return to collect from her."

"*Tiricora has no intention of giving you a thing, naive one.*" Kaimaradan rolled her beady little eyes. "*With two aspects one becomes exponentially more powerful; she will kill us without thought. She is selfish and has no intention of keeping her word.*"

Breowakoe's instincts told him she was right.

"So you think I should go with them?" he asked aloud.

The Grobut and the woman picked up on his hesitation. The woman piped up again.

"You would have a room in the palace, Master Grona is very good to those of us who serve him directly. You will be of a higher caste than most and, and -"

"- And you will not be subjected to the bile. You will remain a free man. You will be allowed to leave whenever you wish," the scholarly Grobut finished her thought.

Breowakoe put his finger down but kept the thripsis charged throughout his body.

"So, you think I should do this?" Breowakoe thought.

"*Must I make every decision for you? Do you think I am your mother? Tiricora is a death sentence - I will tell you that much - but after that, exercise a little agency.*" Kaimaradan snapped.

Breo ruminated a little longer.

"All right. My name is Breowakoe. I will meet your King. But if you try to betray me, I will kill you."

He tried to sound threatening. He felt he had no choice

but to go with these strangers, but had learned the importance of perceived power.

"A pleasure to make your acquaintance, Breowakoe. I would have it no other way!" Turia placated.

Breo climbed into the caravan and sat next to Turia, while Mischa sat across, smiling at him intermittently throughout the three-hour ride. Mischa was attractive, but there was also something disturbing and uncomfortable about her, something underhandedly wicked that even the monster beside him did not seem to possess.

The Way of Service - 8

The light of the sun was fading as their caravan finally came to a halt. A pair of drones opened the door from the outside and bowed as Turia stepped out. Mischa got out next, and Breowakoe followed. He stretched his legs; the sand under his feet was surprisingly cool here. A looming presence caught his eye - to his left, a massive stone gate reaching 500 metres high and connecting to the port wall. He stared in awe at the massive steel grate securing the city.

"Welcome to Gol Paqua, the Kingdom of the Grobut." said Turia proudly, turning back to enjoy the look on Breowakoe's face.

Breo traced with his eyes the towering stone wall that extended far into the desert and out of view behind blowing sand. In the distance along the wall was a large building surrounded by what looked like a Nethriel village.

"What is that?" he asked, pointing to it.

"Ah, those are the Nethriel farms. Our species cannot survive without Nethriel. We need their bodies to gestate our King's eggs and they are also our primary food source. As mentioned, however, some Nethriel are considered to be a protected class, yourself included. Your safety is assured,"

Turia backtracked, hoping not to upset Breowakoe.

"How did you reproduce before Nethriel arrived in the Spoil?"

Breo was puzzled.

"Oh, Nethriel were here before we were. We were created when the Piccaros merged a Nethriel, a Satrian, and a Blonak into one being. We share a third of our DNA with you, incidentally."

Turia began taking slow steps toward the gate and indicated that Breowakoe should follow him.

"Interesting. Who are these Piccaros, anyway, and how many species did they create? I've encountered the Vemanen before, as well," he noted, hungry for the information that this scholarly Grobut was willing to provide.

"They are one of the three original demon races, the goblins. The smallest but perhaps the most cunning," Turia explained.

"I see."

"Your friend there would likely know more about them than I, however," Turia continued, gesturing to Breowakoe's abdomen.

Breo could feel a deep anger inside Kaimaradan at the

mention of the Piccaros. Their small party arrived at the foot of the massive metal bars.

"Behold the opening of the great gate!" Turia cried, as he raised his arms excitedly.

What must have been fifty drones flew out of the gate's interior from windows carved into the stone, taking positions along its base.

"No way..." Breowakoe started, under his breath, as the drones grasped the bottom of the gate.

"Oh yes!" Turia smiled. "As you may have noticed, we Grobut - even the drones - can amass a small amount of thripsis within ourselves to dispel at will."

Without warning, the fifty drones hoisted simultaneously. The power of their collective thripsis thrust the gate two metres into the air, leaving them depleted of energy. The top of the grate poked through the stone at the peak of the structure.

"The drones that work the gate are a sacred order; there are only 250 of them. They release pheromones that allow them to dispel their thripsis in unison, although it's a bit antiquated and ceremonial. Most travel over the wall is now done simply by flying."

"Unbelievable. That must be 10,000 square metres of metal! I don't think an aspect could lift that," Breowakoe remarked, being polite.

"Well, that depends on the aspect – come this way -" Turia led them through the gate, between the raised arms of the drones lifting it, and into the city. "- King Grona can throw it all the way to the top of the stone arch with the aspect of power," Turia finished.

"He is amazing," Mischa swooned.

"He can't maintain it, of course, and after a full discharge like that he wouldn't be much more useful than a drone in a fight. But he would never use it so carelessly."

"Why not?" Breowakoe asked, curious to know why a great King might not have some fun now and again.

"Because he would not recklessly leave himself vulnerable to challenge. Whoever is King of Gol Paqua necessarily holds the aspect of power, so to obtain it one must kill the previous King in unarmed combat - a duel we call the 'right of coronation.' We foragers serve the King directly and among our responsibilities is maintaining fairness in the violent transition of power. I, myself, witnessed King Grona defeat his predecessor, King Geru, in the arena. Geru was in his prime. We thought the succession would not come for years, but Coabra Grona's strength and combat intuition won him the throne. Even a clever drone with a well-placed thriptic blast can best a King with the power to destroy a city. King Grona is the fourth King of Goliah and I believe our strongest yet."

"How do you maintain fairness? How are foragers different from drones?" Breowakoe asked, looking around at the strange, clay buildings they were walking past.

"There is a 1 in 100,000 chance that a flylet will mature into a forager. We are sterile like the drones but responsible for ripening the bile of the drone who defeats the King; we hold the keys to Grobut fertility, and so we are as revered as the King. There are four of us, currently."

"I see."

Breowakoe drifted away from the conversation, peering beyond the row of clay buildings, as their party intersected with a dirt road. They were in a more commercial-looking area, and the colourful signs of several businesses caught his eye. One sign in particular stood out: "The Painted Slave," it read, and was bordered by pink, flashing lights. Something about it intrigued him, but a mysterious flutter in his heart told him it was wrong to look at it for too long.

The party approached an enormous stone staircase at the long foot of a monolithic palace. Its odd asymmetric proportions towered over the city. It looked like some sort of termite hill or ant colony in its design: twisting spires with bizarre gaps and windows. The staircase was not protected by a guardrail, of course, as the citizens of Gol Paqua could fly, but it was wide enough that staying near the middle posed no danger to the walking folk. Breo hadn't noticed he was falling behind when he saw Turia already climbing the steps.

"Come along, Breowakoe; our King awaits!" Mischa bossed. He was annoyed but obediently followed. After a great deal of climbing into the sky, they reached the palace gate. Breowakoe stopped again to look around. From this monstrous vantage the ceiling of the Spoil still looked far away, but he had a clear view of the city. Below, located centrally within the great wall, was a large, circular structure.

"What is that?" Breowakoe asked.

Turia turned. "Ah, that is our arena where battles take place to honour our King and Verivoluae, and where the right of coronation that I mentioned earlier is held."

"I see..."

Again, Breowakoe trailed off, staring into the distance where tiny dots of Grobut were flying over the wall. It was hard to make out, but some of the Grobut appeared to be carrying Nethriel. He turned away and was slightly startled by Turia who was standing behind him, watching.

"All right, sorry. Let's go," Breowakoe said.

Mischa was already kneeling in the foyer to the throne room as the large door opened. Two ceremonially armoured drones with battle axes stood on either side of Breowakoe as he entered, and the floor before him was tiled with what looked like the chitinous carapaces of dead Grobut. Turia looked over his shoulder at Breowakoe and gestured for him to step forward.

"My Lord, I present the aspect of hatred, Breowakoe!" Mischa cried theatrically, further deepening her bow.

Breo timidly stepped into the throne room. It was rectangular, about three times as wide as it was deep. The metal throne, pedestalized upon three stone steps, was surprisingly close to where he stood on the opposing, narrow side of the room. The enormous Grobut atop it rose to his feet. He was half again as tall as the average drone, and yet he looked a lot like one. His carapace was dusty and old-looking.

A score of sparingly dressed Nethriel women orbited the King. They stroked his legs as he stepped off the platform. The stones of the palace shook beneath his feet.

"Show some respect, and bow, Nethriel!" Mischa hissed, a scowl on her face.

Breowakoe glared at her, but again complied, lowering himself into an awkward bow.

"There's no need for that, Breowakoe. That will do Mischa, return to your chambers," King Grona said in a casually booming voice.

"Y-yes, right away, sir."

Breowakoe looked behind him to locate Turia, whom he had grown to like, but he was gone. King Grona walked right up to Breowakoe and stopped about a metre away, eyeing him up and down. From this close it was obvious that he was almost twice Breo's height.

"Does she call the shots, or do you?" the King opened, pointing to Breowakoe's chest.

"A bit of both, I guess," he replied.

King Grona just stared at him while lifting an arm quizzically, impatiently.

"What does that mean? You share control over your

body?"

"Oh... no, I mean, I have control over my own body. I just meant that I take her advice, sometimes," Breowakoe explained sheepishly.

The King of Gol Paqua looked down at him, and Breowakoe could feel his judgement. His thriptic presence was far and above the most imposing he had felt from any aspect or being he had encountered thus far. It took everything Breo had not to take a step back.

"And *you* killed that giant eye? Or was that her?"

"That was me, sir."

King Grona paused for another moment, then turned.

"Walk with me, boy."

Coabra Grona began walking down the length of the room and Breowakoe instinctively hurried to follow. A couple of the Nethriel women left their post at the throne and ran after the massive Grobut, trying to stroke the King's back or elbows, whatever they could do to be in contact with him.

"That's enough," he bid them, and they scurried back disappointed and worried.

Breowakoe felt alarmed at their behavior. They seemed truly brainwashed, as though they had eyes for nothing in the world but their King.

King Grona chuckled to himself, "It's my ripened bile - it brings out the best in Nethriel women."

The mood shifted quickly as the King stopped walking and pivoted abruptly towards Breowakoe, who subtly flinched.

"My envoys tell me you were working for Tiricora," he paused and let the silence ring.

"That's true, yes," Breowakoe replied.

"And do you intend to return to work for her?"

"N-no I don't think I will..."

King Grona's beady eyes narrowed. "Why did you agree to meet with me?" he asked, resuming his slow pace toward a window at the end of the hall.

"I don't know. I'm still learning about the Spoil, I guess - and I didn't want to go back to Tiricora."

King Grona looked over at him with disgust.

"You are not what I expected, at all." The King sounded disappointed. "You sound just like the ones we raise to serve us. Have you been castrated?"

"Umm, no I'm not castrated."

"Bizarre. You speak just like the Nethriel men we capture, after procedure."

Breo couldn't believe how openly disrespectful King Grona was to him, but he hadn't the trust in his own combat skill to stand up for himself. All the talk of Nethriel castration was burning an image of that horror into his mind. He felt angry and humiliated hearing Coabra Grona speak that way about his species, but he wasn't sure why given that Nethriel had treated him terribly since as early as he could remember.

"Well... no matter. I was going to ask how I could trust you, knowing you betrayed Tiricora, but I know you won't betray me, isn't that right?" King Grona primed the aspect of power without discharging it and Breo felt the immense weight of thripsis within him.

"You want me to work for you?" he asked nervously, ready to agree to whatever might end this interaction.

"No, not particularly. You're here to learn more about the Spoil, is that it?"

King Grona stared down at him and he nodded.

"I may not know much about the Spoil, but I can show you our Grobut way of life. I am a generous man. I will do you this favour now, and in the future you may return it, how does that sound?" the King asked with authority, his confidence transforming the question into a demand.

"I-I would appreciate that," Breowakoe wavered.

King Grona began to walk away from the window and into another room. Breowakoe instinctively followed.

"Excellent. I will assign my concubine, Mischa, to be your housecarl and attend to you. There are rooms fit for Nethriel accommodation in my palace."

Breowakoe felt a pinch of anxiety at the mention of Mischa's name.

"As I am being hospitable to you, you will not lay a hand on any of my concubines during your stay."

The King passed through the door and Breowakoe followed into a room with what looked like a swimming pool. There was heat coming off it.

"You may use this bath during the day but at night, it is off limits."

"You called for me, Master?" Mischa's voice crooned from the top of a staircase Breo had not noticed to the right of the bath.

"Yes Mischa, show Breowakoe to the guest room. We have an early morning tomorrow."

Breo hadn't heard a call - it seemed odd that Mischa claimed to have. He didn't appreciate being put to bed like a child, but he was tired. The morning felt so long ago; there had been so much travelling, and such intense violence.

"Yes, sir. Follow me Breowakoe," Mischa instructed.

Breowakoe bid King Grona a good night to no response, then followed Mischa, turning briefly at the top of the steps to watch the King wade into the bath. Silently, his concubines filed in from the throne room to join him. It was eerie, too organized even to have been scheduled, almost as though the King communicated with them telepathically, or controlled them through a hive mind.

"Come along, now," Mischa repeated impatiently, like a stern mother in a grocery store.

He followed her around the corner of the staircase and into a series of tunnels. The interior of the palace was proving to be just as odd as its exterior. Breowakoe had expected many more open areas and branching corridors, but the design was labyrinthine. It was impossible to get lost, but once in deep enough, it might take ages to get out. The staircase, lit by torches, wound around in an unpredictable way. Breo and Mischa bypassed four floors of vertical distance before they finally came to a hallway. The hallway itself zig-zagged, occasionally shooting off into dark, little, doorless rooms. The floor seemed to vibrate, and the air was more moist than Breo could remember air ever feeling. It really did seem designed for insects despite being made of stone. The ceiling was low, barely tall enough for an adult forager to pass through. Mischa gazed over her shoulder periodically to make sure he was still with her. He wondered if he were being led to his death; the air smelt sickly tart, like it was rich with body fluid and nutrient waste.

"Here we are," Mischa said as they reached a windowless room around the fourth bend of the hall. It appeared to be identical to the countless rooms they had already passed.

"The chamber pot is under the bed. King Grona has asked me to tell you not to wander too much; stay in your room and I will get you in the morning."

"How will I know when it's morning?"

Breo looked around for a window, agitated.

"You will know because I will come get you," Mischa said coldly before walking off into the dim hall.

The bed had a flimsy, metal frame with a bit of padding on top. It looked like something a Grobut had impatiently made after glancing into a Nethriel dwelling, like a parody of what a Nethriel would sleep on. Breo lay down on the cot and could feel that odd vibration coming up more strongly from the floor. He lay there for ten minutes as the soft rumble continuously raised his blood pressure.

"Hush, now..." a voice sounded from below him.

It was Mischa, and for a moment Breo thought it was another attempt to boss him. But then a strange, haunting humming emerged through the stone as she began to sing a lullaby. He knew this was not for him. Breowakoe rose from his cot and pressed his ear to the moisture of the floor. Breathing deeply and closing his eyes, he made himself aware of the thripsis around him. He could feel and hear Mischa beneath him, as well as hundreds of thriptic clusters that shared a signature with Grobut thripsis but were much smaller.

"You're going to be ok, little flylet!" Mischa cooed again, lovingly.

Breo realized these must be the King's children sectioned off into a protective part of the palace - those four inaccessible floors he had climbed past. Perhaps the humidity and the heat were for them, also. He was sleeping above a massive nursery of larval children birthed and cared for by Nethriel women. He lay awake in this massive, stone hive most of the night. Examining his circumstance made him insecure and nurtured a feeling of deep helplessness within him. There was no vision of his future in which he saw himself happy, comfortable, or enjoying existence. He was in such a strange, foreign reality - one that was not his own, one to which he knew he did not belong. He had been dragged from situation to fetid, abominable situation, unable to get a grip on even a solid desire of his own.

Kai was already sleeping within him, so he turned onto his left side. Her outline over his ribs and pelvis on the right hurt more to lie on. Finally, in a moment of solitude, he allowed his anxiety to subside. Within that glimmer of peace, he cried silently, pitying himself for his weakness and circumstance. After an hour of sobbing, the confused young Nethriel, alone and in hell, slipped from consciousness.

The Culling and the Reaving - 9

"Get up. King Grona has summoned you, boy."

Breowakoe thought Kai's voice was making its way into some rapidly forgotten dream.

"Get up, RIGHT NOW, Nethriel!" Mischa yelled again, naming her own species as a slur.

She could not have been much older than he, and yet she assumed enough authority to call him 'boy.' Breo felt rested and rose quickly; he had no need to dress as he had never disrobed. He made no attempt to hide his annoyance with Mischa, glaring at her as she led him back into the labyrinth.

King Grona was seated on his pedestal as they entered the throne room, still with concubines in a mess about him.

"Ah, Breowakoe, just in time. We'll get to the arena before the festivities begin!" he said gleefully, rising to his feet and heading to the door.

Mischa rushed to catch up with her King while the other concubines got up, walked quietly past Breowakoe and up the stairs he had just descended. Mischa was clearly held by King Grona in a higher regard than the other concubines, but Breo was puzzled as to why. He hadn't been there a day and was already growing resentful of being corralled around. Grona waltzed out the main door of the palace and Breowakoe begrudgingly followed. On the horizon, over the wall of Gol Paqua, the view of the sandstorms was breathtaking. The interior of the palace was so dull that Breo had forgotten its setting.

"Ahh, it's a beautiful day for the sport! Follow me, Breowakoe!" King Grona shouted before sweeping Mischa off her feet and jumping off the top stone step.

He launched himself over the city with a massive burst of thripsis and landed 600 metres down and a few kilometres starboard into the centre of the arena. Breowakoe was in awe and in the distance he felt King Grona's thripsis explode again as the arena shook. His people's roars of amazement and loyalty could be heard even this far.

"I see, so he released thripsis to survive the landing."

Breowakoe readied himself to jump, but doubt crept in. He worried that he would release too little thripsis and die, or release too much and make a fool of himself in front of the King. He thought about taking the stairs down but figured it could take half an hour on foot to catch up. He closed his eyes and breathed deeply, channelling thripsis down through his legs and arms and pointing his fists to the ground. A hot wind picked up, and Breowakoe was elated as he started to ascend; flying was easy! He shifted his weight to allow the thripsis from his feet to propel him forward into the air over the city as the thripsis from his arms balanced him. Seeing the ground so far below sped up his breathing, which dangerously slowed the stream of his thripsis; he calmed himself to recover power, then confidently leaned more deeply into the space over the Kingdom. Once over the arena, he hovered awkwardly, realizing he needed to narrow his thriptic flow but not wanting to cut it off too quickly. He descended embarrassingly slowly into the middle of the arena next to King Grona as tens of thousands of Grobut jeered.

"...and here is our special guest referee, now! With a *most* dramatic entrance, please welcome the aspect of hatred, Breowakoe!" King Grona mockingly introduced him as half the drones cheered and the other half remained silent or booed.

"What? Guest referee?" Breo worried, realizing he was being burdened with a daunting responsibility to be executed before an unfriendly crowd.

King Grona ignored him and again addressed the audience.

"THE SHOW WILL COMMENCE IN TEN

MINUTES!" he roared, all of his many arms raised. The crowd went wild and the King placed a hand on Breowakoe's shoulder, walking him toward a gate along one of the Arena's stone walls.

"I thought you might enjoy refereeing! It's a front-row seat to view one of the great pleasures of Grobut culture. But before the festivities begin, let me show you the prep room."

King Grona lifted the gate and allowed Breowakoe to pass under his massive arm before following behind. They entered a dungeon that smelled like sweat, and piss, and fear.

"This is where I got my start, you know. I was always a gifted fighter. HA. Well, I'm sure Turia told you all about it," the King boasted.

Breo looked around to realize he had not seen Mischa since the King jumped away with her, but he put it from his mind.

"These are holding rooms."

Breo was led into a small, dark room with two small benches lining the walls.

"This is where you prepare yourself mentally before going out there. HA! Takes me back! Last time I was in one of these was right before I fought King Geru. These holding rooms, here, are for Nethriel, though. In the other corners of the arena, there are holding rooms for Grobut and for the beasts who will do battle."

Breowakoe thought of the enormous stag beetles he had seen dragging Turia's carriage the day before and wondered how they fought. A loud series of bangs erupted from a side room up the narrow stone hallway and King Grona led Breowakoe to it. In the centre of the room, a rickety elevator transporting Nethriel men emerged from a sub chamber. They were naked, shaking, and afraid. Breowakoe's eyes, drawn to the colour red, noticed a few of the men had blood running down their legs. They were freshly castrated. He looked away, thinking he might be sick.

"Kneel before the King!" a Grobut drone yelled, looking surprised to see King Grona.

"Oh, don't mind me. I'm just giving a tour to the aspect of hatred," the King laughed, passing by the drone with a slap on the shoulder. The Nethriel men stared at Breowakoe with a discernible mix of hatred and confusion but none dared utter a word. He could tell they hated him for being both Nethriel and free while being also incomprehensibly in the company of the King. Breowakoe tried his best to ignore them and scuttled up behind the King.

"This is the portal room. These men have just come from the tunnel connecting the arena to the Nethriel farms. Over here they will be outfitted with weapons and armour as the choreographer sees fit."

"Choreographer? Are these not real fights?"

"Oh, they're real, but there is an art to this. Perhaps our oldest tradition, the arena is held once a week. The matchups and armaments are planned to keep things interesting, tell a story. A whole generation of drones will pass by before any matchup is repeated exactly."

"Wow." Breo had trouble comprehending how this could be possible. "So when I'm refereeing, how am I actually judging?"

King Grona chuckled confidently. "The referee is more of a ceremonial role. Almost all fights are to the death. In the case that they are not, you are expected to kill the party that you thought performed worse."

"Oh, ok..."

Breowakoe was disconcerted to imagine deciding life or death in the sacred practice of a people that clearly saw him as an outsider.

"That is all; there's not a lot to the prep rooms. Enjoy the refereeing!" King Grona said sincerely, brushing past Breowakoe and leaving out the way he came.

The drone corralling the Nethriel men was screaming at them as they scrambled to put on thin, leather tunics.

"You won't embarrass me in front of the King; hurry up, swine!" he yelled, as he pinched a man's shoulder, appearing to work his fingers into the joint.

The man screamed, dropping the thin bits of leather.

"Good luck, guys," Breowakoe heard himself muttering under his breath, ashamed to make eye contact as he walked past.

The arena was roaring as he stepped back out into the near-blinding light of Verivoluae. Squinting, he could see King Grona and Mischa sitting in a pavilion that jutted slightly over the battleground. Two foragers sat on either side of them, and Breowakoe struggled to distinguish which was Turia. He started making his way over to them, but King Grona simply pointed away while looking directly at him. Following the King's finger with his eyes led Breowakoe nowhere in particular, but when he looked back, the King was still pointing. So he walked uncomfortably towards the spot in the center of the arena that the finger roughly suggested. A confused volley of boos erupted from the drones in the stands. Breowakoe sheepishly looked back up at King Grona whose finger was now withdrawn. Grona and Mischa scoffed at him, Mischa wagging her finger derisively while the two looked back and forth between him and one another. Breo felt hot in the face and he quickly walked back to the sidelines, still unsure of what he was supposed to be doing. He could feel that he was slouching, stuck deep within his own head. Still amused, Grona now held an open palm to him. His mind raced for a moment, wondering what this was supposed to mean, but he gave up on the signal, reflecting on his humiliation. He simply hung his head until the booming voice of the King echoed through the stadium.

"People of Gol Paqua, the Kingdoms downstream of us are dead. Upstream, the Nethriel Kingdom of Goliah stands as the only other civilization left in these wastes. But WHO ARE THE TRUE HEIRS OF THE SPOIL?"

Breowakoe's ears perked up and he looked into the stands.

"Grobut!" the crowd roared in unison.

"Their men defy us, but their women love us!" King

Grona jeered.

The drones laughed and booed. Breowakoe peered at each of the faces of the bull flies. Each was uniquely hideous, with slobber and glee pouring out of their humanoid mouths.

"Their Kingdom may be bigger than ours, but one Grobut is worth ten, no... fifty! No... one hundred Nethriel men! My drones, I present to you: one Grobut drone, versus one hundred Nethriel men!"

The rumble of approval from the crowd was monstrous. A gate dropped to Breowakoe's left and a drone stepped out, holding a large, pewter club within all four of his hands. He walked with a swagger to the middle of the arena and the crowd could not have been happier. A second gate dropped on the other side of the curved wall and 100 emaciated Nethriel men stepped onto the sands of the arena. They were completely naked and the blood from their recent castrations still trickled down their legs. Each grasped a carved, stone knife and nothing else. Many were limping and sobbing as they clutched their groins, collapsing onto hands and knees. Breowakoe felt selfishly relieved to see that none of the men from the holding room he had visited were among them.

It was clear that nothing about this was intended to be a

fair challenge. It was propaganda for the masses. It was something that the drones needed to believe. Breowakoe couldn't help but wonder why it wasn't obvious to them, though. Why did they need to prove to themselves repeatedly that they were superior to Nethriel? They literally farmed them and consumed them as food.

The gates closed and the few Nethriel that were still walking completed a weak surround of their Grobut combatant. The movement stopped, and all were staring at Breowakoe. He stared back, puzzled. A cacophony of boos started to pour in from the stands.

"On your mark, referee," King Grona's booming voice sounded from the pavilion, and Breowakoe realized that *he* was to begin the fight.

"Oh, ok... BEGIN!" he yelled through a pinched anxiousness.

Immediately, the Grobut in the center swung his pewter club down on two Nethriel men's heads. Breo could hear their skulls crack instantly. Their bodies folded in on themselves grotesquely, leaving the men as bloody disks of tissue and bits of bone in the sand. A few brave Nethriel were maneuvering up from behind the Grobut, but their stone knives simply shattered on his carapace. There was no way for them to win. A brave soul, realizing his knife was useless, jumped on the drone's back, trying to rip off his sensitive wings, but he couldn't budge them. Breowakoe couldn't help but compare himself to these other Nethriel men; he was beginning to appreciate just how much his own strength differed from those without an aspect.

The drone swept the brave soul's leg like a hook and cracked the knees of the two men standing behind him. With one of its four arms, it threw the man on his back to the dust on top of them. It then stepped on their necks, crushing their windpipes one at a time and letting them slowly die. The drones in the stands only continued the sounds of their glee.

The macabre display played out with about half the men simply sitting down and accepting their fate, while twenty-five, or so, made bad attempts to dodge the monstrous club and, after some time, about four surprisingly composed Nethriel men remained. They looked more determined than the rest and were even signaling to each other. Breowakoe felt himself cheering for them internally; with calloused hands and weathered faces, they were up against impossible odds but they kept calm. He wondered what other adversity they had faced, if they had ever known any kind of joy, and was taken aback at how he admired them so deeply, not knowing them.

The four first moved in pairs to surround the drone; two charged from its right and it pivoted to swing at them, batting their bodies to splat against the wall of the arena. This had been a diversion, a sacrifice, as now one of the remaining two Nethriel hoisted the other into the air behind the Grobut. The man in the air sent his little stone knife sailing into the Grobut's left, bulbous eye as it turned around. The crowd gasped and went silent. Breowakoe felt his own heart pounding. A second stone knife was passed up to the Nethriel still clinging to the Grobut's neck as it staggered. A beautiful second swing was heading to its right eye.

The Grobut dropped its club and grabbed the Nethriel by the throat with two hands, crushing his neck until pulp escaped from his mouth. It threw the lifeless body to the ground and removed the dagger from its own mangled eye. The last Nethriel man shuffled backwards like a crab, looking around in search of another dagger. The Grobut stomped on his knees and the man screamed as it then reached between its own legs to direct its abdomen into his face. The Grobut gestured to the crowd whose cheers were starting to hurt Breowakoe's ears. It retrieved its club to raise high above its head. Breowakoe felt the small pool of thripsis within the drone stir. In a lightning-fast swing, it deleted the Nethriel man. Breo's face was splattered with blood from many metres away, and a fine mist of blood rose from the small crater where the man had been. As Breowakoe wiped the blood from his eyes, a familiar, booming, patronizing voice echoed through the stadium.

"Who won, referee?" King Grona mockingly asked.

"One Grobut defeated one hundred Nethriel!" Breowakoe tried to shout officially, realizing this was part of his job.

The crowd was exuberant. Twelve drones emerged on the arena floor to clean up the mess as the victor retired to the Grobut quarters. King Grona moved swiftly onto the next event.

"Two disgraced drones who disobeyed authority now fight for one last shot at redemption."

One of the foragers had flown down from the pavilion, carrying a large drum of something, and made his way to the center of the arena.

"200 litres of driln will be poured onto the arena floor. Should their skin even touch the driln they will forever lose the ability to produce even sterile bile, and there is no chance they may ever become King!"

The drum was placed on the sand and the unfamiliar forager took a step back and pointed at it. Thripsis left his finger. Breowakoe was surprised to see that the foragers were able to channel thripsis as he was, not just simply release it in one burst like the drones. The metal drum corroded and a green fluid spilled onto the sand of the arena. Corroding metal was something Kaimaradan was able to do with her aspect of cruelty, but somehow this creature that wasn't even an aspect could do it. Breowakoe reckoned he should watch his back around the foragers, previously having thought them to be a peaceful or powerless strain of Grobut.

The forager flew back up to the pavilion, and two gates on the Grobut wall of the arena opened. A pair of drones flew into the air without hesitation and were extremely hostile to one another even before the round started. Breowakoe wondered if he was supposed to step in and create civility, but it didn't seem like his place.

"Who will regain their honour, and who will suffer the greatest humiliation a Grobut can endure?" King Grona signed off - Breowakoe looked up to see Coabra pointing at him.

"BEGIN!" Breowakoe yelled, a little more confidently this time.

The two Grobut were tightly tangled into a hovering ball before the word even left his mouth. It was very difficult to tell what was happening; this fight seemed quite desperate. These Grobut were struggling more than he had seen any Grobut struggle before. Finally, the commotion in the air resolved into a lesser calm. One of the Grobut had the other in a headlock, and with its free arms ripped off its wings. The crowd gasped and became still as the now wingless Grobut fell to the sand. The soon-to-be victor followed closely, then dragged its prey face-first into the driln. The victor did not celebrate; he simply walked away. The defeated Grobut struggled a moment to get back to its feet, but then realized its defeat and collapsed back down in the driln. Breowakoe's confusion slowly resolved as he realized the drone was committing suicide. It couldn't bear to face the humiliation of the crowd who still sat respectfully silent.

"Uhh... the winner!" Breowakoe hesitated to announce – gesturing to the Grobut walking away, to no applause.

One of the gates opened and the victor disappeared into the bowels of the arena.

All four foragers now flew down in a diamond formation around the arena's center and placed their hands on the ground. The sand in the middle began to sink, carrying with it the body of the drowned drone and the driln. Sand bubbled up from the sides of the circle to replace what was lost in the whirlpool of dust. One last blast of thripsis leveled the arena floor and the foragers resumed their seats.

"When the Grobut settled these wastes, we had to tame many beasts that wanted the territory for themselves - but what happens when beasts struggle to tame one another?" King Grona set up the next bout.

Breowakoe's ears perked up; he was curious to see what oddities would come out of the animal gates.

"My dear people, I give you six Nethriel men vs thirty badlands jackals!"

The Nethriel gate dropped first and the men Breowakoe had seen earlier, in the holding room, stepped out. They were fully outfitted with a thin leather armour which, although wasn't much, looked like it could stop the odd cut. They had light metal shields and wielded scimitar swords. They appeared to be more capable now than they had in the portal room. They coordinated themselves well, standing a metre apart from each other in a semi-circle that faced the animal gates.

"Nethriel men, prepare yourselves! My dear people, make some noise for this last fight!"

The crowd roared as King Grona lifted their spirits.

"Choreographer, RELEASE THE JACKALS!"

The animal gate dropped and the creatures spewed from the opening. They were the size of coyotes but they looked much lighter, with sharp claws and razor-sharp teeth that barely fit in their mouths. Their lower lips hung open such that they couldn't help but drool and the entire lip was lined with teeth. They moved extremely quickly. These badlands jackals were to dogs what Vemanen were to Nethriel.

The pack descended on the Nethriel men, pouncing at two in the middle. These jackals could jump quite high and extremely far, but easy swings of the men's scimitars put them down quickly.

"Oh, this doesn't seem so bad," Breowakoe thought to himself.

Seven or so jackals had the man on the far end somewhat surrounded; they stalked back and forth and he looked uneasy. They jumped in to attack in unison, seizing his arms and legs. The man screamed, but the other Nethriel were in similar stalemates, unable to attend to him. A fifth jackal jumped at the surrounded man and he cut it down with the point of his scimitar. This motion did not go unpunished, however, as the jackal clinging to his right arm used the opportunity to flay his skin to the elbow. A sixth jackal leapt up and took the man's throat. A gurgling noise sounded as he fell backwards, hitting the sand. He convulsed, but his arms and legs were being stretched apart. A seventh jackal climbed onto his abdomen and effortlessly sheared away the leather and skin from his chest. A second stroke of its lip pulled the muscle away from the rib cage. Although he was unable to scream at this point, the frequency and intensity of his convulsions increased. The seventh jackal pushed its claw between his ribs and punctured the left ventricle of his heart. Blood shot about six feet into the air and all the starving jackals came running to feed.

While the jackals were distracted the other five Nethriel men were freed up to counterattack. They killed six jackals in a matter of five seconds, but the jackals regrouped and two more Nethriel men were taken down by the throat. The three remaining men continued to fight, throwing caution to the wind - fueled by adrenaline.

Breowakoe counted as twenty-two jackals became fifteen, and three men became two; then fifteen jackals became nine, and two men became one. This one man clearly had some combat experience. He played it safe but always chose the perfect opportunities to strike.

A pair of jackals broke from the pack and bounded over to Breowakoe who now realized they saw him as just another potential meal. He was afraid of killing them, upsetting the balance of the sacred duel. But his sense of honour fled quickly when the jackals jumped in tandem toward his throat. A thread of thripsis from Breowakoe's gaze sliced them in half. He was becoming quite adept at controlling the energy.

A chorus of boos from the ugly faces in the stands broke over his ears. While he was distracted, the Nethriel man still fighting had taken out another three jackals, and only four remained. The man was smiling, clearly believing he would win.

"Favouritism!" a drone called from the stands.

"Not fair!" "Even the score!" "Break his leg! Break his leg! Break his leg! Break his leg!"

The chanting became louder as more drones joined in.

The man glanced in Breowakoe's direction with fear in his eyes. A jackal pounced but was knocked to the ground by the Nethriel's shield. The chanting in the stands got louder still.

"Break his leg! Break his leg!"

Breowakoe really didn't want to do that; the man was fighting well and deserved to win. It didn't seem fair; he was sure this one would have made quick work of all nine jackals if Breowakoe himself hadn't been forced to kill two. Two jackals were not a balanced trade for the man's leg. The man slew the jackal he had stunned and picked himself up again just in time to block another leap.

"Break one of his legs, Breowakoe." King Grona's stern voice boomed over all the noise, delivering the command Breowakoe had been dreading to hear.

Looking over, he felt both angry and afraid to see that King Grona was standing up. He dared not find out what would happen if he disobeyed, so began taking steps toward the Nethriel man. Tears of livid anger flowed down the man's face as he watched his own kind come to kill him.

"You piece of shit, traitor!" he yelled over the three remaining jackals. The man maneuvered around them again, this time to close in on Breowakoe. He struggled to maintain the stalemate with the jackals but slowly maneuvered closer.

Breowakoe weighed his options. If he killed the remaining jackals he would most likely die. He knew that even with the aspect of hatred he couldn't handle this many angry Grobut, let alone their King, the aspect of power. Breowakoe was so lost in thought that he barely noticed the man charging him, shield raised, screaming in a deep rage. The jackals followed him close behind and the man swung his scimitar at Breowakoe's neck. Channeling thripsis into his palm, Breowakoe was able to catch the blade with only a small cut. With a swift kick he knocked the man's left knee.

The man looked shocked and nearly held himself upright, but gradually succumbed to the loss of balance. Two jackals pinned his arms with little hesitation, and the third - with its horrific, toothed lower lip - replayed the pageant of gore experienced by every other Nethriel that had encountered these creatures.

Breowakoe was overwhelmed with guilt as the man screamed in acute suffering. He had not deserved this outcome. Breowakoe couldn't stomach any more rage. With a flick of his wrist the jackals were in flames. They collapsed as the man continued to scream; another flick of Breowakoe's wrist and the man was decapitated. He knew that censure was coming and he didn't want to hear it. He turned and walked toward a less populated area of the stands between the Nethriel and the Grobut gates. He just wanted to get out of there.

Then the jeers and the boos started. Breowakoe quickened his pace. Ten drones jumped out of the stands to intercept him, so he stopped in his tracks. A deeper anger emerged in him and, for a moment as they towered over him, he believed he could dispatch them all. He channeled his thripsis radially, with all the current he could muster.

The Grobut before him winced in the intense heat, but they were not in range to burn. Breowakoe looked back toward the rest of the stands, a savage look on his face, in that moment he was willing to die. Unexpectedly, the crowd went silent. He looked into each one of their faces and realized they were afraid of him.

Breowakoe's outburst subsided and he came to his senses, he was in the heart of a foreign culture, mocking it with his freedom. He stopped channeling thripsis, freshly alarmed at the horror he had brought upon himself. Once again fearing death, he didn't know what had come over him. The ten drones were now marching on him, and he no longer had the will to defend himself. The scorn from every direction was so abundant that he felt he deserved whatever fate was now his. There was an explosion in the sand and the smashed pieces of drone body parts flew.

"ENOUGH!" King Grona roared, having just decimated ten of his own people. "The referee has decided that in the battle of the beasts, there are no winners!" Grona excused Breowakoe's behavior poetically.

The crowd cheered – so fickle – unwilling to disagree with their King.

"The aspect of hatred displayed excellent judgement today, and I thank him for the role he played in this sacred tradition. In fact, in light of his performance, I have made the decision to name him honorary Grobut!"

Again, the crowd cheered, and Breowakoe was happily shocked, failing to understand why or how the King had come to this decision. Was Grona really beginning to like him? Just an hour ago he was mocking him from the pavilion. Perhaps Grobut really *did* value strength above all else? Or was he playing some longer game?

"Good job. I know that wasn't easy," the King said, slapping Breowakoe on the shoulder.

It felt good to be praised by someone so strong and sure of himself.

"I wanted to see if you would be loyal to Nethriel, and how you handle pressure. I want to offer you more for your services in exchange for handling sensitive diplomatic issues for me in the future. I always reward the loyal, especially when they are strong, and I could give you a good life here. If you serve me well, I may even grant you a Nethriel concubine of your own one day."

Breowakoe was intrigued at that prospect, but having spent his adolescence clamoring through corpses in the waking nightmare of the Squalor, he was too poorly "socialized" to understand his attraction to women.

"So, what do you say?" the King asked warmly.

"I'll work for you, my King." Breowakoe said, feeling good about himself.

He glanced at the pavilion to see that Mischa was watching him keenly, but he ignored her.

"Kneel before me, then," King Grona said resolutely. "You will not receive the bile, as I promised you earlier, but a formal pledge is necessary."

Breowakoe dropped to one knee.

"I pledge myself to your service, King Grona."

"Good. Now, rise, honorary Grobut."

King Grona smiled. "Let me tell you about a little problem you can help me to solve."

The Piccaro Files - 10

The next morning Breowakoe awoke as an officer in the King's army. He marched down the great, stone steps of the palace carrying a strange bit of material - halfway between paper and sponge - that he had been told contained pheromones from King Grona's fertile bile. It was a signature of sorts, an official document that could be interpreted only by Grobut.

Making his way to the barracks by the great gates, Breowakoe ruminated on the problem King Grona had outlined the prior evening. In the Nethriel farms, the Grobut had been using the most obsequious Nethriel males as bulls - men that from capture had done as they were told or even without prompt had acted in unsolicited service to the Grobut. In many cases, these men had fathered three generations of Nethriel in the farms, creating a stable supply of subservient concubines for the King and more tender males for consumption. The most subservient of those males were set aside not to be castrated, and they fathered many of the current generation of farmed Nethriel. But continuous inbreeding meant that genetic abnormalities and miscarriages were starting to become more commonplace in the pens. To maintain the health of the

Nethriel farm, and to expand their sources of Nethriel, King Grona needed 'wild' sources of Nethriel, which he lamented were not easily come by. Goliah was the most obvious source, but it was under Tiricora's protection and was also currently in a civil war. Previous attempts at raiding Goliah had resulted in many Grobut casualties and overall was considered by the Grobut generals to be undoable.

There were other Nethriel settlements, however, some as far downstream as Gol Paqua and some even farther. But for unknown meteorological reasons, those regions were constantly enshrouded in sandstorms. The patrol that originally encountered Breowakoe had been looking for such settlements.

In his heart, Breo had forgiven King Grona for his rude capture. It felt good to be useful to someone, to be a part of a community and a cause. He noticed that the busier he was, the less abhorrent his reality seemed.

He made it to the base of the great stone steps and approached a building matching the description of the barracks. Just down the narrow road, he saw the familiar pink sign with flashing red lights: "The Painted Slave." The sign had captured his attention so completely when he last stood here that he hadn't even noticed the giant stone barracks in front of it. He paused with his hand on the door of the barracks, still gazing down the street at the little clay building.

"Not today. I don't have time today, but I'm a free man now. I'll go explore it tomorrow," the little voice in his head chirped.

The door he was touching flew open and Breowakoe jumped back, startled.

"What are you doing, Nethriel!? This is the barracks of Gol Paqua; where is your handler?" the angry voice of a grizzled old drone sounded.

"I am the aspect of hatred; King Grona has told me I am to be an officer." Breowakoe said proudly, handing the old drone the King's signature.

The drone's expression changed to a snarl as quickly he acknowledged the scent of the fertile bile.

"Come along, then," he hissed, retreating into the building.

Breowakoe followed swiftly. This building seemed to be designed like the palace in that it was more of a labyrinth than a logical arrangement of hallways and rooms. Two drones were stationed as guards at the entrance and there was a desk at the back of the lobby with a chair looking casually discarded a metre behind it. He followed the old Grobut a short way down a barren hallway and into a room where two other Grobut sat on opposite sides of a desk. The one behind the desk looked just as old, and far more weathered than the receptionist. He was already sniffing the King's signature as Breowakoe walked in, and the two seated Grobut glared at him.

"This Nethriel... a lieutenant, eh?" the Grobut behind the desk growled. "Well, I'll assign him to your team, Thrakarnid."

The Grobut on Breowakoe's side of the desk was shocked and angry.

"Please Colonel, you can't be serious..."

"That's enough lip, captain. Were you not JUST telling me you were undermanned for today's mission? I'm willing to call this a 'sign.'"

The Colonel raised his two left hands and waved his fingers about.

"What is it, kid? You an aspect or something?" the Colonel asked, staring directly at Breowakoe's misshapen torso.

"Yes, sir, I am the aspect of hatred."

"There you go, Thrakarnid - he will be the most useful guy on your team."

Thrakarnid looked positively alarmed.

"How can I trust a Nethriel aspect on my team? What the hell is going on?"

Thrakarnid looked to the old secretary in the doorway for support, but the old Grobut turned and walked back to his post.

"If King Grona trusts him, that's all I need to know," the Colonel said, and then snarled, "Would you disobey the King's order? Get the hell out of my office! Get to the rendezvous, and get your new teammate acquainted with how we do business."

Thrakarnid got out of his seat abruptly and checked Breowakoe, knocking him aside, while storming out of the room. Breowakoe regained his balance and glanced over at the Colonel, who simply gestured to the door. Breowakoe chased Thrakarnid down the hall and into the daylight. Thrakarnid took flight in some childish attempt to lose the Nethriel, but he wasn't much faster in the air. A group of three other drones were waiting for him just inside the great gate.

"What happened?" one of them asked. "Whoa, whoa, whoa, where's your handler?"

Another drone put his hand up, shuffling to intercept

Breowakoe who was charging up to them.

"Ignore him; let's go, now," Thrakarnid said hurriedly, taking off higher into the sky. The other three Grobut obeyed. Breowakoe found this to be entirely amusing as he channeled thripsis through his arms and legs, taking off after them.

"Oh, shit, he's an aspect; we should report this to the King!" one of the lower-ranked drones alarmed.

"The Colonel just told us I am on your team; Thrakarnid isn't taking it well," Breowakoe called up impatiently as they passed over the top of the giant wall.

Thrakarnid button-hooked in the air, grabbed Breowakoe, and shook him off balance, slamming him into the patrollable walkway on top of the wall. It happened so fast that Breowakoe couldn't react. Thrakarnid was gripping his throat, pressing him violently into the stone.

"I don't know how you convinced our King to let you into our ranks but while you are in this team you are under MY command," Thrakarnid growled.

Breowakoe nodded, knowing it didn't make sense to fight this guy. Thrakarnid let go of Breowakoe's throat and he stood up. The other drones were hovering in the air, mixed looks of satisfaction and surprise on their faces. They followed their leader to the ground outside the city where four large, pronutum-saddled stag beetles sat with trainers holding their reigns.

"Hatred, you're going to have to share with Penma."

Thrakarnid pointed to one of the drones who looked quietly unhappy to have been chosen. Penma got into the saddle first, looking uncomfortable as he tried to make room at the front of the saddle for Breowakoe. Climbing into position in front of the beast, Breowakoe and was immediately disgusted with every bit of this. Penma smelled terrible and was about a head taller, so he breathed hotly and heavily into Breowakoe's hair at the back of his head. The creature they rode atop looked deadly, with its giant pincers, and made a lot of very precise clicking noises as it turned its massive head. Penma took the reins of the stag from the handler, holding them in a half-hug around Breowakoe's body. Kaimaradan, who hadn't spoken to him in days, scuttled under his skin – he had almost forgotten about her.

"Surrounded by bugs, within and without," Breowakoe thought to himself, shuddering.

The reins were whipped and the beetle's wings flew open. There was a deep vibration as the powerful paper-like sheets beat the air. All four beetles levitated in unison. Thrakarnid at the front yelled, "Yah!", and they all took off, flying upstream at about three times the flying speed of a Grobut.

Breowakoe almost began to enjoy himself as the hot desert wind whipped against his face. It gave him a vague feeling of freedom, although something felt unstable or imbalanced about the way these beetles flew. The troop continued in a straight line along the port wall of the Spoil.

"So, what are we doing?" Breowakoe called out to no response.

They were all likely pretending not to hear, but they had the wind as an excuse.

It was difficult to reason how flying along the port wall would lead them to discover any new settlements, but shortly they arrived at the base camp where Breowakoe was first held by the Grobut. The journey was about four times faster flying on the beetles than it had been when they were towing him. The stag beetles landed and everyone was eager to stretch their legs. Breowakoe made note of a particularly uncomfortable back sweat that could only have been produced by another guy's body rubbing up against him. All four Grobut wasted no time in entering the large tents. Breowakoe stayed outside looking towards Goliah; the sandstorms were lighter today and he wondered if he would be able to see it on the horizon.

Peering into the tents, all four Grobut were looking for something and one by one they gave up.

"I don't think he has arrived yet." Thrakarnid breathed.

"Who hasn't arrived yet?" Breowakoe was intrigued.

"Shut the fuck up, please..." Thrakarnid sounded exasperated.

"The Colonel asked you to get me up to speed with what's going on. I am a member of the team; I should know what's going on."

Breowakoe felt annoyed as he didn't want to let King Grona down. Thrakarnid made a beeline toward him, though, a fury in his eyes.

"There is nothing more sickening in this world than a Nethriel who doesn't know their place."

Breowakoe stepped back and coincidentally found himself pressed to the same rock he had been tied to days earlier. The same feeling of overwhelmed desperation began to overtake him. Stressed, he channeled his thripsis at its base level, controlling the flow. This captured the attention of the whole team, who looked on in fear as Thrakarnid hesitated.

"I see our King forgot to castrate you, swine," Thrakarnid said as he reached for his abdomen and an axe off his belt.

Breowakoe cocked his head to the side and gritted his teeth. He opened the valve over his body of thripsis further, so that the heat was just barely scorching Thrakarnid's carapace.

"I am not your enemy, but I will not let you harm me," Breowakoe said, voice wavering, afraid for himself in his novel social status.

Thrakarnid growled as he let his axe slide back into his belt. He released the hold of his abdomen. He turned and walked away, so Breowakoe stopped channeling thripsis. The other Grobut looked somewhat relieved.

Not too far from the camp, something emerged from the sands as though it had just deactivated a cloaking device. It was a creature of about three feet tall that had pointed ears and a large nose with green skin.

"Is that a goblin? Was it watching us?" Breowakoe thought to himself as he looked around for any other potential threats.

The Grobut noticed the goblin and Thrakarnid walked

out to intercept it.

"*Piccaro...*"

A chaotic thripsis emerged from Breowakoe's abdomen. Kaimaradan was in a rage unparalleled by anything she had previously revealed. The goblin did not seem to notice, but all the Grobut looked over at Breowakoe in horror, once again. Breowakoe maneuvered behind the boulder apologetically.

"Kaimaradan, calm down! What's the problem? What's going on?"

"*That creature is a Piccaro, the clan that slaughtered my people.*"

Breo craned around the boulder and gazed across the short plain to see the creature hand a file folder to Thrakarnid. It didn't wear clothes. It looked feeble, like it had no musculature – just organs and bones. After seeing how effortlessly Kaimaradan tore apart Nethriel, it was hard to imagine these small creatures slaughtering anything. Breowakoe didn't know what to say; he didn't want Kaimaradan making any more of a scene when he was already on thin ice in present company.

"*They played upon my better nature, crafty devils... They will not rest until they alone rule the Spoil. I surmise they created the Grobut to that end. To them, the Grobut are a tool to unearth the root of Nethriel. The entire Oxalthry insurgency in Goliah is their doing, as well, I am sure of it. That was what they did in Satria; they convinced half my people that they were something other than Satrians and spread fear of authority. That said, the chief Piccaro, Stynia, and his aspect of cunning will not break Tiricora so easily. She is not as kind as I."*

Breowakoe rolled his eyes at the thought of Kaimaradan being kind. Thrakarnid and the Piccaro glanced over to where Breowakoe stood with his head poking out from around the rock. He felt self conscious and it took him a moment to register that he was doing nothing wrong.

"I wonder what's in that file folder," Breowakoe pondered as his new friends withdrew their gaze.

"*Not anything good,*" Kaimaradan mused.

The handoff concluded and the Piccaro's body became transparent with a raise of his hand and a twirl. He vanished into the sand. Breowakoe emerged from behind the rock and approached the band of drones, who were conversing quietly.

"What's in that file?" he asked, earnestly.

To his surprise, Thrakarnid replied politely.

"Hey, hatred, that was chief advisor Ghoul, and this is a schedule of future rendezvous where he'll give us information on the whereabouts of Nethriel settlements. Now that he trusts us he'll return to the camp in half an hour to deliver the first round of coordinates. I'm going to deliver this schedule to King Grona; you stay here with the others and wait for Ghoul's return."

"Oh, ok. Thanks for telling me."

Breowakoe felt good to be kept in the loop and regretted that he had to flex his aspect of hatred to receive that basic respect. Thrakarnid mounted his stag beetle and flew off in the direction of Gol Paqua.

The mood in the camp was very different from the joviality of the mission at its start. None of the Grobut were speaking or even looking at each other. Breowakoe wanted friendship but felt too alien to ask them something about themselves. About half-an-hour had passed when Penma suddenly looked over at him.

"Want to learn how to fly the beetles while we wait?" he asked, with a slight smile.

Breo's heart fluttered as the warm feeling of inclusion spread throughout him.

"Yeah, that sounds really fun!"

Breowakoe and Penma walked side by side around the boulder to the spot where the beetles were parked. The other two Grobut followed.

"So, as a Grobut, when you first encounter a beetle you must bond with it before it will respond to your commands. We do that by massaging our bile against its jaws, so it picks up the faint scent of our pheromones over the course of a few days."

Penma did this, as he spoke, and the beetle's breathing slowed. Breowakoe noticed that behind him the other two Grobut were doing this with their beetles, as well.

"Since you don't have bile, feed a very slight current of your thripsis into his jaws."

Breowakoe felt nervous but did as he was told. The beetle seemed agitated and clamped its jaw shut. He jumped back.

"That was good; he just isn't used to bonding this way, but he felt your energy and will become familiar with you over time. Next comes a show of trust: you get down between his jaws like this and stroke the top of his head while looking him in the eye."

Penma backed up his words with action, crouching to place his head between the beetle's jaws.

"Oh, wow... I don't know if I can do that."

"It won't bite; it knows the signature of your thripsis," one of the other drones piped up from the back.

As Breowakoe looked over, he saw that all the drones had that level of trust with their beetles.

"But don't I need to give it a few days to get used to me first?"

"No, with thripsis it gets acclimated much faster," Penma answered, brushing off this concern.

Somewhere in the back of his mind Breowakoe suspected this might be a hazing ritual, but he was eager to be accepted so he manoeuvred over into the beetle's massive, sharp jaws. Kaimaradan stirred inside him; the pain was shocking, and he hesitated.

"What are you doing?" he thought, his breathing becoming more rapid with the pain of the centipede shearing through the muscle in his chest. Kaimaradan injected something into his heart as she had days earlier, and the familiar prickling sensation tore through his arteries.

"You're doing well - just get a little lower," Penma

encouraged from over Breowakoe's shoulder.

Breowakoe stood completely in the jaws of the beast, but resisted kneeling as the prickling in his blood continued to disturb him.

"*I see you are still as naive as ever, herilli,*" Kaimaradan hissed.

Some sort of whistle blew behind him, and the jaws of all three stag beetles came down on him simultaneously. Breowakoe felt both humeri snap immediately and any of his ribs that Kaimaradan's armour was not shielding cracked. He was stunned but remained grounded enough to inhale deeply. Craning his neck, he saw that the arms of his new friends were charged with thripsis. All three were in the process of bringing their massive, super-powered clubs down on his head.

Breowakoe exhaled coldly. The eyes of every extra-dermal insect in the vicinity burst. Hot steam poured out of their mouths at such a rate that a cloud formed over the camp and their black shells fell to the ground, empty. His legs were now weak as he stumbled out of the pile of bodies without the support of his arms. Stray cinders ventured into the camp and set the tents aflame.

"Why?" he asked out loud, feeling frustrated and choking

back tears.

"*Thrakarnid does not trust you. Is this truth not obvious to you?*" Kaimaradan crowed condescendingly.

"Well, it's not up to him," Breowakoe growled, limply marching back towards Gol Paqua - he took a moment to register Kaimaradan's attitude - "...and you know what, if you hate me so much why do you keep saving my life? Just let me die already."

"*No. I want to make sure you suffer as much as possible.*" Kaimaradan replied as coldly as ever.

Breowakoe could feel that she really meant it but he was still too flustered to care. Even as he scolded her, he realized that he had participated in saving himself this time, but wasn't sure why. Perhaps he was led by an instinct. He quietly wondered if he really wanted to die.

-

Night had fallen by the time Breowakoe made it back to Gol Paqua. His arms, still healing, flopped limply at his sides. His toes were blistered from walking on sand for hours. He felt nervous as he approached the great gate, wondering if

Thrakarnid had turned the King against him. Was Thrakarnid even allowed to report to the King? He seemed too lowly a soldier for that. He stared at it in silence for a moment, and the gate opened for him. Nervously between the gate drones, he walked into the quiet city.

Once within the walls, he hobbled over to the barracks, but it was pitch black inside. He tapped on the door with his knee, but still saw no movement through the window. Down the road he saw the inviting pink and red lights of "The Painted Slave," but pushed the shameful thought away, knowing this was no time to indulge in fantasy. He marched up the great stone steps of the palace, channelling thripsis into each stride to bound five steps at once. At the top, he knocked on the gate of the palace with his knee. His heart pounded, wondering what Thrakarnid had told the King. He was furiously eager to prove his loyalty.

A guard opened the peep hole and shut it; then the gate opened. The guard stopped him in the doorway.

"Welcome back, Lord Breowakoe. Please do not disturb King Grona at -"

Breowakoe walked past the guard brusquely. There was no way King Grona didn't want to hear from him. The throne room was empty, and Breowakoe could hear subtle splashing noises as he approached the truss to the bath.

"Thrakarnid tried to have his men kill me!" he voiced as he burst into the room.

Breowakoe readily regretted his intrusion upon seeing King Grona's abdomen retract from inside one of his concubines. Every one of the concubines was there with him, sprawled out dramatically across the far side of the bath. They looked like they belonged in a painting, staring at him from across the room. King Grona staggered back into a seated position in the shallow bath, a satisfied look on his face.

"Oh... sorry for interrupting, my King..." Breowakoe sheepishly recoiled.

King Grona laughed.

"There's nothing to worry about, Breowakoe. Thrakarnid has been demoted to a foot soldier. He was told by Colonel Cert to inform you of the mission and he did not do so."

Breowakoe squinted, failing to understand the calm in the King's voice.

"Not only that, he tried to have me killed!" Breowakoe protested, hoping further action would be taken.

"Thrakarnid didn't trust a Nethriel who had been made a

Lieutenant in the blink of an eye with information on the whereabouts of Nethriel settlements. Most Grobut can see Nethriel only as the obsequious breed, and they don't understand exceptions. I can't blame Thrakarnid for that. But the good news for you is that you will be taking over his rank of captain. If it's retribution you seek, I promise you, that will sting him more than you know."

Breowakoe wasn't sure how King Grona had uncovered the truth of the matter on his own, knowing what tales Thrakarnid had likely tried to fabricate.

"So, that's what those files were? The coordinates of Nethriel settlements?"

"Yes, and they were recovered safely; good job, today. Now, go enjoy yourself. Enough with all this fussing," King Grona smiled, and waved Breowakoe away as he tilted his head back and let his concubines nuzzle into him. The warmth of the compliment washed over Breowakoe's squalid heart.

Mischa came down the stairs to Breowakoe's right, completely nude, shot him an expression he did not recognize, then waded into the bath. Breowakoe lingered in the doorway in an uncomfortable calm. The only sound in the room was a few playful splashes echoing from the long side of the bath.

King Grona seemed to be high or intoxicated.

"King Grona... my lord..." Breowakoe started.

"You're still here?" the King muttered without budging or looking back up. One of his concubines began pouring a fancy glass of something into his mouth.

"May I go to The Painted Slave?"

There was a pause. Grona had a confused look on his face and Mischa whispered something in his ear.

"Oh... of course, of course you're free to explore the Kingdom."

"But... but what if Grobut there tell me to get lost? Can I have one of those… things that tell people that I have your permission?" Breowakoe asked longingly, like a kid asking his crush to a dance.

"Oh, you don't need that..." King Grona's head tilted lazily to the other side. "If anyone gives you trouble just kill them," he added, a big smile on his face, eyes still closed. He seemed to be drifting off to sleep.

"Oh, ok, thank you, my King," Breowakoe answered awkwardly, as he turned and left the throne room.

He bounded down the stone steps excitedly, for he felt respected and free. He was developing a feeling of deep love for Coabra Grona, who always seemed to be in his corner. Breo turned down the street by the barracks. The night was still so quiet, the sand still held a glimmer of warmth in the pitch black, and in the mid-distance he saw the familiar sign with flashing red and pink lights. His heart fluttered as he approached the small clay building, and its door pushed open for him with ease.

There was a loud noise inside, a series of patterned reverberations. It must have been music for Grobut, and it made his head spin. He ascended a short flight of steps to see a flood of pink lights and magical, spinning tubes that glowed. There were Nethriel women wearing next to nothing walking everywhere, dancing on platforms, and many drones seated at tables. A particularly large Grobut put his hands on Breowakoe's chest and shoved him. "Get out. No Nethriel inside."

"What? I see Nethriel here..." Breowakoe tried to reason with the fellow as he stumbled to regain his balance on the bottom step.

"No Nethriel MEN, genius."

The bouncer descended the stairs to see him out the door, but the next time he lay hands on Breowakoe he was boiled alive in his own fluids. His husk fell just inside the door at the foot of the stairs and no one seemed to notice. Breowakoe climbed back into the establishment with a twinkle in his eye. He felt a little out of place, and the looks he was getting confirmed that he was. The Nethriel women working there looked shocked, and the Grobut in the booths were gesturing angrily and looking around. The girl behind the bar raised a hand as he approached. She looked afraid even to be seen near him.

"We don't serve Nethriel men. You need to leave."

"I am the aspect of hatred and I am working directly under King Grona; he told me I could come here."

"Time to go, swine."

Some of the Grobut from the booth closest to the door had come over and put their hands on his shoulders.

"All right," Breowakoe said under his breath in frustration. He rose to his feet and turned to face the entire bar.

"King Grona told me I could come here. I don't want to bother anybody; just pretend I'm not here!" he pleaded.

"NO NETHRIEL MEN! IT DOESN'T MATTER IF YOU'RE THE ASPECT OF HATRED!" a distressed Grobut yelled from the back.

"You're full of shit! You don't know the King!"

A punch to the back of the head knocked Breowakoe over; his noggin bounced off the bar, twisting his neck. The two Grobut who had been standing behind him began stomping him out while he was on the floor. His mostly healed arms extended and grabbed one of each of their ankles. Their eyes exploded and the room went silent. The 'music' stopped, and Grobut standing way at the back stood up to see what was going on. Breowakoe picked himself up and again addressed the room.

"I don't mean anyone harm, but by permission of the King, I'll kill anyone who stands in my way!"

As the patrons realized Breowakoe really was an aspect, a grim acceptance took hold of the bar. Several walked out and many of the staff made a start toward the door, looking back nervously. Breowakoe sat down at the bar and rested his cheek on his knuckles. The remaining Grobut looked categorically unbothered, high or drunk out of their minds. The staff calmed down when Breowakoe did, proving himself not to be a continuing threat.

"All right... what can I get you?" the bartender asked tentatively as the peculiar music started up again.

"What do you have?" Breowakoe asked with a smile, his excitement to be out doing something picking up again.

"Uh, well... we have blood from Nethriel men. Uhm... we have ghom, which is this, uh... it's like a drink from this root plant from the downstream tar sands -"

"Sound's lovely! I'll take one," Breowakoe said with a laugh.

He looked around at the Nethriel women who had resumed their dancing. A glass of what looked like mud was placed in front of him.

"Thank you!" he said cheerfully.

The bartender walked to the far side of the bar to tend to a Grobut patron. Breowakoe didn't know what he had been expecting in coming here, and it was a far cry from his wildest fantasies, but it wasn't bad.

"E-excuse me," a female voice broke through his train of thought.

A new Nethriel bartender was before him.

"The King said I could come here -"

"Oh, I know, I don't mind that you're here," she said apologetically.

Breowakoe was unfamiliar with someone being polite to

him, so he just stared at her like a barbarian, hoping for her to lead the interaction. She had hair the colour of the sands and a scar on her chin, but she was beautiful. Within him, Breowakoe identified a new feeling blossoming inside Kaimaradan. He could feel that she didn't like the girl, or, more precisely, she didn't like how he liked the girl.

"Are you the aspect of hatred?" the bartender continued, nervously.

"Yes, I am. Why?"

The girl looked around feverishly and sank below the bar where Breowakoe couldn't see her. Moments later, she surfaced.

"I have something I want to show you; it's in the back room there. Go, and I'll meet you in a few minutes, ok?" she instructed timorously.

Breowakoe felt blindly hopeful, at first, with no understanding of where this was going. The girl put on a fake smile and began tending to other patrons.

Breowakoe had an inkling that this could be a trap, and while waiting in the back room he readied himself for combat. There were purple lights in the room that made everything look interesting. Volumes of time passed and his anxiety grew. Just as he arrived at restlessness, the girl emerged. She was breathing a little heavily and that made him uncomfortable, but he smiled when she entered. She knelt before him and was fiddling with something in her bra.

"Ok, so there's this drug the Grobut use; we sell capsules of it here but it's very expensive because it's hard to find in nature, so I had to steal it from the safe."

"Oh, y-you didn't have to do that for me," Breowakoe said, a bit confused, a bit excited, and a bit apologetic.

"- But on Nethriel it has a different effect," she continued, ignoring him. "I caught a whiff of it once while serving a wealthy patron, and I've never been the same. It makes you remember things... things that happened before."

Out of her bra she pulled a familiar object. It took him a minute but Breowakoe recognized it. It was a capsule of essence, the reward Tiricora promised him for helping her find Globramora.

"Is that -"

Before he could finish his sentence the girl broke the object in front of his face and traces of a faint, familiar smell entered his nostrils and murmured in the back of his mind. The girl threw the pieces of the capsule to the side. She was trembling, looking at him with half a look of horror and half a look of hope. She took Breowakoe by the hands and gazed intently up at him.

"You have to save us. You have to remember who you are," she whispered aggressively, the sound in her voice becoming more panicked.

Breowakoe's heart was pounding. He couldn't remember anything and didn't know what she was talking about.

"I'm sorry; I don't; I can't... I don-"

"Please, PLEASE. I've been a slave here for hundreds of years. This place - it makes you forget what time is. Some of these girls have been here for a thousand years, and every day they live it as new. They have no idea. Please, you have to save us!"

The girl poked her head out of the curtain of the private room to make sure no one had overheard their conversation. Breowakoe felt a deep sense of dread of the burden she was placing on him.

"I'm sorry. I don't know what you're talking about - I want to go."

He tried to shuffle around her awkwardly as she clung to him, begging.

"The Grobut are demons, DEMONS. We are in hell right now, you died... probably a long time ago! You need to remember, please! PLEASE!"

Breowakoe looked down at her and pushed past her back into the main bar and out the door into the cool night. He was horrified and felt like he was going to be sick.

He stumbled up the stone steps to the palace and through the throne room. He was relieved to find the great bath empty as he passed it. He made it through the winding, moist tunnels to his room and collapsed on the bed. The echoes of Mischa's singing haunted him as, for much of the night, he lay wide awake. When at last the lullabies stopped, and the darkness lost its shape, Breowakoe slipped under a curtain of sleep only to be tormented in dream.

<u>Obsequious Breed - 11</u>

"Two hells below, no heaven above," Mrs. Barrister's voice echoed through a blackened room.

Dunstan could see nothing - not the walls, nor the floor, nor the ceiling.

"Two hells below, no heaven above."

A click sounded overhead, shining a spotlight on Dunstan in his desk.

Mrs. Barrister's face appeared before him, leaning over him and whispering, "Two hells below, no heaven above."

Dunstan felt like he wanted to cry. A dog was barking somewhere.

"Below us, the Squalor," she declared as her face morphed into the face of the old hag from Goliah "- and below that, the Spoil."

The barking got louder and louder as Dunstan fell back in his chair, into a cold, thick fluid. He sat up, gasping for air, rising out of the mud. Pus spewed from his infected knee and Mr. Doggy was licking it. Mr. Doggy went still, growled, looked up, and barked loudly in Dunstan's face. Dunstan jumped back, then found himself sitting in his parent's kitchen; they sat across from him at the table, stone faced. Their lips did not move, but their yelling echoed into the room from another part of the house. Both their faces transformed into that of Mrs. Barrister.

"To the Squalor go the good," Dunstan's father said, blankly.

"To the Spoil goes evil," his mother contributed.

A loud gunshot sounded, and the world went dark. Dunstan felt an intense, moist heat and the sensation of falling. He was back at the dig site.

"There is no god. The Katharnians discovered the hells thousands of years ago. They were an ancient civilization far more advanced than we, but their weak King led to their demise."

Dunstan blinked and was in the court of a palace. The humans around him were mutating, becoming monsters. His heart was pounding.

"What's going on!?" he screamed in a deep, adult voice.

Everyone was screaming, becoming insectoid, eyes falling out, flesh deliquescing into heaps.

"What's happening!?"

Dunstan rose from his throne. A woman was holding his face, lovingly, staring into his eyes. She was beautiful. She *took his hand and guided it to her pregnant belly. The woman looked back up to his face and smiled. Her face hollowed, and she began to scream. Her arms retracted into her body. her fingers peeling apart once they reached her shoulders. Her eyes became smaller, beadier, blacker. She miscarried and, on the floor, the carcass of a large, misshapen bird sat in a pool of blood. The beauty's legs fused together and her pinky fingers grew as they slid down to her knees. Her hair fell out. Her ring fingers grew as they slid down to her hips. Her skin turned brown and she scuttled away, a massive centipede. Dunstan vomited and fell into it, then plunged into a great, deep pool. His eyes opened and he now stared out from a vat, the hag of Goliah leaning over him, reaching to the top of his head and lifting him out of the water to throw him into a novel darkness. Barking resonated through the moist, hot column and at last he hit the sinew of human carcasses at the top of the pile.*

-

Breowakoe burst awake. He couldn't breathe. He was choking on his own vomit. He keeled over as it spilled out of him. He was shaking violently. As strong as he had become through ten years and a week in the hells, he felt like the scared child who had died only moments ago. His heart was racing as never before - even in all the torture he had endured. He vomited again, looked around, and for the first time realized that he was *in THE Spoil* - literally in the hell Mrs. Barrister had spoken of - and in the palace of a demon King. He got up and ran to the doorway, then changed his mind, and went to the back corner of the room to curl up in a ball. It felt like his heart was going to explode. There was nothing he could do. He had died many years ago. He was already dead. Breowakoe's body went numb; his head smashed into the wall and slid down with him as he passed out.

Some hours later, Breowakoe woke up on his face, still in the corner of the room. He got up and sat with his back against the wall, reflecting on the time when he had lived. He checked in with his own thripsis and was pleasantly surprised that he could still feel it. The energy of the hells was more potent than that of the living world. Breowakoe felt so present living here, so much more alive. He placed his hands on himself to feel that indeed he had a physical form, as did the floor, as did the wall. Another stark realization hit as he felt the giant centipede coiled around his torso just under his skin -

how had he become so accustomed to the feeling of Kaimaradan at her perch? He started to lose it again with panic, as any human would to realize this plight. He could still feel her thripsis; it felt surprisingly calm. She was quiet, but he knew she was awake and wondered if she had been observing his thoughts.

"Did you see my dream?" he asked, in thought.

Kaimaradan remained silent for a time.

"*I did not see your dream; I awoke as you vomited,*" she replied plainly.

Breowakoe got the sense that she knew things that she was neglecting to share. He recalled the centipede he had seen in the dream and wondered if those had been her memories, but the centipede in the dream had been much larger than Kaimaradan with a brown carapace rather than black and red.

"Kai... was there ever a time that you were human?" he asked.

The silence in his mind was deafening.

"*No. I have always been a Satrian,*" she replied simply, seeming to choose her words so carefully that Breo became more suspicious.

"Would you get your lazy ass to the throne room,

Nethriel! King Grona has summoned you!" Mischa yelled from the doorway. "What are you doing in the corner? … Oh, look - you made a mess!" she fussed, pointing to the vomit. "You better clean that up later; I'll make sure to rub your nose in it!"

Breowakoe sighed and rose to his feet. He followed her through the narrow halls to the throne room where King Grona stood with the Colonel and several other apparently military Grobut.

"Oh, good, you're here!" King Grona exclaimed. "I have assembled our entire armed forces and we will leave to invade two smaller Nethriel cities within the hour. General Rogba will take the bulk of the forces to the further, but larger city, 'Thelise,' and I would like you and Colonel Cert to pillage 'Hurst.' Remember, as we discussed yesterday, don't kill any of the Nethriel women, and try to limit the number of men killed, especially if they appear to stand down readily. Those are the most obsequious and we will use them to father the next generation in our farms."

Breowakoe was barely listening. His head was still spinning, racing through memories.

"Glory to Gol Paqua!" King Grona shouted triumphantly,

a fist in the air.

The Grobut in the room echoed his sentiment and began filing out. Breowakoe looked around nervously, trying to remember what he was supposed to be doing. He worried that the Grobut could tell he now remembered the living world, but nothing suggested that they did. He would have to deal with those memories later to be sure they remained private. He spotted old Colonel Cert toward the back of the line, summoned his focus, jogged up beside him, and walked him out.

"I'm sorry about Thrakarnid; his demotion was a long time coming, though, to be honest." Cert said, staring straight ahead.

It took Breowakoe a moment to remember the eclipsed events of yesterday. "Oh, that's all right."

"Make us proud today, honorary Grobut!" Cert said roughly, patting him on the shoulder.

There was a great swell of noise from the top of the stone steps. Breowakoe could feel the thripsis of thousands of Grobut in the distance, on the far side of the wall. Even this far away he could feel the vibrations of their marching in place and the thunder of their voices in unison. The military higher-ups flew over to the wall, and Breowakoe followed in his own way. From atop the wall, he could see the army. There must have been 50,000 Grobut drones arranged into five massive phalanxes of 10,000 each, facing the starboard wall of the Spoil. The backmost line was difficult to see, veiled by a distant sandstorm.

General Rogba flew ahead, and in three minutes was hovering in the air before the third company. Colonel Cert followed closely behind, hovering before the fifth. Using the store of his thripsis and focusing it into his lungs, General Rogba shouted.

"What we do here today will secure the existence of the next thousand generations of our people! Today Verivoluae smiles upon the Grobut! Today Verivoluae honours its chosen as they make their mark upon creation! First through fourth companies, we fly for Thelise; fifth company flies with Colonel Cert! Fly my drones!"

The swarm roared in jubilant agreement and ascended in a deafening collective hum of their wings. The juddering was dizzying and concussive and jolted Breowakoe out of his thoughts. Despite it being an army of demons on their way to enslave humans, there was something about the fury and power he saw before him that filled him with awe. He channeled thripsis near full capacity, rocketing up to the front to be with Colonel Cert. Somehow in that moment, he felt that he belonged. Cert kept his eyes on the horizon as they traveled fearlessly into the storm, even into near blindness.

After an hour, there was a distinct mood shift. They were flying into a storm that seemed to have no end. Regular Nethriel had no thriptic presence so the Grobut had no way of knowing if they were traveling in the right direction. This whole operation depended on the accuracy of one report by a single Piccaro - creatures known for their lies. Colonel Cert never seemed to lose faith and although he kept it to himself, Breowakoe could feel that they were traveling in the right direction.

He found that he was aware of everything around him, every object and person: the walls, the sand, the ceiling, the entirety of Goliah, and deserted cities downstream that he had never seen before. Breowakoe closed his eyes, puzzled with the sudden emergence of this new ability. This was far different to the awareness of large bodies of thripsis he had experienced the past few days. He gasped to realize that he could no longer feel the presence of Verivoluae - at least, not thriptically. He could see its light and feel its warmth. He could feel Tiricora's presence easily from kilometres upon kilometres away in her tower, but he could not connect with the source of all energy in the Spoil.

"What's going on?" Breowakoe thought to himself, goosebumps emerging on his arms. "Is this because I took the capsule of essence?" He directed the question to Kaimaradan, who stirred, but remained silent.

A dark figure caught his attention on the sand below; Colonel Cert seemed to notice it, as well: a Nethriel male, wearing a brown robe. Colonel Cert's thripsis burst through his lungs.

"DESCEND!" he bellowed.

The resonant beating of wings slowed as the fifth company landed heavily on the sand. The Nethriel man before them was kneeling on the ground with hands folded together in front of him. The army took a quiet moment to observe him; he seemed so at peace, flecks of sand billowing against his weathered cheek.

"MARCH, MARCH AND TAKE WHAT IS OURS!" Colonel Cert bellowed.

A drone wasted no time in scooping up the obviously

weak and subservient praying man to fly him back in the direction of Gol Paqua. The faint lights of buildings poking through the silica haze in the near distance were their guide, now. The Grobut roared as they piled into the village.

Some Nethriel men ran out of their straw huts with pitchforks and swords, only to be cut down instantly and packed to bloating with sterile bile. Their bellies were so stretched they began to tear. The manifold horrors were only beginning and it was difficult to focus on any one of them as the fifth company ripped through Hurst. Countless drones ran right past Breowakoe and into the homes of his fellow humans. The screams of women, of men, and of children were all around him and yet were faint because the wind blowing against the buildings made monstrous moans. Lament brewed - suspended in the sky, the deep light of the sun was unable to kiss the town through the weeping sand.

Breowakoe knew that his skills were not needed here. These Nethriel had no means of defending themselves. He approached a metal lamppost who's lulling ring drew him out of the chaos. A larger building was in front of him, with swinging saloon doors flapping open and shut with the constant flow of drones into the building. He could see a

Nethriel woman being raped with each opening of the doors, and with each closing, Breowakoe tried to find a peace that never came. He strolled over to the building himself, reading above the door that it was an orphanage. He entered a large room to find a second woman in a similar predicament, being taken next to a pile of colourful blocks. Both women appeared to be in their 50s or 60s; they must have been the children's caretakers. Breowakoe saw Grobut pouring into the back halls of the orphanage. It made sense that children soon to be raised in slavery would likely become the most subservient. It was strange, then, that no Grobut were returning from the back halls.

Breowakoe made his way back there to investigate and saw a large bunking room filled with Grobut feasting upon children - some already dead, some still in the process of being eaten alive. Some Grobut ate quickly, with a great, furious hunger, while others savoured their meals. The screams were bloodcurdling. In their engineering, Grobut had inherited the teeth of Nethriel, which were not particularly sharp, but they had large heads and jaws that with their insect eyes must have made a truly nightmarish death. One Grobut was taking his time, biting each of a nine-year-old boy's fingers off like carrot sticks; another took messy, barbaric bites out of a child's arm and calves, their elastic, young skin stretching about a foot before ripping off the bone.

"What are you doing!? Children will grow into the best slaves!" Breowakoe found himself yelling, trying his best to stop the madness. His voice suffocated in the cacophony.

"Hey, look, I'm your nanny!" a drone joked as he entered the room wearing the skinned face of one of the 50-year-old women from the front.

A little girl holding a toy truck burst into tears upon seeing it. The Grobut crouched down to give her a closer look.

"Don't be rude, now, you're up well past bedtime, aren't you?" he mocked, speaking in terms he must have thought a Nethriel would use.

He grinned a huge grin as her sobbing escalated into a scream of despair; he then opened his jaws wide and bit off her face in one powerful motion.

Breowakoe had seen enough. He stumbled out of the orphanage and puked into the dust. A dog was barking in his left ear, then his right, and his head was spinning. He crawled a few metres through a side street and up behind a house to try to break free of the madness. He picked himself up, having found a quiet place, but through the window of another house he saw parents being devoured in front of a young boy who screamed as he looked on.

How many drones were actually following orders? Most of these Nethriel were supposed to be captured and yet without authority's gaze, the drones just got off on defiling Nethriel. Breowakoe walked up to the window as the mother was killed with a bite to the throat. Her slippery eight-year-old boy somehow freed himself of the clutches of the Grobut, as the drone leaned back in laughter. The boy ran at the drone eating his mother, with violence in his eyes, so the one eating the father paused and dispelled his thripsis with a kick to the boy's patella, breaking his leg backwards.

And for a moment Breowakoe could feel only his own knee, broken backwards in that same way while he had tried to defend Mr. Doggy. A bitter recollection of his own powerlessness morphed into self-disgust to realize that he still felt like a victim when he no longer needed to be one. He had accepted an image of himself as frail and confused, but the essence allowed him now to let that die - that image and that self. If Grona were to kill him, so be it.

Breowakoe tore open the wall of the house. He was not

channeling his own thripsis, as he found himself suddenly able to control the thripsis that flowed freely in the environment. The Spoil itself now seemed another limb he could control with a newly awakened level of consciousness.

After creating a vacuum around the heads of all three laughing drones, Breowakoe delighted as they suffocated. When they tried to flee the void, he manipulated the air to move their bubble with them; and when a Grobut tried to make one last dying attempt on the boy's life, Breowakoe increased the air pressure outside its bubble, causing its head to explode.

"What are you doing!?" a bitter voice sounded behind him.

Breowakoe turned coldly, not caring about his own life in this hell. Thrakarnid ground his teeth in fury, making a direct challenge. Without hesitation Breowakoe moved on Thrakarnid, ready to enjoy himself to the fullest.

"I knew you were a traitor. Our King will kill you, fill you with his ripened bile, and you will serve, castrated, for the rest of your days, watching your women and children enslaved!" Thrakarnid said savagely.

Breowakoe had heard it all and wasn't phased by sick talk, or tough talk, or any other kind of talk. He imagined

Thrakarnid's legs cut off at the knees and in moments the energy of the Spoil made it so. The bug screamed as sand got into its wounds. Breowakoe then opened Thrakarnid's abdomen effortlessly with his hand, channeling a bit of his own thripsis. In his left hand he held the back of the bug's head and with his right forced its abdomen into its own mouth. It was satisfying to feel each vertebrae pop and dislocate as he went. Controlling the small well of thripsis within Thrakarnid, Breowakoe then had the creature pump its own sterile bile into its lungs. He smiled into Thrakarnid's face, stepping on two of his flailing arms and watching his eyes roll back in its head as he drowned.

Standing up, Breowakoe realized he was surrounded by Grobut. Some in the skies, others on the ground. They kept their distance.

"It seems Thrakarnid was right about you after all, traitor." Colonel Cert crowed confidently from the roof of a nearby house. Breowakoe looked up at him, saying nothing, and feeling calm. They were positioned just outside the range of his own thriptic channeling - it seemed they had more intel on him than he had suspected. Perhaps King Grona had not trusted Breowakoe as fully as he would have had him believe.

"Axes!" Colonel Cert yelled. Grobut all around him oiled their blades with sterile bile, hurling them at Breowakoe. Breowakoe breathed deeply and channeled his thripsis. The powerful current of air repelled the axes and set fire to many of the houses around him. He knew better than to stop channeling and stared up at Colonel Cert, trying to devise a plan.

"You sure are the aspect of hatred," Colonel Cert commented. "I guess it won't be easy to find an opening."

Colonel Cert recollected his thoughts for a moment, then called out, "Attack formation C!".

Breowakoe expanded his awareness and noticed a long line of Grobut flying directly above him, powering into the gravity. Each drone held the shoulders of the one before him, their free hands dual-wielding biled axes. It was a suicide charge, a hopeful attempt to have a single axe connect with their target. Breowakoe found an unexpected respect for the Grobut knowing they were willing to give their lives for the sake of their Kingdom.

As the first Grobut hit the outer perimeter of his channeling, Breowakoe realized his current output was not enough to stop them. The first few bodies, already scorched, were ploughing through the blast of his thripsis like an unstoppable force. He was forced to stop channeling radially and instead dispelled energy upwards from the crown of his head. A thin torrent of fire and radiation shot up in the air like an arrow, making it a quarter of the way to the ceiling. The Grobut in the suicide charge didn't even have time to scream before they roasted. Breowakoe jumped out of the way as a heavy pile of carcases came crashing to the ground.

A sudden pain jolted into the back of his right ribs. He looked to see an axe plunged snugly into his side between the wrapping helices of Kaimaradan's form. His ability to channel thripsis was leaving his body, and he began to panic.

"And... checkmate!" Colonel Cert laughed from the roof, still unwound from the speed of his throw. "You did not die in vain, Brothers..." he continued under his breath, jumping to the sand from his perch. "This is a historic day. In the thousand years the Grobut have existed, we have held only the aspect of power. With three aspects, we will dominate these wastes for the next 10,000 years."

Kaimaradan had already maneuvered towards Breowakoe's heart, injecting him with the prickly cold.

Colonel Cert, attuned to what was happening under Breowakoe's skin, delayed his advance. He was watching

Breowakoe like a hawk, and over time, a small smile crept across his face. Sure enough, even after Kaimaradan's injection, Breowakoe was still unable to channel his own thripsis. His panic deepened with the understanding that the Grobut higher ups were aware of Kaimaradan's toxin, and had developed a countermeasure.

A frenzied worry took hold of Kaimaradan, seeming herself to be unable to generate thripsis. Breowakoe turned and started to run, but the wall of Grobut surrounding him had not budged. Colonel Cert ran towards him now, axes drawn back and ready to deliver the final blow. Kaimaradan scrambled under Breowakoe's skin. He calmed his mind and summoned the thripsis of the air into him. As though a singularity had spawned in the village, the air of Hurst rushed toward the core, kicking up more sand and blinding the Grobut.

The radiance of Verivoluae itself shone through Breowakoe's body, destroying the bile toxin in his cells. Colonel Cert stopped moving metres away from Breowakoe, staring at him, dumbfounded.

Breowakoe infused both his own thripsis and the environmental thripsis with the aspect of hatred. There was a moment of profound stillness.

"Are you... are you THAT Breowakoe?" There was real fear in Colonel Cert's eyes. "Are you the false god!?"

The air itself combusted as Breowakoe released his vacuum hold on it. The flames were so intense that from a distance, through the storm, it must have looked like a second sun. All buildings and Grobut within sight burned so quickly that to the eye they simply vanished. Ten metres of sand underneath Breowakoe's feet were pushed away, exposing a Spoil-rock floor beneath that he had never seen. The sandstorm had vanished, muscled out of the sky by the expanding wall of torrid air. Burning debris from structures and the flesh of Grobut and Nethriel who had been at the edge of the blast rained down from the sky. The metal lamp posts distant enough that they weren't uprooted were melted and bent deep to the ground. They formed an eerie, metal crop circle leaving one last impression that a town had once been here.

At last, Breowakoe felt peace. He climbed out of the pit he had dug for himself and began walking downstream in what remained of his clothes.

"*Breowakoe... is it really you?*" Kaimaradan asked, for the first time calling him by name.

"Yeah... what do you mean?" Breowakoe asked, but he

knew what she meant. He had heard that name somewhere before, even before his death, but couldn't place it.

"No... it is not you. Sorry, I do not know. There are some mysteries I may never understand about this hell..." Kaimaradan trailed off. *"Breowakoe, where are we going?"*

Her tone was so different, almost sweet - he was so unaccustomed to it.

"I'm going to go kill the rest of the army."

"Why?"

"I'm not sure. Even though the humans here are wicked, it feels right to protect them." Breowakoe paused to think about this answer. "Or maybe it just feels good to make my own decision, and live with it."

Breowakoe channeled environmental thripsis through his legs and arms to fly into the desert at ten times the speed he had been capable of before.

"I see," she replied simply.

Becoming more confident in his new power, Breowakoe believed he could harness even more environmental thripsis than he had just done in Hurst. He could feel the first, second, third, and fourth companies of the Grobut army still many kilometres ahead. He could feel Thelise, a city about twelve times the size of Hurst, its many people unaware of the advancing doom. The army had not adjusted its flight path; it seemed they had no idea what had just happened to the fifth company – they could not sense thripsis as Breowakoe now could.

His heart beat a little harder. He had had a close call just now, fighting a piece of the fifth company after many drones had already left. Now he was about to face ten times that number of drones with a General, rather than a Colonel, at the helm. He was closing in on them quickly and could feel the deep vibration in the storm, the furious beating of paper wings.

Then, he saw them. The monstrous army, still a half an hour's flight from Thelise. Some turned their heads, noticing him in return. Breowakoe drew his focus into a line and cut a deep inferno - one kilometre long - into the ground. The four companies came to a halt perplexed by the molten glass ahead of them. Breowakoe dropped to the sand behind the molten line, directly facing General Rogba.

"Aspect of hatred, what are these actions!?" General Rogba's voice boomed through the sandstorm.

Breowakoe closed his eyes and placed his hands on the fine sand.

"This is your last warning, hatred!" the clueless General threatened.

Breowakoe inhaled the energy of the vast desert around him, of the crystals in the air. He grappled with the prodigious heat from without and from within himself, channeling all of it into the line he drew. Molten glass built, and swelled, and rose like a great wave, embellishing General Rogba's view of him in an orange hue and blocking any axes flung his way. He could hear that the General was yelling but could no longer make out the words in the roaring wind. The drones flew higher, trying to get over the wave, but it lifted too quickly. Through convection, intense heat tore at the wings of the drones nearest to him. The tsunami of molten glass expanded until it had reached half the height of the ceiling, and drones on the other side realized they could not outpace it. They scattered in every direction, breaking formation, in pandemonium – but they could not escape the breadth of the glass wall any more than its height. The general was horse with yelling to get his soldiers under control, his thripsis exhausted.

Realizing they could not escape him, Breowakoe closed his eyes once more. He channeled untold energy to bring the lava to a crest. The sound of wings beating the air diminished as screams crescendoed to dominate all hearing. One by one the Grobut army became like any other bug found trapped within amber.

Breowakoe allowed himself to indulge in the silence and, when the light on the other side of his eyelids finally faded, 40,000 Grobut lay dead under a beautiful, cool, smooth sheet of glass extending almost as far as eyes could see. Rising to his bare feet he walked with pride along it - his beautiful creation. He saw some faces perfectly preserved in horror, for eternity, while others looked rather expressionless, as though they had simply accepted death. It took some time to find the General.

"Ha! Died yelling. Died doing what he loved most!" Breowakoe joked aloud to himself.

It was a long walk to Gol Paqua, but Breowakoe wanted the time to strategize. The storms of the morning were a distant memory as Verivoluae's light faded and a cool breeze cleared some of the soot from Breowakoe's skin, soothing away his ailments in the haunting dark.

"*Are you going to fight Coabra Grona?*" Kaimaradan piped up.

"Yes. I am."

"*Well... I am sorry to say it, but I think he will kill you.*"

Breowakoe rolled his eyes. The nerve of this nagging centipede.

"Did you not see what I just did? There was an old woman in Goliah just before I met you. She told me I had two aspects within me. I don't know what I have other than hatred, but whatever it is - I think the capsule of essence awakened it. King Grona stands no chance."

"*Coabra Grona is the aspect of power, not some drone foot soldier. It does not matter how much thripsis you throw at him, the density of it is unlikely to be enough to kill him. Even if you are channeling at your capacity, if he lands one good hit, you are dead.*"

Breowakoe stopped walking.

"If he scares you so much, you are free to go. Are you afraid of Tiricora? She won't come after you in the middle of this desert."

"*You are also free to go; Coabra Grona will not leave his Kingdom to come after you.*"

"Where would I go? I am a boy who died and went to hell. If I go to Goliah I'll end up fighting Tiricora, according to you. I don't know what I want. I think about my parents' suffering, and my only friend, Mr. Doggy, in the clutches of that monster and I just feel a burning wrath. I want to go to the Planelands. I want to live again, and do right by the world above. I want to kill Mr. Doggy's owner. But here I am, dead. So instead, I'm going to kill every piece of shit sadist in this world. That's all I can do. I am trapped in death, and you know what? If King Grona kills me, at least I'll be free of the Spoil."

Kaimaradan remained silent. She made no attempt to leave, and Breowakoe's walking resumed. Moments of silence passed in the quiet blackness.

"*Beyond the sun there is a moon that does not glow or shine.*

Verivoluae, our gracious host, imprisoned him behind.
Creation is a trick of light, but truer forms exist at night;
Reflect upon the spoiled sight, until destruction's time."

"What's that?" Breowakoe asked.

"*It is a poem, roughly translated from Satrian. My sister, Fairglow, used to sing it to me when we were larvae. She was gifted, more attuned to the deeper ways of the Spoil.*"

"Oh. Ok..." Breowakoe felt uneasy with how friendly Kaimaradan had become.

"*Breowakoe, do you know what Verivoluae is?*"

Kaimaradan continued. *"It is a great, furious, ego."*

"What can that possibly mean? Every time something is explained to me I only feel more confused," Breowakoe lashed, frustrated.

"The Spoil is a realm very unlike the Planelands. It is a deep, disturbed consciousness. Verivoluae, the aspect of creation, is its ego, the greatest fragment of that consciousness. We aspects comprise its other parts."

Breowakoe's mouth fell open as he was beginning to understand.

"It is common knowledge that there are seven aspects, in addition to Verivoluae, the aspect of creation; they are cruelty, hatred, power, cunning, control, and apathy. But my sister's poem speaks of an eighth aspect - a piece of the Spoil's consciousness so forsaken by the ego that it was imprisoned in an impossible space. It is said to exist infinitely far downstream, behind Verivoluae in the never-ending tunnel."

The hairs on Breowakoe's neck stood on end.

"That fragment is the 'deep self' or the will of the Spoil: Yoorkapala, the aspect of destruction. It is not aware of the world; it merely acts in it. That action is said to be what will terminate the Spoil. I do not know how, but I suspect that even

before you awoke in the Squalor you possessed the aspect of destruction, and it was because of the aspect of destruction that you were able to resist the Cultivator and awake at all."

Breowakoe scrambled for understanding.

"*I never imagined I would see it, and I never imagined it would be so intertwined with Verivoluae's own consciousness. It seems you can freely control the very thripsis of creation... Breo, I want to test something. I want you to try to control my thripsis.*"

He stopped walking, intrigued. He closed his eyes, identified Kaimaradan's aspect of cruelty and tried to bring it out of her. It was as futile as trying to move someone else's arm using one's own mind.

"Ok, good to know. I can't control other fragments of the consciousness."

"*Interesting... What is also interesting is that although it served you passively, you were unable to activate it until remembering your time in the Planelands, until you remembered who you were.*"

"Yeah, I don't know..." Breowakoe trailed off, remembering both components of his dream. It felt like two sets of memories existed within his mind. His life as Dunstan seemed almost less real than the chaos he had witnessed in that throne room of his dream.

Immolation - 12

Dawn broke as Breowakoe reached the Nethriel farms on the outskirts of Gol Paqua. He was surprised to see that it was a massive operation. None of the Nethriel imprisoned here appeared to have been given clothing. All were kept in pens with chain link walls and rooves. Women at various stages of pregnancy and those with young human babies sat in the mud of some cages, while other cages housed older children, women who did not appear to be pregnant, men who appeared to be castrated, and men just freshly captured from Hurst. The air - overwhelmed with the sour smell of feces and sweat - also reverberated with the various shrieks, moans, and gurgles of each stage of life.

"And how did you get out of your pen, piggy?" a high-voiced Grobut taunted as it approached. Breowakoe barely looked at it before decapitating it with the Spoil's thripsis.

Venturing further into the farms, Breo found himself in a steel-roofed underground section that must have been within or under the great wall of Gol Paqua. The sand bank sloped down, transitioning into a cooler clay - perhaps this whole area was a former clay mine for many of the buildings he had seen in the city.

Underground, Nethriel men were lined up in cuffs and chains off to the left, and there were strange little huts deeper into the cave on Breowakoe's right. Behind the huts were surgical tables over large drains that appeared to be for butchering and collecting blood. Shrieks echoed from the head of the line on the left, and leaning around a corner Breowakoe saw drones with paring knives performing castrations. As men approached the front of the line, they would often panic and try to run, only to be beaten or find their bondage inescapable. But most seemed to accept it, having already been brainwashed into thinking obedience was the only route to a better life. Perhaps, in their circumstances, the brainwashing was actually correct.

Ahead, Breowakoe identified the tunnel that led up to the arena, but before leaving the farms he sat cross-legged on the ground, making himself aware of every fence and chain and shackle in this vast flesh factory.

"Kai, do you see them?" Breowakoe asked.

"*You want me to corrode them?*" she confirmed.

"Yes, please."

"*Ok Breowakoe, I will do this for you if that is your desire, but that will take most of my thripsis, I will be unable to aid you in fighting Coabra Grona."*

Breowakoe said nothing and Kaimaradan began her task. He waited for the sound of chaos to break across his eardrums, but none ever came.

"It is done," Kaimaradan told him.

Still puzzled by the lack of commotion, Breowakoe stood up to look around. The cages were gone and yet the Nethriel still stood within their shadows. The men in line to be castrated continued walking forward. Children stopped their play at the shoulder of the dirt paths between muck pens. Breowakoe walked over to where the cages had been, looking one of the Nethriel men right in his eyes.

"Run, you're free, get out of here."

The Nethriel man became visibly upset and looked around frantically.

"No one's looking, just go!" Breowakoe reiterated impatiently.

The man took a step onto the dirt path and took his foot off. He simply shook his head, no, and turned away.

"They are too far gone. This is all they understand. Many of these people were born here and have lived here for generations."

Breowakoe realized Kaimaradan was right and a deeper fury burned within his heart as he marched deep into the tunnels. A pair of drones seeing him moved in to intercept - both were decapitated.

Breowakoe flew up the elevator shaft. Grobut tried to accost him in the prep rooms of the arena - decapitated - and he made his way outside. Gazing up at the great stone palace, his heart was pounding.

"Here we go..." he said to himself, channeling thripsis to his legs and blasting himself over much of the city.

He landed gently at the top of the great stone steps and knocked on the palace gate. The peep hole opened and a guard let him in. He marched into the courtroom where King Grona sat on the throne, his harem sprawled haphazardly about him.

"Breowakoe! What happened to your clothes? How did the raid go?"

King Grona sounded genuinely intrigued. He did have a real charisma that Breowakoe couldn't help but hate him for.

"Coabra Grona. I challenge you for the right of coronation."

King Grona stared at Breowakoe, looking at first to be perplexed. The concubines giggled and Mischa's cackling was particularly distinguishable. From a gallery up high on the wall behind him, the four foragers floated softly to the ground, channeling thripsis through their feet the same way Breowakoe did.

"A Nethriel may not challenge for coronation," Turia said, coldly.

"Be silent, Turia." King Grona's look of confusion had become a look of deep anger. "What happened in Hurst, Breowakoe?"

The room was silent; even Mischa looked tense standing next to the throne. Breowakoe felt fear as King Grona towered over him even at a distance; he briefly thought to accuse Colonel Cert of attacking him first but instead chose to own his actions.

"I killed everyone in the fifth company."

King Grona clenched his jaw and exhaled deeply. The concubines formed a line and left the room.

"Then, I flew to the rest of the army, still on their way to Thelise, and I killed all of them, too."

King Grona stepped off the platform and walked towards Breowakoe with thunderous steps. Breowakoe wasn't taking any chances. He channeled his thripsis and the heat of the room increased rapidly.

"We cannot allow you to fight him alone, King Grona. Breowakoe is a threat to our people's existence," Turia cried as he flew into a rage that Breowakoe had not suspected he possessed.

All four foragers channeled thripsis and Breowakoe felt his legs become heavy; his feet seemed glued to the ground. His blood pressure rocketed- mobility was the most important thing he had in this fight.

"ENOUGH, TURIA!" King Grona roared, in a flash bounding towards the foragers and punching a hole straight through Turia's chest.

Turia looked as shocked as Breowakoe as he dropped to the ground, dead. The other foragers stopped channeling, and tried to tend to their fallen colleague.

"Breowakoe, I accept your challenge. I will take great pleasure in killing you. The arena - now!"

"What if he wins!? We cannot ripen the bile of a Nethriel!" one of the remaining foragers pleaded. King Grona wasted no time in crushing its throat with one of his giant hands.

"You dare suggest I would lose to a fledgling Nethriel?

No. I will make him regret his betrayal."

King Grona turned to Breowakoe.

"I should have castrated you the minute you first walked into this room. I should have made you drink of my ripened bile and raise my young flylets to dominate your species for centuries to come," he said, taking a step closer. "I promise you, Breowakoe, I'll make you suffer before I kill you and take your aspect of hatred for myself. If there is anything you love in this world, I find it, subjugate it, or destroy it."

Breowakoe said nothing. He was trembling but tried not to show it.

"To the arena, now! I want my people to see how their King deals with betrayal," King Grona repeated.

Breowakoe turned and burst through the gate, flying like a falcon and diving into the center of the arena. Not a second later, a massive shockwave rattled him as King Grona landed a few metres in front of him.

"PEOPLE OF GOL PAQUA, I HAVE JUST LEARNED THAT THE ASPECT OF HATRED, WHOM I MADE HONORARY GROBUT, HAS BETRAYED US! COME TO THE ARENA AND WATCH YOUR KING ANSWER THIS BETRAYAL."

His voice rumbled into the sky, as he paced back and forth, never taking his eyes off Breowakoe. Bells tolled throughout the city. Even absent the 50,000 who were now gone, the arena filled quickly and with unparalleled uproar. Breowakoe was unsure just how to prepare himself - dread was building in his chest. He could feel Kaimaradan's worry within him. He jumped up and down in place, getting acclimatized to being on the balls of his feet and testing the speed of his movements while channeling into his legs.

"Ha! I'm actually excited!" King Grona grinned. "This may be the worthiest fight I have ever had. Try not to die too quickly, Breowakoe."

Breowakoe remained silent. Bombastic trash talk would not serve him, so he refrained from it, as always. This was a fight for survival and he could not afford anything but the purest focus. He made himself calm as the two surviving foragers floated to the arena pavilion from the palace. The arena was overflowing now.

"By the way, you - cruelty, centipede. I have no fight with you. If you want to live, you should get out of Breowakoe now. I can't promise to avoid you as I kill him," King Grona reasoned. Kaimaradan did not stir.

"ENOUGH STALLING. LET'S BEGIN!" King Grona roared, looking furiously at his foragers – one of whom mustered the courage to speak up.

"King Grona has accepted the aspect of hatred's challenge for the right of coronation; the winner of this match will become or remain the King of Gol Paqua and inherit the rights of ripened bile!" The forager hesitated before continuing. "This challenge is to be solely unarmed combat and it may end only in death!"

In the stands, the crowd was confused. King Grona waved one of his hands in an exasperated fashion.

"Without further delay, let the right of coronation begin!" the forager squeaked out.

Breowakoe channeled his hatred-infused thripsis to its fullest extent. King Grona, standing three metres away, winced and stepped back. Breowakoe had expected him to charge, to go for the kill shot right away, but the King moved like an experienced fighter, measuring up his opponent's capabilities.

King Grona kicked sand into Breowakoe's eyes, obstructing his vision. But why? Coabra Grona must know that Breowakoe did not need to see him. Any aspect could readily sense the thripsis of power before them. King Grona kicked the sand up again but Breowakoe's channeling was just pushing it away. He wondered when and how he should use the aspect of destruction. It didn't increase his power much, and its benefit of extending his range would be of little consequence in this arena.

King Grona must have realized that whatever he was trying wouldn't work and charged directly toward Breowakoe. He had excellent thriptic control in his feet and was lightning fast. There was no time for panic before the distance was closed and Breowakoe was punched in the face. He flew back a few metres onto the ground. He was in shock and the crowd roared. King Grona had not released his store of thripsis - if he had, Breowakoe would certainly be dead.

Wasting no time, the King advanced the attack, dropping a knee toward Breowakoe's neck. Knowing he could not roll out of the way in time, Breowakoe expelled thripsis from the left side of his body to slide across the sand. He got up as quickly as he could, expecting another rapid attack. It felt like the orbital bone was broken around his eye; he was seeing double - possibly a concussion.

To Breowakoe's surprise, King Grona was still kneeling, a trickle of blood running from his nose. Breowakoe felt hope that Grona wasn't immune to the effects of the aspect of hatred radiating at close range. He attempted to kick the King while he was down, vacuuming the air away from his face as he had done to the Grobut in Hurst. But King Grona's own thripsis had too much influence over the air around him, and he rose again. Breowakoe could see on his face that the King had a plan. He looked determined; he had figured out that he would lose the long game to the aspect of hatred. Breowakoe's dread returned. King Grona was likely to try to end him as quickly as possible.

Breowakoe directed his thripsis in a straight line, concentrating radiation toward the King to faster destroy his body at the molecular level. Suddenly, there was a precipitous heaviness in the air that Breowakoe recognized as an aspect being activated.

Space seemed to bend around King Grona's legs, and he leapt forward. In four milliseconds he closed the distance to Breowakoe who felt a sharp pain in his knees and in an instant was blinded, losing all sense of direction. He was flipping through the air. After three full revolutions he landed on his rump. His shins and feet lay on the sand ten metres in front of him. To his horror, King Grona still had 75% of his total thriptic pool and was calmly marching on towards him.

Each step seemed to rattle Breowakoe's brain, shaking the whole world. He couldn't believe this was happening. He tried to stay calm and plan an escape, but he was accustomed to flying by channeling thripsis through legs he no longer had. He was helpless, stuck in a seated position.

His hearing was completely shot but for a dull ring. He isolated the noise, trying to make sense of it. It flowed within his head, and his head was its source. He was cut off from reality when he was in the sound, and it morphed as he resolved it. The ringing became a haunting melody played by a strange stringed instrument. It sounded so sad, so beautiful and twisted – as though it belonged at the funeral of a great hero. Then it was no longer coming from within; the soft strums kissed the walls of the arena.

Breowakoe looked around for the source of the music and, on his right, he found it. A tiny, skeletal creature, with the legs and spine of a human baby but the wings, claws, head, and beak of a songbird. Its entire body was not larger than a human head, and it played a small harp... no, a lyre. Breowakoe could only stare at the tiny phantom as he emerged from the same confusion he had seen in so many he had killed.

"The bone child."

He mouthed the words, letting them land. He was going to die in less than ten seconds. It was really happening, just like that. The fight had barely started - his adventure had *barely* started. He was just beginning to like himself. He had grown so much and become so powerful, just to be defeated so swiftly. He thought about what Kaimaradan had told him the day before. He could have just walked away and lived in the desert, found some meaning, but instead he got cocky and charged into danger.

"I'm so stupid..." Breowakoe sulked.

He wanted to cry. Kaimaradan had always been right. He was a naive little boy from the beginning. The tremors of King Grona's approaching footsteps echoed through his crippled body.

"*ENOUGH OF THIS. READY YOURSELF!*"
Kaimaradan was screaming in his mind. It sounded like she had been talking to him for a while but he had no memory of it. "*ENOUGH SELF PITY, BREOWAKOE! YOU ARE THE FALSE GOD. I WILL NOT LET YOU DIE HERE. SUMMON ALL THE THRIPSIS OF THIS LITTLE HELL. IT IS YOUR BIRTHRIGHT. IT DOES NOT BELONG TO*

COABRA GRONA OR ANYONE ELSE!"

She spoke with an impassioned tone that Breowakoe had never felt in her before. She tore new pockets of his skin from his muscle to reposition herself. He gasped in excruciating pain but quickly snapped out of it. He realized he had not been channeling thripsis and did so immediately, summoning everything he could find in the environment. The aspect of power was inhabiting King Grona's four arms along with the totality of his remaining thripsis. This was it - he meant to end it all in this one attack. Kaimaradan re-aligned herself with Breowakoe's spine and locked her sharp, strong legs into the spaces between each vertebra. It actually felt good - for the first time in forever his back had no load. Like a living, metal splint, with what little thripsis remained within Kaimaradan, she braced for the impact.

"*You survive this, you win,*" she whispered, resolutely.

King Grona leapt into the air, arms all above his head, hands all in fists. Breowakoe reached up to block the hit. He gnashed his teeth, knowing this would probably kill him but enjoying the feeling of giving all he had in his final moment - he was no one's slave. In this moment he was living to the fullest. This moment was all that had ever mattered.

Breowakoe lowered his head instinctively as the impact snapped through his arms, then made much more solid contact with his cervical vertebrae. The sand beneath him was blown away and he felt his tailbone hit the rock floor of the Spoil. The aspect of power overwhelmed. He felt his vertebrae crack. Kaimaradan's legs, brittle and hard, were shattered and, finally, Breowakoe folded in half, losing all feeling from the neck down. His ribs were next to break, puncturing his lungs – he lay a crumpled heap of flesh, completely unable to move, bones sticking out every which way in a puddle of blood. Even Kaimaradan had partially burst at her seams, her guts spilling into his in a grotesque concoction. Barely clinging to consciousness as the pressure finally let up, Breowakoe noticed that Kaimaradan appeared to have passed out. The trauma was so great that he was completely emotionless, like a lower order organism fighting to exist in harsh surroundings.

He could feel King Grona standing above him, could hear him panting, probably thinking that Breowakoe was already dead. It wouldn't be long before the King realized his error, though. In the greater awareness afforded him by the aspect of destruction, he identified the state of his body and lungs; although the nervous connection to his diaphragm was lost, he forced air in and out of his lungs with environmental thripsis, just barely clinging to life.

King Grona looked down quizzically into Breowakoe's glazed-over eye, then collapsed to his knees, vomiting blood onto the floor of the Spoil. Breowakoe's left eye followed him to the ground, and they met each other's gaze one last time. Seeing the horror in King Grona's eyes, Breowakoe cracked the slightest of smiles. He had never stopped channeling the aspect of hatred from his head, and without his own pool of thripsis to safeguard him, King Grona was feeling its full effects, almost to the extent a regular drone would.

A terrible heat was building inside the King's large body and his eyes burst, their humours vaporizing. In what should have been his last scream he could only moan as he boiled away from the inside. Minutes passed, the moaning stopped, and King Grona's body lay still.

The call of a great thripsis descended upon Breowakoe's mangled body, imbued with the warm light of the sun. He could feel his afflictions gradually righting themselves as he was lifted into the air in a great whirlwind of chaos and sand. His ribs popped back into position and his lungs healed. His spine and the column of nerves it protected were straightened and his neck snapped back into place. His flesh mended around Kaimaradan uncomfortably, in that her unconscious body was crumpled up in a heap within the skin of his back.

In the eye of this tornado, Breowakoe could see with ease over the far wall of Goliah and even over the great stone palace. A higher vantage than he had ever had in the Spoil, he was above the sandstorms, and Verivoluae shone bright in the far downstream, pulsing blue. He saw the familiar shockwave travel down the walls and ceiling. The great haunting war horn that rattled space itself sounded, and within himself Breowakoe felt an absolute colossus of thripsis emerge. The aspect of power belonged to him.

Breowakoe was lowered gently to the ground and Verivoluae resumed its orange glow. Climbing out of the hole, he noted the silence of the crowd. The foragers rushed into the pit to see the corpse of their former King. They dragged his body out of the pit and stretched it out upon the sand. There were anxious murmurs in the crowd.

By right, Breowakoe was now King, and yet his foragers still tended to Grona's lifeless body, attempting to heal him. Breowakoe snapped his fingers and the corpse burst into a great pyre of blue flame. He was pleasantly surprised.

"With the aspect of power, the aspect of hatred burns even hotter..."

The orange flames of the aspect of hatred alone weren't able to melt a Grobut's exoskeleton as these blue flames now did. The foragers leapt back, hanging their heads and weeping for their people. Feebly, one of them lifted his head.

"Hail, King Breowakoe!" he called to the crowd, fulfilling his duty.

Not one Grobut cheered. Breowakoe couldn't care less; he had no desire to rule over these demons. They had a difficult decision to make, now: to respect their former way of life until they died out, or to ripen the bile of a drone not chosen by the right of coronation. Perhaps the foragers would ripen the bile of some random drone, or hold a tournament. Without the aspect of power, however, the Grobut posed no threat to Breowakoe, and never would again.

He turned and silently left the stadium, bringing Kaimaradan into his awareness. Using Verivoluae's thripsis he pushed her spilled innards back and cauterized her wounds.

There were three things he wanted to do in Gol Paqua before leaving it forever. First, he found himself back at 'The Painted Slave.' Before he even entered the building, he suffocated patrons and staff alike in their own personal vacuum bubbles. As he opened the door all but one dropped to the floor, a Nethriel woman behind the bar. She covered her mouth with her hands as she looked upon the massacre quavering, wondering what was going on. When she saw Breowakoe she looked hopeful and started to say something.

"King Grona is dead. Leave Gol Paqua immediately."

"Y-You're saying it's safe to leave? How will I get past the gate?" she asked hesitantly.

"I'll get rid of the gate for you."

"Oh... ok... where should I go? Goliah? I don't know how to get there..." The woman was clearly very worried, but at least unlike the Nethriel in the farms, she had thoughts of her own.

"Goliah is no place to live. Go to Thelise - never been there, personally, but it's gotta be better than Goliah, closer too."

"How do I get there?"

"Walk due starboard. If you see dead drones under a field of glass, you're going the right way..."

"Ok - thank you so much."

The girl ran into one of the back rooms. Breowakoe

went outside and walked to the great gate. He lifted his palms and infused Verivoluae's thripsis with both hatred and power. Great blue flames enveloped the wondrous structure and, as the steel melted, it collapsed in great globs into a heap on the sand.

"ORDER OF THE GREAT GATE, YOUR SERVICES WILL NO LONGER BE NEEDED. YOUR ORDER IS DISBANDED."

His voice boomed to the drones living in the wall, who rushed out holding their heads, beside themselves, their life's purpose gone in an instant.

Breowakoe approached the large, cooling pile of molten steel and flung it so far into the desert that it could not be seen. A pair of small footsteps came running up behind him. A small, soft hand landed on his shoulder. An unfamiliar part of his brain lit up as he gazed down at the beautiful server from The Painted Slave.

"Thanks again, so... did you remember the Planelands?"

"Yes, thanks to you."

"Oh… g-great. Well, I don't think many people do. Come find me if you ever want to talk about the time that you lived."

She smiled up at him. Breowakoe was perplexed, still so unfamiliar with kindness that good feelings made him uncomfortable, but he wanted to like them.

"Thank you, maybe I will..." Breowakoe said and awkwardly forced a smile back.

She turned and started to head through the open gate until his voice stopped her.

"One more thing - walk upstream about a kilometre before you turn starboard, steer well clear of Gol Paqua..."

There was a tone of doom in his voice that he didn't necessarily intend, but she got the message.

"What will happen to Gol Paqua?" one of the drones behind him cried out.

Breowakoe identified every Grobut within earshot and suffocated it.

Unconditional Honour - 13

Breowakoe climbed the great stone steps to the palace. He didn't want to fly to the top. He wanted to savour the sensation of approaching the throne room. He was deep in fantasy, smiling to himself as several different retribution scenarios played out in his mind. He even imagined that he didn't know where he was and was coming upon the palace for the first time.

At the top of the steps, Breowakoe knocked on the gate and the guard let him into the throne room.

"Is King Grona…?" A look of concern came upon the guard's face.

"I won. He's dead," Breowakoe said impatiently, looking around the throne room.

Both guards looked well taken aback, not sure of what to do with themselves, then rushed out the gate in a hurry. Breowakoe continued into the throne room. He was looking for Mischa but was not willing to use the aspect of destruction - that would be no fun. He gazed at the stone throne on the platform and allowed his curiosity to carry him over to it. He sat down and let his feelings wash over him. A soft pitter-patter wafted into the throne room from the bath.

A young flylet entered the room, skipping and dancing about. It was the first flylet Breowakoe had seen. It looked just like a Grobut but had not yet developed its hard, outer carapace. Although all Grobut were male, there was something distinctly feminine about its movements. Mischa emerged from the bath, following the child. She glided across the floor in a long, flowing dress. Breowakoe stared at the side of her head for a minute until she took notice of him sitting there. She raised an eyebrow.

"Shouldn't you be a paste on the arena floor by now? My, my - you're even less of a man than I thought, cowering all the way up here after challenging King Grona."

A smirk crept across Breowakoe's face. It was difficult not to laugh, but he held the corner of his mouth down to keep the look sly. Mischa rolled her eyes and rasped a sigh of exasperated disgust.

"You're not even half a man! You're a pathetic Nethriel man, fit only to serve the Grobut; a Nethriel who doesn't serve the Grobut is nothing but trash!"

Her temper grew hotter as Breowakoe continued his silence. She began at a pace to the port side of the room, her eyes fluttering about.

"Where are the guards?" she asked, bothered.

Breowakoe said nothing. After checking the doorway, she turned to him directly.

"WHERE ARE THEY!?" she screamed, stomping up to him and stopping below the steps of the throne.

The sound echoed off the walls and faded. The soft patter of Mischa's effeminate child making-believe coloured the intensity of her gaze. He had been dying to see what she would become with her support gone, stripped of even the air of power.

"YOU SPEAK WHEN A CONCUBINE OF KING GRONA SPEAKS TO YOU, BOY!"

She lurched toward him, raising a fist. Breowakoe remained still and she brought herself to rest two feet from him. He couldn't help but blurt out a chuckle. Mischa leaned back, shifting physically and mentally into a less aggressive stance.

"You look filthy, by the way, and you're covered in scars - are those from the sand? Did the sandstorms tear through your soft, Nethriel skin, pussy-boy? Looks like your centipede friend abandoned you, too."

Breowakoe played along, looking down at his body.

Verivoluae's treatment had left a lot of visible scar tissue. He turned in his seat to reveal Kaimaradan's outline within the skin of his back - an outline that had become an odd source of pride. Breowakoe checked in with her, her brain was operating at base level, but she was still unconscious, unable to see what he was doing. Without warning, Mischa forced a cackle.

"You aren't even half a Nethriel man! Wow! A Grobut defines himself by the number of adoring concubines or Nethriel slaves he owns. The Nethriel define themselves by how well they serve the Grobut, and you can't even stay outside as the other Nethriel men do without ruining your delicate skin!" Another over-acted shriek of glee left her lips. "Look at you, playing King! That's so pathetic! Have you ever done a day's work in your life -"

Breowakoe rose to his feet; her arrogance was getting to him. Mischa winced, and jumped back. He was a head taller than she when standing on a flat surface but towered over her from the steps. For a moment she looked terrified, then regained her composure.

"What? Are you going to hit me? Ha! You should do it! It won't hurt; you're just a little bitch! Normally I'd think it was wrong for a man to hit a woman but seeing as you aren't a -"

Breowakoe turned to face the downstream door and walked down the steps. When Mischa finished wincing again, she continued to try to emasculate him with incessant, tedious ranting that he simply tuned out.

He gazed upon Mischa's playing child. It was so delicate in its movements that for a moment it softened his heart. He approached the flylet and took it by the hand, guiding it into the bath. The wee flylet danced and twirled under his arm. It was undeniably cute.

"What are you doing? Where are you taking my son?"

Mischa had a new kind of fear in her tone. Breowakoe didn't know what he was doing. He was acting on impulse, not yet having formulated how Mischa would pay for her cruelty. He trod softly down the steps of the bath into the water. The child resisted following him, tugging back against his hand but not releasing it, gingerly fluttering its little antennae.

"STOP. He can't swim! LET GO OF MY CHILD, SLAVE! GUARDS - HELP!"

Breowakoe yanked the child's arm, dislocating it, and caught the top of its head in his other hand. Staring curiously into Mischa's frantic eyes, he dunked the flylet's head underwater.

"NO-O-O-O-O! NO-O-O-O-O-O-O-O!" Mischa screamed, jumping into the water and bounding toward him.

The child flailed and thrashed about but Breowakoe barely even noticed the resistance. Mischa clawed at Breowakoe, trying to dig her nails into his neck, trying to kick him in the knees, although her foot's momentum was slowed by the water. Breowakoe was horrified at what he was doing. He floated in and out of the present as Dunstan's memories kept flooding his mind. His hands were holding onto this child. He was killing it. Is this really how it felt to kill a child? Was it really this easy? Had he been this easy to kill? Why would someone do this? Why should someone so strong waste their time doing this to someone so powerless?

He hadn't noticed his skin tearing as Mischa's claws got under it. He was bleeding; why did it barely hurt? He looked over to her, stupefied as she went about it. Continuing to hold the child with his right hand, Breowakoe balled his hand up into a fist and tapped Mischa's solar plexus, releasing a small burst of thripsis. She buckled instantly and popped up two feet in the air before falling back into the water gasping for breath.

The movement under his weathered hands clocked down to a perfect stillness and Breowakoe looked down at his work.

He released the back of the child's head. The tiny creature floated away from him; he watched it go. Mischa was still retching and Breowakoe turned to stare at her, expressionless in the tranquil ripples.

Mischa could feel her face was red from coughing as she looked back up at this unruly slave. He was looking right at her with tears welling in his sunken eyes, head cocked. He looked out of place, confused, as though he didn't know where he was. In all this time he had not uttered a single word and he didn't appear to need to. Her child by the demon King - so dearly loved - bumped repeatedly into the filter on the far side of the bath. Terror mounted in her heart as Mischa realized her Coabra was dead.

Mischa scrambled to climb out of the bath and was yanked back in by her hair. She was given no chance to plead, and no stage for wit. Breowakoe palmed the back of her head and held her face just under the water. Her eyes were oscillating between surfacing and being submerged but her mouth and nose were fixed. Mischa tried everything to free herself, pushing off the shallow bottom, scratching at Breowakoe and trying to kick him off, but eventually she gave up her bubbles. He held her in the lull for another few minutes to make sure she was dead before leaving her to float next to her boy.

Breowakoe was leaving the palace as the foragers returned. Article after article they were addressing him about the business of the Kingdom. He looked up at each of them. With such prudence they spoke; they really expected him to rule them, to guide their people into the future. He could barely even make out their words - he was too disturbed. They were honouring their customs even though he was a Nethriel, even though it meant the extinction of their people. Guilt overwhelmed him, he deserved everything this hell had served him. What if Mr. Doggy had seen what he'd just done in the bath - he would surely yelp and run in fear.

Breowakoe tried to make himself focus on the forager's words; he wanted to - they spoke so passionately. They wanted to trust him, they wanted him to care, but he couldn't bring himself to. Mr. Doggy was not watching. Kai was not watching. Breowakoe was done with Gol Paqua; he was done with the Grobut. He just wanted to be alone.

He pushed past the foragers, further onto the platform atop the great stone steps overlooking the city. He took flight and hovered over the Kingdom's center.

"Where are you going, King Breowakoe!? These matters are urgent!" the foragers shouted, chasing after him into the sky.

Breowakoe closed his eyes. He released a steady, unwavering stream of pure, crimson thripsis vertically into the air. The energy carried all the way to the roof of the Spoil, enveloping it, and the Kingdom fell under a deep haze of heat. The foragers, having nearly reached him, instantly vaporized. The windows of every building shattered and people outside screamed all over the sweltering city, taking to the skies and fleeing to try to get to safety, unsure of what was oppressing them. The Nethriel here were better off dead. The Grobut, too. Breowakoe had lost all interest in paying them back by torturing them; he just wanted the peace of mind that only their extinction would bring.

He now drew air to himself as he had in Hurst. He was able to pack the air much tighter with the aspect of power complementing the aspect of destruction and, infusing hatred into the mix, he released it. The clay buildings - the majority of the structures in the city - burst the second the blast hit them and Grobut within the stone structures came running out, screaming as blue flames melted their carapaces. The wall over the Nethriel farms appeared to be less stable – being dug under – as it came collapsing down on the farms. Breowakoe could sense that inside the palace the flylets and concubines were roasting alive in the heat... yet the palace still stood.

This simply wouldn't do. Breowakoe blasted at a high speed back toward the palace and delivered a punch to the wall with the aspect of power. A deep crack led to crumbling and as Breowakoe flew away, the palace collapsed onto the city, its spires poking deep holes into the sand. The structure rolled, coming apart piece by piece, until at last it crushed the arena.

The city fell quiet. Breowakoe felt peace. He flew into Verivoluae's golden light as it dimmed and, when it finally went out, dropped to the ground to continue on foot.

Breowakoe was beginning to love the cool of the night, and the subtle winds that moved him on these walks through the desert. He hadn't slept in nearly two days and yet, he didn't feel tired. He felt accomplished and at ease, having earned a moment without purpose. In that moment he wanted to explore further downstream; something was drawing him there. He wanted to be alone with himself and his thoughts, and he could feel that in doing this, something worthy would emerge.

A sharp leg twitched in his back as Kaimaradan awoke.

Within, Breowakoe could feel her gasp as the moment she had lost consciousness caught up with her. She tried to reposition herself as the coil around Breowakoe's abdomen but she was still healing, still too weak to move.

"*Consider me surprised. I did not think I would awake into the light of this warped star, again. Well done, Breowakoe.*"

"Thanks to you," he said.

"*In truth, I thought you would lose. I was ready to die and let our aspects become one in Coabra.*"

"I thought you were against stockpiling aspects – 'vulgar' you called it."

"*Things have changed. Tiricora broke that seal. Also, the fact that the aspect of destruction is here among us suggests things are about to change forever.*"

Breowakoe raised his eyebrows but remained silent, putting his hands behind his head as he strolled deeper into the dark.

"*Breowakoe... you killed Coabra Grona on a whim, but what is it that you want now?*"

Breowakoe sighed.

"I don't know. I feel directionless. The only possible

guide I have is this feeling of longing for the Planelands. I keep thinking about my friend, Mr. Doggy. I worry about whether or not he is ok, or if he's still alive. It's been so long. I still can't believe I'm dead; something about knowing that feels so lonely."

"*I see. Why are you walking downstream?*"

"Just felt like it, I guess. To explore what's down there."

"*There is nothing for you downstream. At least not yet,*" Kaimaradan trailed off.

"What do you mean 'not yet'?"

"*My civilization, The Satrian Mounds, was very far downstream, as far as civilizations in the Spoil go. It was second only to the First Tar Sands – the home of the now extinct Blonaks.*"

"- the aspect of apathy was a Blonak?"

"*Correct, Globramora was the last of them. Any further downstream and Verivoluae's heat became unbearable to live within. None have explored much further downstream than that, not even aspects can handle the heat, and of what I was able to explore I found only nothingness - blistering deserts and high winds await.*"

"So, there's nothing but ruined cities out that way?"

"There was one structure that I encountered during my voyage. Six perfectly straight, immovable swords that descended all the way from the roof of the Spoil and came to their points one metre above the sand. The outer five are arranged in a pentagon with the sixth running down through its middle - but what makes these swords more interesting is that they appear to lead to a gap in the roof of the Spoil. Globramora knew of it, too. He called it 'The Silo Blades'."

Breowakoe was pulled out of his stupor. The more he learned about the Spoil from Kaimaradan the more intrigued he became.

"If you were unaware, it is widely known that the brown stone walls, deep floor, and roof of the Spoil have been utterly immovable and unbreakable from the time this hell spawned. This material is known as 'Spoil rock.' Coordinated attempts to move or damage the stone have all failed and the only other case of a gap was the one that the Cultivator's eye was born into, so the existence of the Silo Blades is not trivial."

Breowakoe remained patient.

"Globramora tried to climb the blades once, well over 1000 years ago, but when he was only ten metres up, skewered on the blades, Verivoluae's heat became so intense that he

caught fire even while channeling thripsis. He told me he barely escaped with his life. Globramora believed that just as the Squalor connected the world of the living to our world, so climbing the Silo Blades would allow one to return to the Planelands."

"That's amazin -"

"But think carefully on what I said, Breowakoe, for it is not that simple. Globramora studied these blades for many years and determined that Verivoluae's heat is most intense halfway between the floor and ceiling of the Spoil. He calculated that the thriptic output required to survive the climb was greater than that of all six available aspects flowing through one individual. I never told Globramora of my sister's intuition about the moon behind the sun, and so he died having gone mad, believing that the blades were there only to taunt. But you, Breowakoe, with all aspects flowing in you plus the aspect of destruction - you are the one true rival of Verivoluae, or as Cert put it, the false god. I am certain of it."

Breowakoe stopped in his tracks. His breath was deep and heavy and he turned around to face Goliah.

"So, I need to kill Tiricora," he said aloud.

"That is correct. Including the aspect of destruction, and

not including creation itself, you already have 3 of the 7 aspects that you need. You also need to kill the chief Piccaro, and you need to kill me."

An unexpected twinge of shock and sadness flowed into Breowakoe's heart, but he pushed it to the side. He began slowly walking back upstream.

"Do you think I have a chance against Tiricora as I am now?"

"The aspect of control is by far the deadliest in one-to-one combat. But you might be able to overwhelm her."

"Would my odds increase if I took the aspect of cunning first?"

"Marginally. Neither cunning nor my cruelty is a very strong combat aspect. You already possess the next-best three aspects for combat."

"I see... Why is control so deadly?"

"Think of that little trick you do with your aspect of destruction where you pull the air towards yourself and release it in an explosion. That takes very precise thriptic control. Tirocora's thriptic control is 100x greater than yours. From the other side of Gol Paqua, she can fire bullets of air from each of her fingers that would rip through you, and she could make

them so small that you couldn't even see them. Of course, without the aspect of hatred she would lose a long fight - if you could survive her attacks she would run out of thripsis, but she can use the small pool that she has extremely efficiently. With the aspect of apathy, she will not feel pain, but I do not imagine pain ever stopped Tiricora before."

Breowakoe laughed. "That makes sense. So, I would want to channel all three of my aspects pretty much non-stop."

"If you wanted to have a chance at living, then yes. It is likely that she can also channel her own thripsis around her epidermis to protect against hatred's radiation, so it could be a long fight. Now, if I were to fight alongside you we could give each other openings. She would likely go for me, as I would be more vulnerable, but if she takes the bait and you can land one good hit, she will certainly die."

"Hmm. You're more clever than I thought, Kai."

"I could not have lived as long as I have if I were not."

Breowakoe leapt into the air and rocketed back towards Goliah. They flew in silence over the ruins of Gol Paqua as his mind stewed. The arena was still partly visible under the rubble of the palace. He could feel Kaimaradan's surprise at the state of Gol Paqua. He tensed as he felt her come upon the memory of his moment of bloodlust: drowning Mischa and her flylet, but Kaimaradan said nothing. She did not judge him or ask any questions. The night swallowed the silent moment, replacing it with countless others.

"Kai, how is it that I saw the bone child, but I didn't die?" Breowakoe hadn't considered this up until this point.

"*I am unsure. But if I had to guess it is because through your eyes, I also saw it, and I changed my behaviour accordingly. I was not initially planning to help you in that fight. The bone child appears to those whose courses of action will lead to death in the next ten seconds; you had all but given up and I intervened with my own course of action. You may not have noticed, but the moment I snapped you out of your funk the bone child vanished.*"

"Kai, I have to ask once more. Why are you helping me? You aren't just keeping me alive to suffer, and I'm not naive enough to think you are just curious about me anymore."

"*Well, my curiosity is still genuine; it is your choice not to believe that. If you are looking for something more to my answer I will tell you this much. Once Tiricora is dead, I may have a favour to ask of you.*"

He tried to dig into her mischief. "What's the favour?"

"*Once this is done, Breowakoe...*"

The Loft of the Deceiver - 14

There was an eerie quiet as Breowakoe flew into Oxalthry territory, downstream Goliah, in the wee morning hours. He descended to the warm sand and closed his eyes to open his mind. Tiricora was not in her tower, but perhaps stranger was that he could not sense any aspects in the Spoil besides Kai and himself.

"Do you feel that?" he asked aloud, albeit quietly.

"*Yes, I do not know how they have hidden, but the fact that both are gone suggests collusion. Tread carefully, Breowakoe.*"

Breowakoe returned to his mind, searching even more furiously for anything useful. He gasped, realizing he had flown over something on his way in. It was about 80 metres into the desert behind him, walking away from Goliah. He whirled around to see only sand but didn't need to see the invisible voyager. He leapt forward and seized it in his left hand. His nails dug into the feeble creature's shoulder and it screamed and showed itself. It was the Piccaro from the Grobut outpost, Chief Advisor Ghoul.

"You!" Breowakoe growled, his thoughts racing too quickly to articulate.

"Breo, hold him still. I will take delight in coaxing his master's whereabouts from him!" Kaimaradan piped up.

Breowakoe finally caught up to the relevance of this find. This Piccaro worked directly under the aspect of cunning.

"Quickly, place your hand on his head."

Breowakoe did as she bid and the flow of space bent to Kaimaradan's will. Ghoul's mouth hung open further and as he appeared to enter a waking nightmare, his eyes rolled back in his head. His muscles twitched haphazardly and he intermittently screamed. Breowakoe had no idea that Kai's aspect of cruelty could be used for interrogation.

"Hurry, ask him something!" Kaimaradan sounded strained.

Breowakoe, put on the spot, scrambled to remember their goals.

"Where is the aspect of cunning?" he half-shouted, flecks of spit falling onto the possessed goblin's face. The Piccaro grunted.

Ghoul's thoughts appeared in Breowakoe's own mind, even as the creature struggled to vocalize. He appeared to be visualizing a network of tunnels, racing through the halls to several more open chambers. It was no place Breowakoe had seen before. Ghoul's thoughts shifted to the surface, to a village of small brick dwellings against a wall and backlit by Verivoluae. Breowakoe could tell this was the port wall via its orientation to the sun.

The thoughts were cut off. Blood was spurting out of the mouth of the Piccaro and his eyesight had returned. He was grinning with a gaunt, creepy little smile and spat blood in Breowakoe's face. Surprised, Breowakoe released his grip on the goblin. Ghoul had bitten off his own tongue, and now pulled a small shiv from his cloak and stabbed himself in the neck four times.

Breowakoe had barely reacted when the little shit died with a smile on his face. Kaimaradan hissed in frustration. She had finally recovered enough to right herself and slithered into her old spot, wrapping around his torso with her head over his heart. The pain caused by her movements was less intense than it once had been.

"*Who knew Stynia's dog would be so loyal?*" she mused.

Her inner voice trailed off as Breowakoe's attention shifted to a memory of his own. Before being captured by the Grobut, while witnessing Tiricora fighting the aspect of apathy, he had sensed two strong thriptic presences that he could not identify - one downstream and one on the port side of the Oxalthry district. The downstream presence he now knew to be the aspect of power, which meant the Oxalthry presence must have been the aspect of cunning; at least, this was consistent with Ghoul's thoughts. He turned and walked back into the outskirts of Goliah.

"We can find Tiricora later. I have an idea of where to look for the aspect of cunning," he said aloud to put an end to Kaimaradan's bellyaching.

Breowakoe looked around cautiously as he took his first few steps into the district. All the shanties on this side of town appeared to be barely standing strips of sheet metal, fastened together crudely. There were holes in the walls but it was too dark to see inside. He sensed that while many were empty, others had Nethriel - or Oxalthry as they called themselves on this side of Goliah – within. The huts were arranged roughly into crooked rows with just enough space between to see all the way down. There was little evidence of the war that had been raging here not long ago. Through haze and light, Breowakoe could make out downtown Goliah and Tiricora's tower far in the distance. Surely, Tiricora would return there eventually. Breowakoe fantasized about fortifying a position there to wait for her, but this was dashed by the realization that she might already be doing the same - hiding away in her tower for his arrival.

After half an hour of walking Breowakoe noticed, in the periphery of his senses, a change in the makeup of the city towards the port wall. There were several houses that were made of stone rather than sheet metal. They had construction that seemed more precise than anything he had seen in the Spoil apart from downtown Goliah, and they were a third the size of the Nethriel houses. This was promising.

Beneath these houses, under the sand, he perceived an intricate series of tunnels and rooms. Every single small house was connected in a giant network that made up a large city in and of itself. There appeared to be a variety of structures underground that must have served different functions: stores, great halls, dwellings. Sure enough, there was even a tunnel that appeared to run under the city toward Tiricora's tower. The dwellings were densely populated by small, humanoid creatures with crooked noses and pointed ears.

"Piccaros," Breowakoe smiled, thinking himself clever.

He could feel Kai's anger building as she observed his

thoughts.

"Calm down. You aren't useful if you're flustered," Breowakoe demanded of her.

Kaimaradan quieted her thriptic flow. Breowakoe took another worried look in the direction of Tiricora's tower and then out to his right toward what he now knew was the Piccaro district. He walked between the meandering rows of shanties for a while longer before emerging in that district. It looked cute, like a village for gnomes with little pointed rooves and neatly carved trusses. There were precise stone corners and even little, round, glass windows – out of which little goblin eyes peered. The buildings looked out of place in the Spoil. He continued through the village toward the port wall. In the shadows, tiny forms darted indoors and out of view. He could hear them whispering: "Don't go outside! That's Breowakoe, the false god."

"The aspect of destruction, come to end us..." a soft little voice in another direction muttered.

The more carefully Breowakoe listened, the more of a quiet uproar he heard around him, as though he were being passively bullied by a catty clique.

"*This is not good,*" Kaimaradan expressed.

"Yeah, it kind of feels like the Vemanen district all over again, doesn't it?"

"No, well yes. But what I mean is that they know you are the false god. Piccaros are not like Grobut; they cannot sense thripsis. If they know you are the aspect of destruction, then everyone in Goliah knows, including those you hoped to surprise in killing."

Breowakoe's lips tightened. It did *feel* as though he were walking into a trap, but how they could possibly have known he would come here. He had needed to interrogate the Chief's advisor for that information - information the little shit had died to protect.

Gazing into the distance at the port wall, Breowakoe noticed something strange, but he couldn't make sense of it. It appeared to be a series of structures, although they were much less diligently put together than those in the town. He continued closer to the port wall, ignoring the murmuring around him. The structures he had seen from a distance weren't structures, at all. They were shapes carved into the face of the port wall. Wait, no... that wasn't possible; as Kaimaradan had recently confirmed, the Spoil rock that made up the walls, floor, and ceiling of the Spoil was immovable.

Breowakoe closed his eyes to see the structures more closely. He confirmed that the rock of the Spoil wall had not been carved, but the strange shapes stacked near the wall were definitely made of Spoil rock. Something was gravely wrong. It would be unwise to explore any further.

"Kai... is there a way to create new Spoil rock?"

"*This is bad. We need to leave.*" There was an abrupt panic in her words.

"Why?" Breowakoe started to back up.

"*This is technology that should not exist. This defies what should be possible.*"

Two large, thriptic presences appeared behind Breowakoe as though spawning freshly out of the sand. He turned to see an old looking Piccaro who had a small, hoop earring and a nose ring both on the left side of his face. He had a long, thin, grey beard and his eyes were sharp with intellect. In the foreground, standing a few feet away from Breowakoe, was Tiricora.

Breowakoe breathed to start channeling.

"Too slow!" Tiricora teased, tapping his shoulders with each of her index fingers.

It felt as though he had taken the fully charged swings of

two Grobut drones. He sank into the sand; the shock interrupted his breathing and for a moment his head was submerged before he arrived in an underground chamber. Sand from above caved in on top of him, but it wasn't enough to bury him alive. Breowakoe struggled to the top of the tomb and readied himself, sending a crimson beam of thripsis into the ceiling just as a heavy trap door rumbled to a close above him. He could feel that the energy flowing from him was rebounding at an alarming rate. The sand in the small chamber was blown through two fist-sized holes to reveal that he was encased in a two-by-two metre prison made of Spoil rock. Breowakoe's heart nearly skipped a beat. He lunged toward the windowed wall and hit it with everything the aspect of power had to offer. The wall remained. The force didn't even reverberate; the wall simply absorbed 90% of it. Breowakoe screamed in frustration and fired his thripsis through one of the openings, obliterating a strip of distant city.

"My, my - you've gotten scary," Tiricora's smirking voice sounded through the openings as Breowakoe's channelling stopped. "What happened to the soft, eager young man who stood in my office and asked for a capsule of essence?" she continued to tease.

Breowakoe had nothing to say to her; she had only her life to offer him.

"Ooh, the silent treatment, is it? Well, no matter. I don't know how you found us. I guess you really are the false god, after all! One of the great mysteries and all that, yes, yes. I'd like to stay and play a bit but I made a deal with Chief Stynia. The war is over. Goliah is mine, once again, and in return I help deliver to him four delicious aspects all wrapped up in a neat little bundle," Tiricora crooned haughtily.

"What? Sounds like you're getting ripped off!" Breowakoe almost chuckled, the trade was so absurd. Why would someone as intelligent as Tiricora barter near-limitless power for phony peace?

"*This is one of the facets of the aspect of cunning,*" Kaimaradan explained. "*He will have smooth-talked her into this, despite her better judgement.*"

Breowakoe could see through the small hole that Tiricora was walking away. To her left stood Chief Stynia, hands on his cane.

"Tiricora, you know once he gets these aspects he will just come kill you, right? The war will resume almost instantly!" Breowakoe tried to reason.

"*Just stop - it is fruitless,*" Kaimaradan stymied Breowakoe as Tiricora ignored him, bounding off towards her distant tower.

The Chief walked up to the foot of the cage he had constructed for them. The whiny, nasally voice of an old man chirped up.

"Thank you for your sacrifice, my dear advisor, Ghoul," he smiled. "Kaimaradan, I believe we've been acquainted only at a distance."

The rage within Kaimaradan boiled up to the point of seething.

"Although I suppose there wouldn't have been much to say face-to-face; you Satrians weren't gifted with the ability to speak, were you? It's been so long since I've seen one, you must forgive me if I'm mis-remembering."

Kaimaradan's razor legs twitched, slicing at Breowakoe's muscles, causing him to flinch and growl.

"I did have one interesting conversation with your sister. Fairglow, was it? Once she learned that it was I who orchestrated the revolution within the Satrian kingdom, she begged that I spare you the wrath of your own people. She offered up her visions to me as payment, but I killed her all the same."

Breowakoe was bewildered at the insatiable hatred this goblin had for Kaimaradan, even after slaughtering her people. It seemed that these two knew each other better than Kai had let on.

A dagger came flying through one of the openings. Breowakoe, noticing barely in time, deflected it with a burst of energy.

"I knew I couldn't kill you in a fair fight, but the outcome will be just," Stynia said.

Another dagger approached the right opening but was repelled even before entering the chamber. "You little rat… How is this just?" Breowakoe grunted.

"Oh? What's the matter, Breowakoe? Do you not like how it feels to be trapped? Good. Is it just that I am here? Trapped within your rotting mind?"

"What?" Breowakoe tried to make sense of this covert accusation.

"I despised you even when you lived; I did everything I could to undermine you. I want you to know that."

With no time to wonder what Stynia could have had against a nine-year-old boy in the Planelands, Breowakoe felt a sharp pain dart through his shoulder. The thripsis he was releasing was so dense that he hadn't noticed a long, curved spear reaching around from a spot outside the prison that his thripsis could not reach.

"You have always disgusted me, even more than Kaimaradan. My greatest regret is that I wasn't there to see your face as all you loved melted before your eyes."

Breowakoe pushed the spear away and cut his hand in the process. The spear was made of Spoil rock.

"Of course. That's why I wasn't able to repel it…"

Stynia plunged the spear deeper into the chamber and Breowakoe focused his thripsis on dodging it, but it was a losing game. He could not escape. Goblins on top of the chamber were giggling as the false god danced beneath them.

"Stop struggling, Breowakoe. Give up your aspects. I have all the patience in the world. Just relax, give your aspects to me, save yourself some time, and atone for what you've done in this small way."

Breowakoe felt utterly helpless, but the fury within Kaimaradan had boiled over.

"*Enough of this. I have longed to kill Stynia for as long as this plane has memory. Do not aid me, Breowakoe. Give me the small pleasure of killing him alone. For the sake of my sister and my people, and you.*"

Kaimaradan extravasated from her perch - slicing through the skin over Breowakoe's heart - and climbed adroitly up the Spoil rock to the hole not in use. She looked too big to fit through, as she was about the width of two fists, when the same distorting thripsis he had felt in the couple's shack burst forth.

"Ere ghit - everything fits," Breowakoe thought to himself as Kaimaradan's body contorted through the opening.

He heard the old goblin shriek outside the chamber, and the spear dropped into the cell. Breowakoe rushed up to the left hole and peered through to see Kaimaradan locking her legs around Stynia's feeble body, spraying acid in his face. She was about twice as long as he, so it looked like an easy kill until another dreadful, unfamiliar thripsis rode the air. Determined to survive, the elder Piccaro scowled, pushed the acid back out of his melting face with the energy of the Spoil, and tumbled out of view. Breowakoe was pressed tight against the wall, trying to find a more comfortable position when he was yoked abruptly to the twisted thripsis of cruelty. His joints bent in difficult ways and his bones cracked oddly, but somehow, he glopped through the wall and his body righted itself on the other side. He was free.

"Kai, you're incredible," he breathed.

Stynia was scrambling away to safety while a horde of his fellows, wielding ice picks, jumped in to aid him. They took aim at Kaimaradan as she was distracted to free her comrade, so Breowakoe released a small burst of thripsis that ignited them. Their screams evaporated as they dissolved into cinder. It would have been easy to kill the chief as he scrambled into a small stone house and into the tunnels, but Breowakoe wished to honour Kaimaradan's request. He thought it was foolish, but she had suffered the greatest losses of her life to that creature, and it wasn't right for him to butt in. Kaimaradan looked up at him once more with her beady, black eyes.

"You better not fucking die. But if you do, I promise I'll kill that little shit," Breowakoe told her resolutely.

She nodded and moved like a snake into the sand. Breowakoe felt her shift away in pursuit of her life's hatred. She was even faster underground than on land. It made him wonder about the Satrian civilization, mounds upon mounds of dexterous centipedes, tunneling beneath at incredible speeds.

"Ew..." he shuddered and paused another moment to sense her entering the tunnels, gaining ground on Chief Stynia. Again, he felt a moment of worry. "No - she is strong. She will win. I trust her with that. I have my own mountains to climb."

He gritted his teeth, looking toward downtown Goliah and the loft of the deceiver, then flew to Tiricora's tower at top speed. Newly loose abdominal skin flapped in the wind.

Retribution for the Extant - 15

The little goblin was close enough that Kaimaradan could feel him on the other side of the wall, scampering through the hallways and bowling over other Piccaros, making an obstacle course of his subterranean Kingdom. Breowakoe's strong presence faded rapidly until she could no longer feel him.

"Good."

Feeling relieved to be alone with her past, Kaimaradan flowed through the sand as though it were water and pulled ahead of the place she sensed Chief Stynia. She turned and pierced the outside of the stone tunnel with her pincers. Anticipating her movements, Stynia turned down a branching hallway just as she burst through. The inside of the tunnel was lined with a paper-like film so thin that a generous amount of sand spilled through with her. The few civilian Piccaro roaming the tidy, white, hospital-like hallway screamed and fled as the demon centipede appeared.

Kaimaradan took a moment to register Stynia's change in direction. She climbed over a desk to cut a corner and forged down the darkened hallway after the twisted wretch. On the hard tile, the sound of her footsteps was a symphony of clicking. Lit rooms periodically illuminated the red stripes of her back as she passed, but in the distinct fluorescent flashes, her legs appeared to move as a single wave. The hallway led to a short, steep staircase and Chief Stynia leapt straight to the top, breaking his momentum against an unsuspecting Piccaro. Kaimaradan followed, gaining ground, clicking up the stairs and right past several terrified Piccaro clustered together on the floor.

Chief Stynia released a series of guttural noises that seemed to resonate through the entire network of halls. Kaimaradan, accustomed to identifying movement underground, immediately recognized this as a summons - as from every corner of the deep came the rumbling of thousands of little footsteps. Stynia passed quickly through the short, rectangular room and bounced off the wall with both hands, taking a right down a long, tight ramp, sliding and pushing himself using his thripsis. His giggling echoed eerily through the novel stretch of black hall, but Kaimaradan was deterred by nothing: he was her prey and she would have him.

At the bottom of the ramp, the first of her new assailants emerged, taking a stab with a dagger along her sleek, armoured body and hoping to catch her by surprise. The metal couldn't even scratch her hide. The carapace of a Satrian becomes only denser with age, and now, after surviving for so long, only an aspect could hurt her.

She ignored the many assailants whose knives she deflected passively, following Stynia's trail left into another, larger, dark room. Several Piccaros popped out of nowhere and dog-piled onto her, each holding one or two of her legs. Sacrificing themselves for their chief, several Piccaros were trampled and cut up, but the few who hung on did slow her down. Kaimaradan was forced to take a moment to turn and lacerate them - nearly to ribbons in the case of a particularly tenacious and resilient fellow.

The dark room was filled with rows of tables - a cafeteria of some sort - and Chief Stynia awkwardly maneuvered around the corner of one row before sprinting to the door on the right. Kaimaradan was low enough to run under the tables, making up for some of the distance she had lost. Stynia looked over his shoulder once upon reaching the doorway and groaned in frustration to see that she was still hot on his heels. He was running out of thripsis; he couldn't afford to conserve it any longer. Expelling what remained, he burst down the next long, narrow hallway, and Kaimaradan had to burn her own thripsis to keep up.

With thriptic power, her feet cracked through the tile beneath her and the clicking noise became a crumbling. With both aspects expending thripsis, the gap between them merely narrowed.

The deep light warped the air as the aspect of cruelty activated fully. Cruelty had a power that Kaimaradan had never revealed to a single soul. It was a subtle time-dilation effect that allowed her to trap an individual by causing them to experience the passage of time fifty-percent more slowly. She believed that in the design of the Spoil, this power was intended to draw out the suffering of her victims - but she had discovered young that, strangely, she could make people experience the passage of time fifty-percent faster, as well. She had had many fights, protecting her colony, where she had overwhelmed her enemy, seeming to them to be moving at blinding speed while finding themselves stuck in a lethargy. She had lied to Breowakoe when she told him her aspect was weak in combat. Although she knew it would benefit his fight with Tiricora, deep down she feared death and, still deeper, she wanted to spend more time with him.

"I had better see you again, Breowakoe," Kaimaradan

worried. Chief Stynia looked around in horror at what to him was a whirring burst of speed from the insect behind him. She appeared blurry, his eyes receiving mixed signals of light, telling a conflicting story of two different points in time. He took a left and Kaimaradan turned to clamp down on his heel, narrowly missing as the feeble creature leapt into the air. Stynia made it onto a large chandelier and hoisted himself up.

This was a large room. It looked like a banquet hall and had multiple fancy chandeliers over large, round tables. Kaimaradan reared up on her hind legs, but the nearest chandelier was out of reach. She stopped channeling her thripsis and looked around for a way up; she was no jumper.

The falsely gleeful goblin grinned and giggled mockingly as he swung from the ceiling. They were totally alone, the war band he had assembled had evidently lost them, and he realized it wouldn't be effective to summon another.

"Well, I see I was right not to face you on the field that day!" Stynia admitted.

Kaimaradan kept an eye on him as she moved away to the nearest wall.

"He doesn't look like the Breowakoe we knew, does he?" Stynia panted. "It sure feels like him though, doesn't it? The aspects work more easily through him than they do through us."

Kaimaradan began climbing the wall. She wanted to ignore him but, as she considered his words, she found herself agreeing.

"I guess you're determined to kill me. Why? To impress him? You know, Kaimaradan, even though I always hated your guts, I thought we shared a mutual disgust for Breowakoe. I thought that was your one redeeming quality..." Stynia paused to pant, as Kaimaradan was now diligently making her way onto the ceiling. She was glad she had convinced Breowakoe to leave them, glad not to have him hear this dirty laundry.

"To see you now, chasing him around like a schoolgirl with a crush, surprises me."

Kaimaradan began making her way down the metal chain of the chandelier and Chief Stynia hurried to the next. His feet swung out awkwardly from the jump and he barely managed to grab onto the bottom of the chandelier. Kaimaradan backtracked onto the ceiling as he used his legs to swing, building up some momentum. She hesitated before descending the chain and, sure enough, he jumped to the next chandelier. He was breathless, sweat dripping down his face.

Kaimaradan was salivating. It wouldn't be much longer before she had her jaws on him.

"When I was meeting with Tiricora, I hadn't anticipated having to use that trap so soon. I hadn't thought I would need measures to deal with you. I thought only to make it for the false god." His voice was raspy and hoarse; he sounded defeated. "To make a mistake like that at this age is unforgivable. I hadn't imagined Tiricora would just walk away, either. I haven't felt this foolish since the day I died."

Chief Stynia swung onto a gallery that overlooked the dining hall and made a break for the next door, desperately channeling what thripsis he had remaining. Kaimaradan dropped from the ceiling, landing on his shoulders and dismembering him down to the torso in two swift motions.

The Piccaro screamed as Kaimaradan cauterized his wounds with acid.

"YOU BITCH!" Stynia now laughed out of his scream. "So, this is why he manifested you as the aspect of cruelty!"

Stynia's head shook violently in the delirium of his intense suffering. Kaimaradan sat on top of his helpless abdomen, enjoying the shallow rasps he struggled to produce. She actually wanted to let him catch his breath; in an odd way she was enjoying this one-sided conversation with her old associate, and touching him, she could now participate in it."

"*He is not the Breowakoe we remember. That Breowakoe is the sun that burns over our heads. This Breowakoe is merely a child from the Planelands; he died not long ago. THAT is the life he remembers, not the one he shared with us.*"

Stynia's breathing slowed. "How is that possible? Who called him Breowakoe?" Stynia asked, genuinely curious.

"*I do not know. If you had longer to live, you might be able to figure it out, with all your cunning,*" she mocked. "*I have seen inside his mind, though, and somehow he does store the memories of the Breowakoe we knew, but he cannot access them. I would not have you bring them up before he is ready.*"

A light in the room burnt out and crackled in a silent pause.

"My god - you're so in love! What madness I have ended up living to see!" Stynia's giggling erupted into a coughing fit.

"*This deep-self of his is something I seldom saw. It is nothing but drive, it is hopeful ambition, despite the challenge of existence. This boy, in concert with the true Breowakoe's will, is atoning for the sins of the man we knew. I intend to guide them both as they right those wrongs. You, on the other hand - you are the same selfish little creature in death that you were when you lived. Perhaps if you had advised him, guided him, rather than conniving for power behind his back, we could have brought this side of him forth in the Planclands and spared ourselves 2000 years of this hell."*

"So dramatic. You sound like your sister," Stynia spat out.

Kaimaradan was in a position to act out upon the object of her rage. She leaned in and spat acid into Stynia's eyes. His musical squeal echoed into the quiet hall as she held his thrashing torso in place. She hooked a pair of legs through his cheeks and under his jaw to prevent the acid from spilling off his face with the turns of his head. She wanted to be sure his eyes melted completely.

"Did you think I had forgiven what you did to my family? The rest of them, perhaps, but my sister's consciousness was not a fabrication. You deserve to suffer for that more intensely than even I am gifted to provide for you in this reality."

Kaimaradan waited many minutes for his little Piccaro breaths to stop again, a small part of her wanting the conversation to continue, a part of her hoping for an apology or an admission of guilt.

"What are you waiting for, you wicked cunt - just kill me," Stynia hissed.

Kaimaradan realized she needed to stop toying with her food. Breowakoe may have been in combat as she spoke. She chose to conserve her thripsis, as much as she wanted to slow Stynia's perception of time.

In a series of little movements, her legs pulled apart the skin of his abdomen, then ripped apart his intestines, unravelling them imperfectly as she went. His screams echoed through the dark until his voice went so hoarse that he could scream no more.

At last, to seal her efforts, Kaimaradan closed her pincers over his throat to decapitate him. She leaned back to behold the satisfying conclusion of her handiwork. In a way she felt sad; she had never liked Stynia, but to see the death of someone you had known for so long was never easy.

Suddenly, a foreign thripsis enveloped her and unearthed this room of the subterranean civilization, blowing away the stone roof of the hall and the sand above it. She was bewildered for a moment as she had forgotten that Stynia was an aspect, and that she was still in the Spoil. The great tornado of energy and dust took her up into the air as she faced the blue, pulsing sun. As she donned the aspect of cunning she could see into the deep downstream. A heavy, crimson thripsis was exploding from floor to roof, partially eclipsing Verivoluae. Kaimaradan's armoured heart skipped a beat - this could have been emitted only by Breowakoe, but how was his battle so chaotic that it had reached this far downstream? It appeared that it was well past Gol Paqua, almost at the Arid Necropolis.

The horn sounded, pulsing along the column and rattling the city beneath her. Kaimaradan found that her thripsis was restored in full and to a greater amount than she had with just the aspect of cruelty. To have experienced 2000 years at the same level only to upgrade this far into the game felt so strange.

Feeling unstoppable, she flowed at top speed downstream through the sands, excited soon to be back by the side of her love.

Ire Under the Overworld - 16

Verivoluae's glare reflected off the tower. Breowakoe squinted, shifting his course to the right. He could feel her presence at the top, in her office, standing behind her desk and looking out the window. He considered the possibility that Tiricora was aware of him, too. Breowakoe knew there would be no perfect surprise, but as much surprise as possible would be ideal. Thinking to change his entry point at the last second, he zipped midair to the furthest side of the tower's top and then flew full speed through the outer wall. He sailed through multiple rooms, moving so fast that Tiricora's henchmen were totally unreactive until they were out of his field of view.

There she was on the other side of her office, just starting to turn around as Breowakoe landed metres from her. He took two long, measured strides, winding up to strike her core. Tiricora wasted no movement. In the last moment she raised a hand and caught the blow, balancing perfectly against the aspect of power with a precise burst of her own thripsis. She was expressionless in that brief moment of time as he launched her out the window, shattering it loudly. Her body was perfectly rigid as she flew into the far downstream; she had balanced the momentum evenly throughout her body and suffered no damage. Armed Nethriel men were running into the room, taking aim at Breowakoe. He ignored them, instead carefully observing Tiricora's trajectory. As he had seen King Grona do, with a powerful leap he launched himself into the far downstream. Pushing off on his right foot, he collapsed the tower behind him. The distant screams of the dying evaporated into space only seconds after he took to the air.

The rock ceiling above was a blur as the two moved beyond Goliah's air space and were soaring over the Grobut outpost. Breowakoe assessed that he was moving about a third faster than Tiricora, having assumed a more aerodynamic position and was now close enough that he could see her smirking at him. It was an unnerving sight; her body remained rigid, and she remained calm after being launched two thirds of the way to the ceiling.

The air was roaring past his ears over the ruin of Gol Paqua as Breowakoe closed in on Tiricora. She readied herself for another blow by extending her arms in front of her. He still took the swing, transferring all his momentum to her, spiking her into the deep desert, further downstream than he had ever been.

In the distance she made impact with the ground; the

sand exploded and a visible seismic wave surged all the way to the port wall. Breowakoe flew to that distant spot, but upon his arrival Tiricora simply stood there, arms casually at her sides, amused. He danced about in the air, not wanting to be an easy target, and raised his right index finger to blast her with a beam of radiant purple energy. Just as Kaimaradan had predicted, Tiricora didn't need to block the beam. She was expending thripsis in a tiny, invisible layer around her skin to protect herself. So arrogant was Tiricora that when Breowakoe flew behind her, she didn't bother to turn around.

Breowakoe dropped to the ground. He channeled all three of his aspects at once, and a deep crimson energy erupted in every direction, even lapping against the ceiling of the Spoil. He rushed her blind spot, leaving a dollop of lava in each footprint, and brought a fist down. Tiricora turned at the last second and blocked the blow. The force carried her out of sight under the sand with the sound of a candle snuffing. Breowakoe knew he couldn't let up, he needed to capitalize on her having underestimated him. Placing his hands on the sand, he expelled a spate of blue fire into the ground, trying to boil Tiricora alive. The sand near-instantly became molten within a 100-metre radius, and Breowakoe hovered over the vast lake of fire searching for her.

Tiricora was moving oddly through the lava beneath him, maneuvering her body like a worm. She surfaced a metre upstream of Breowakoe, shooting a tiny bullet of thripsis from her index finger as she appeared. It ripped through the air and the sound barrier making a loud crack and, momentarily, a cloud formed around Tiricora's finger. The bullet nearly connected with Breowakoe's cheek but was lifted by the upward current of thripsis and carried safely to the ceiling. Breowakoe recognized that if the shot had been point-blank at his head, he might have been killed. He flew higher to put more distance between himself and Tiricora. Over the loud, prickling noise of his energy output he could hear that she was trying to catch her breath. A shockwave emanated from her, and the top layer of the entire lake cooled into glass. She pulled her legs out of the glass and stood up calmly in front of Breowakoe.

"Well done; well done, young man!" she called over the crackling sounds, applauding with her trademark smirk. "A 'Hello!' would have been fine, too, by the way… How did you get out of the Spoil rock cell? Wait, let me guess... it couldn't have been you... Remind me, what are the abilities of the aspect of cruelty again?"

"Kai can contort things and change their shapes, we slipped through those holes."

Breowakoe didn't mind talking as he kept dosing Tiricora with radiation; he just needed to keep an eye on her legs to make sure she didn't try to rush him.

"'Kai?' Awwwww, do you two have little nicknames for each other now? I guess love really is blind," Tiricora mocked.

Breowakoe got comfortable, as there was nothing she could say that would rile him up. He cocked his head back and mirrored her smirk. With a glance he re-melted the glass under her feet. Tiricora looked shocked for a moment as she began to sink, but leapt out to safety masterfully.

"My, my, well isn't that a neat little party trick."

Breowakoe laughed.

"I'd like to know what *I* could do with the aspect of destruction." Her expression soured. "Playing the long game, are we? You think I'll run out of thripsis, don't you?"

Breowakoe said nothing.

"Well, you better point that finger at me again, this is a pitiable amount of radiation you're expelling. My natural accumulation of thripsis exceeds the amount I use to block it."

Tiricora wasn't smiling. She seemed serious and Breowakoe's heart sank, wondering if she was bluffing. He had never seen her in a mood that wasn't phoney or gleeful. It seemed believable, though, that even in the long game she may have the upper hand. He scrambled to think of another way to defeat her: maybe if he could distract her, somehow, and hit her with the aspect of power in a blind spot, he could get a kill shot - but her own kill shots were so effortless, the tap of a finger.

"Why did I challenge her..." Breowakoe began doubting himself. "Kai was going to join me in this fight. Why didn't I just wait?"

"Breowakoe, why do you want to kill me? Do you not like me, or is it for my aspects?"

He blinked. "Your aspects, obviously."

"- and why do you want my aspects? As you are, you could rule any land in this hell - except for Goliah, of course." She smiled, then continued. "You could live like Coabra Grona, dominating and taking concubines. What could my aspects of apathy and control give to you that you could not already seize for yourself?"

Breowakoe stared at her, trying to figure out if there was

a way she could use this information against him.

"I'm genuinely curious."

She sounded sincere, and appeared unimposing, placing her hands on her hips as she leaned to one side.

"I want to climb the Silo Blades. I want to go back to the Planelands."

Tiricora's look of amusement returned.

"You found a capsule of essence on your own, I see... What do you recall of the Planelands? What would you do there?" she continued to pry.

"What's the point in telling you," he replied, after a long pause.

"As you know, Breowakoe, I was one of the first 'Nethriel' in the Spoil. Born into this hell as an aspect, naturally I remembered my time alive without needing a capsule of essence."

Breowakoe was puzzled. Tiricora assumed that he knew this. How could he - was she implying that Kaimaradan had once lived in the Planelands? Dunstan had never even heard of a creature like her at age nine. But how odd that Kaimaradan had never spoken as though she recalled her past life; she reminisced only about the early days of the Spoil - even admitting that she had always been a Satrian. And yet, since recovering his memories, Breowakoe was aware that many had been confusing him for someone else - some *other* Breowakoe. Kaimaradan, Stynia: both had spoken to him as though they knew him or knew some other iteration of him, but when he searched the memories of his existence, he could find them nowhere.

"For my first 50 years here, I had no desire to return to the hell above. This one below seemed much better to me. But one day, when I heard from a Blonak envoy of the existence of the Silo Blades, I realized that the reason I hadn't wanted to return was actually that I didn't believe it was possible. Focusing on the negative of my life above was how I accepted that I would never get it back. My husband in the Planelands, Beratu, spawned into the Spoil as the aspect of power. I thought that to be so odd; he was an emotionally strong man but I wouldn't say he had any particular power in his presence or otherwise.

Upon learning of the Silo Blades, I expanded my influence further. I learned about the other aspects and which I might have the best chance of killing first. The demon races in the far downstream lived in terrain that suited them and where they might have an advantage. The Cultivator seemed to be a sitting duck. Beratu and I spent years beneath it, studying it. We tried to penetrate its stem with our thripsis, channeling thripsis through it; I even climbed up the stem on many occasions, but the back of the eyelid was as invulnerable as the optic nerve from which it nonsensically sprouted. I tried to fit things in the space between the eyelid and the Spoil rock, but it was air-tight. I removed the sand away from the base of the nerve, but that, too, was rooted in Spoil rock. It was as if it had been put there, so close to my territory, just to taunt me."

"You knew, though, that you needed all the aspects to climb the Silo Blades. You were willing to kill your husband to get back to the Planelands? Why? And why are you telling me this?"

Tiricora looked annoyed to be interrupted.

"Obviously I felt conflicted; in every scenario I concocted, he was the last aspect to die, and deep down I thought I would never get to the point where I actually had to do it. I guess I expected to fail. After all, there was an aspect needed to climb the blades that at the time did not exist in the Spoil. I know you know how it feels. You're going to have to kill your 'Kai,' after all, Breowakoe."

Breowakoe quickly shuffled the idea out of his mind.

"Beratu was such a sweet man. He would gladly have given his consciousness for me to reach the Planelands." Tiricora choked, looking close to tears. "But obviously, it would never come to that. Giving up on the Cultivator, my sweet Beratu and I set our sights on the aspect of cunning. Chief Stynia seemed the most frail, and his territory - 'The Network' - was, as you know, a series of tunnels under where Gol Paqua now stands."

Breowakoe thought about the Nethriel farms dug under the wall of the city, realizing that they were the remains of an old Piccaro civilization.

"It was easier to deal with than the first tar sands or that Satrian hive. 800 years after the Spoil was created, Beratu and I set out together with a small group of soldiers for logistical support. When we arrived at The Network I could feel Stynia's presence beneath me in the tunnels, or at least I thought I could. Beratu hammered the ground in places to try to cut off Stynia's path and I fired thripsis into the sand to deliver the kill. I thought I got a clean hit, and we both felt the source of the thripsis fade. We were overjoyed and embraced one another, but I didn't feel any different. I was confused and dug my way into the tunnels to confirm the kill. What I found was not the body of a Piccaro, but a strange machine on a rail cart that had been refracting and modifying our own thriptic signatures. That was when I understood the power of cunning. He didn't have to fight to win.

I rushed back up to the surface to see my beloved Beratu on his knees, tears streaming down his face." Tiricora choked again, it was uncomfortable for Breowakoe to listen to this. "He was convulsing and the veins in his forehead were bulging. Three large creatures surrounded him. They were hideous monstrosities, unlike anything I had seen before. One of the Grobut had its abdomen in Beratu's mouth and was distending his throat, filling his lungs with bile. I couldn't move. I didn't understand at the time how this creature had bested my aspect husband. I didn't know how the bile worked. These demons were biological weapons created by the Piccaros to kill aspects.

At last, the light in Beratu's beautiful eyes died and the sun turned blue. I thought it was weeping for him, but instead the creature that killed him was being rewarded with his power. A syringe poked into my arm - Stynia was behind me and had stuck me with the Grobut bile. I fought through its effects; with my aspect of control I was able to stop its spread throughout my body, but I was unable to use one of my arms. I was forced to flee as at last the Grobut smashed my husband's head like a melon."

Breowakoe was surprised to be feeling sympathy for Tiricora.

"Since that day I gave up on my dream of returning to the Planelands -"

"Why would you work with Stynia after tha -" Breowakoe started, but was interrupted by a pulse of air rattling his body from behind. He gasped - had she attacked him somehow while distracting him with her story? Was any of it true? He turned to see that Verivoluae was blue and that the mystical horn was blasting through their reality. He whirled around to face Tiricora again and sure enough, upstream by the port wall of Goliah, a tornado was visible. It was too far away to see who rested atop it and he was too preoccupied with his own circumstances to be able to sense who the victor was.

"Ooh," Tiricora crooned. "Who do you think won?"

She smirked. Breowakoe felt a jolt of anxiety at the thought of his only friend in the world being dead.

"Stynia has an answer for everything," Tiricora taunted.

Breowakoe's worry turned to anger and he glared at Tiricora.

"Well, I guess we'll know soon enough who won. Whoever it is wouldn't want to miss out on this little party would they?" she said confidently, gesturing to the geyser of energy coming off her opponent.

As slim as his chances were, they would only become worse if Chief Stynia were to arrive. Breowakoe realized he had no choice but to press the attack – he needed to make Tiricora burn through her reserves and accept the risk to himself. He pointed a finger at her and channeled exclusively through it, taking down his shield to sharpen his spear.

Tiricora looked alarmed, as though she had expected him to simply give up. The beam of charged thripsis broke across her face and, lightning fast, she pivoted, appearing right before Breowakoe, ducking under his arm, her index finger raised and pointed toward the underside of his jaw. He was ready for this and brought his left arm down on her head. Again, she looked unprepared, her finger re-positioned and fired a bullet of thripsis into his wrist. Breowakoe's fist connected with her skull, shoving Tiricora through the glass and into the lava below.

With his left wrist on fire, Breowakoe couldn't feel his left hand – had she cut through nerves from the inside? There was no time to panic; he had to finish the job. Focusing under the lava, he continued firing the beam of thripsis from his right index finger wherever he sensed her presence below. With his thriptic shield down, Tiricora could now move toward him rapidly through the molten glass. He moved away - he couldn't allow her to close the gap again. He gnashed his teeth trying to follow her with his finger at the ready for when she surfaced. It was subtle, but he could tell she had increased the thriptic output from her skin to tolerate the focused beam.

Tiricora resurfaced and fired a bullet of thripsis that struck Breowakoe in the left shoulder, narrowly missing his neck. It tore through the front just over his collarbone, clipped the subclavian artery, and exploded his trapezius muscle out the back. He grunted and, in a huff, became defensive, once more sending the violent, prickling flow up to the Spoil rock ceiling.

The searing pain in his neck brought Breowakoe to one knee. It felt as though his left arm was almost falling off. He reached with his good arm to clasp his shoulder, and was shocked upon withdrawing it at the amount of blood soaking his hand. Hyperventilating, he worried that she had hit something vital but tried to calm himself down.

"Well, I'm not bleeding out in the next ten seconds at least..."

"That was a great little bout!" Tiricora laughed, snuffing out the cinders in her short hair.

In her unpreparedness, she had actually been hurt. The left side of her face was badly burned and her neck was clearly broken. Her head was hanging off to the side unnaturally with some vertebrae hiked up disturbingly high just under her skin. Tiricora joined Breowakoe in taking a knee as she tried to crack her head back into place. She was incompletely successful, and although she had pushed it back to being upright, it still looked somewhat awry.

Blood was running down Breowakoe's chest and dripping onto the ground; he was trying to apply pressure to the wound and hold the blood in with his thripsis, but he lacked the thriptic control. He wondered if Tiricora's spinal cord had snapped and whether she was puppeting her own body with her thripsis. It would be impossible to tell without using the aspect of destruction.

"Oooh, looks like I got you pretty good, too!" Tiricora

squealed, as she glanced at his neck. "Do you see the bone child? You want to try me again?"

Tiricora stopped her taunts and looked upstream over Breowakoe's shoulder, disgust rising on her face. He thought she might be baiting him to look the other way, and remained focused on her. But then he sensed her, and an open-mouthed smile crept across his face.

Kaimaradan smashed through the fire and glass and vomited some tincture onto Breowakoe's neck. The pain might have made him pass out if it hadn't been spiked with adrenaline. An elastic, red, scar-tissue-like film developed rapidly over the wounded area and when the intense pain came to an end, he had regained control of his left hand.

"Thank you, Kai," Breowakoe beamed, rising to his feet and looking down into the beady eyes of his dear friend, who at hip height gazed back.

Breowakoe worried that at this range his thripsis would be harmful to her - but on second thought, he recalled that even when she resided under his skin she never seemed to be bothered by it. Perhaps her Satrian carapace was resistant to channeling thripsis.

Tiricora hissed, she was frustrated, even a little afraid.

To no one's surprise, Tiricora wasted no time in raising her finger to fire a bullet of thripsis at Kaimaradan's head. Kaimaradan anticipated the attack as she dove back into the lake under the glass, swimming through it at speeds Breowakoe could barely keep track of. Tiricora desperately shot thriptic bullets into the liquid fire but could not land a direct hit. She looked tired, her movements slower than usual, less precise. Breowakoe remembered the plan and sprinted towards Tiricora. Kaimaradan was already beneath her feet, popping up through the glass repeatedly and trying to slice at Tiricora with her sharp pincers. Tiricora dodged the attacks, but it was becoming more difficult as the glass continued to break. Handspringing backwards, she travelled downstream towards the sand and away. The demon centipede followed the scent of the Nethriel tyrant's thripsis.

Tiricora, midair, fired one off at Breowakoe as he charged in, but the bullet was carried into the air by his torrent of thripsis. She wasn't even looking; she seemed so preoccupied with Kai. The gap closed, Breowakoe was one metre away, his arm cocked, ready to take Tiricora's head off with the aspect of power. She grinned, having been feigning preoccupation with Kaimaradan, and lifted a finger to

Breowakoe's temple. In that moment, Breowakoe knew he was dead.

The reality-bending, intoxicating thripsis of the aspect of cruelty erupted into the air. Breowakoe thought he was imagining things as the giant centipede corkscrewed up Tiricora's leg and abdomen, injecting something into her neck. Why was Tiricora hesitating to kill him? This movement seemed extremely fast even for Kaimaradan. Kai was too close to Tiricora's face and Breowakoe, fearing friendly fire, instead sweep-kicked Tiricora at the quads. She spun for several dozen revolutions in the air. Her legs came flying off just above the knees: one ventured into the far downstream and the other in its frenzy of violent spinning caught Breowakoe in the ribs. Kaimaradan clung tight, wrapped around Tiricora's whirling upper body, which, as it came smashing to the sand, caused a large burst of crystal dust that fell back to the ground flatly, like dry earth after a mortar shell explosion.

Kai crawled away from the body, seeming to want to dig, or no... head downstream? She seemed disoriented. Breowakoe halted his channeling and planted his foot in front of her. Kai was startled and bit Breowakoe's leg with her pincers. He was surprised at how little it hurt - it barely broke the skin.

"Kai, it's me. Get in."

She looked up at him and withdrew her pincers. He actually found her cute when dizzy, trying to focus her little, beady eyes. She finally climbed up his leg and reopened the wound in his right, lower abdomen. She sheared the skin from his muscle to resume her old post; it was painful, but oddly satisfying.

Tiricora groaned and rolled onto her back; she seemed concussed and struggled to sit up.

"Not so talkative now, are we?" Breowakoe finally had the upper hand and a chance to mock Tiricora. "Anything you want me to do for you in the Planelands?" he continued.

This seemed to catch Tiricora's attention as she looked up to him, now vulnerable and with wrath in her eyes.

"I told you, I'm not interested in the Planelands," she snarled.

"What did you even want? You never finished your weird story." Breowakoe was genuinely curious and in a playful mood now, savouring the kill before him.

"*Posturing costs lives, Breowakoe. Just kill her.*"

"What do I want the aspects for? To put an end to this

miserable existence once and for all. To kill that monster who traps us all in here."

Tiricora pointed to Verivoluae. Breowakoe was taken aback. He could hear in her voice that Tiricora was losing emotional self control, something he didn't think possible.

"You always were so selfish and naive, Breowakoe. You made the living world not worth returning to, and even now in death I shall suffer for eternity for YOUR mistakes. You are a NEGLIGENT, ARROGANT CHILD."

Tiricora was screaming at this point looking back and forth between Breowakoe and the sun at the end of the tunnel.

"I served you for twenty years and you never heeded my words! And yes, I abandoned you when I could see what would come of your weakness!"

"What are you talking about? Who ARE ANY OF YOU talking about when you talk about Breowakoe!? I was Dunstan Briar in the Planelands! Take this shit to someone else!"

Breo was getting heated himself. So sick of these people accusing him of things he didn't do. Accusing him of being someone he couldn't remember being. Even still, he was alarmed by the passion in her words.

"Of course you don't know," Tiricora said defeatedly.

"How convenient for you. What a joke… CURSE this JOKE creation of yours, and CURSE YOU, BREOWAKOE." Seething in anger, she spat her words toward Verivoluae: "WHY BRING ME INTO IT!? HAD I NOT SUFFERED ENOUGH?!"

"All right, I've heard enough of this," Breowakoe said as he took steps toward Tiricora who now looked at him, agitated and afraid. She looked down to her right and gasped.

"Oh, no... the bone child beckons to me now, does it? No, Breowakoe, you fucking fool! No, no, no, no - it's not fair! IT'S NOT FAIR!" Tiricora screamed, her face turning red. "Breowakoe if there is any good in you at all you will kill Verivoluae and give up on your dream of reaching the Planelands. It's just another childish fantasy; it won't be as you imagine when you actually get back. You are not who you once were. Kaimaradan, tell him! YOU RESENTED HIS WEAKNESS IN LIFE, WHY DO YOU NOW CODDLE HIS INDIFFERENCE? HE NEEDS TO PUT AN END TO THIS!"

Breowakoe hesitated. He could feel Kaimaradan's discomfort. He furrowed his brow; it was clear that Kai still kept so much from him, but he decided it shouldn't come from Tiricora. He would ask Kai himself. He was getting increasingly annoyed with Tiricora's screaming. She looked to the ground again and saw in the presence of the bone child that she wasn't changing any minds.

The ground peeled away abruptly as Breowakoe's thripsis spewed violently around him. Tiricora now sat passively, facing Verivoluae. She was muttering words under her breath, her eyes closed. Breowakoe raised his arm and brought it down on the top of her head. A gale swept over him as Verivoluae pulsed blue twice, sounding its doom horn and shaking the walls of the Spoil.

Arid Necropolis - 17

Breowakoe marched silently deep into the downstream as Kaimaradan relaxed under his skin. He didn't feel much more powerful with another two aspects, but he noted that his control over thripsis had slightly increased. Perhaps it took practice to achieve mastery of the aspect of control. Breowakoe wondered if this was something he would ever have time or the need to do.

It was another one of those beautiful nights he had come to love: the easy warmth of the sand and the comforting caress of the breeze. Breowakoe had considered making the small journey to Thelise to spend time with the waitress he had rescued in Gol Paqua, but he changed his mind. Thelise was out of the way, and there was no reason to reminisce about the Planelands when he would soon return there. His time with Kai, on the other hand, was limited. She had become a treasured friend, and he wanted to learn all he could from and about her before the inevitable.

"So, what will I find next, downstream?" he asked aloud.

"*The ruins of Satria, what people now call the Arid Necropolis.*"

"Will we get there tonight?"

"*At this pace? Unlikely. Unless you wanted to jump there instantly,*" Kaimaradan replied, condescendingly.

"All right, then. No, I think I'd rather savour the journey."

Breowakoe plopped onto the ground and lay on his back, allowing himself to stretch out fully, yawning.

"How far downstream from the Arid Necropolis are the Silo Blades?"

"*Very. Structures and cities are much further apart from each other the further downstream you go,*" she continued, forlorn.

Breowakoe listened to her answer but wasn't concentrating on its meaning. Her responses sounded automatic, as though her mind were elsewhere. He wondered what she could be thinking about.

"Thanks for helping me kill Tiricora. I would probably have lost without you."

"*Of course; her death was long overdue,*" Kai said, matter-of-factly.

The two of them stewed in a moment of awkward silence.

"Kai... who was Breowakoe?"

Kaimaradan had been anticipating this question, but still took time to choose her words carefully. After a long pause she answered.

"*It doesn't matter who Breowakoe was. All that matters is right now.*"

Naturally, Breo was frustrated with this response.

"Do you think I'll take it personally? I won't be insulted. I know I'm not the real Breowakoe. Some old hag in Goliah just gave me this name. My real name in the Planelands was Dunstan."

Inquisitive feelings crept into the centipede's mind. Kai seemed like she was about to say something, but didn't.

"Fine. Answer me this instead: do you remember your time living?" Breowakoe asked.

She seemed conflicted, as though a part of her wanted to answer and another wanted to remain silent. Breo closed his eyes and kept his mouth shut, giving her a space to fill.

"*I was a Queen,*" she ventured, seeming to be deeply reminiscing.

"Oh, interesting... Are there Satrians in the Planelands, as well?"

Kaimaradan felt a jolt of anger. "*No! I was human. I was*

Queen in the most powerful civilization the Planelands had ever known."

Breowakoe was surprised; the suspicions his conversation with Tiricora had awakened were correct.

"Why did you lie to me before?" He could feel her confusion. "Why did you tell me you had always been a Satrian?"

"*I do not know. I suppose I wanted to protect you.*"

"Protect me from what?" Breowakoe was puzzled.

"*From yourself. From what I thought you might do with the knowledge of your history.*"

"What might I have done?" Breowakoe pressed her, becoming more irritated.

"*It doesn't matter anymore. You turned out not to be who I thought you were - you may recall I thought you to be a foolish boy, and I thought you would act as such once you remembered your past.*"

Breowakoe laughed, forgetting in the moment that she was still avoiding the question. "Was the original Breowakoe a foolish boy when he was alive?"

"*Yes -*" Kai started again, but cut herself off, unsure of how much she should tell him.

"So, this place was created by Breowakoe before he died?" Breowakoe reasoned from Stynia's description of the Spoil.

"*You could say that; it is a long story that I do not wish to tell.*"

Breowakoe sighed, frustrated.

"Kai, I don't know how much more time we have together," he blurted out.

She was silent and he could tell that she was hurt, as they both imagined how he would kill her. Underlying the affection she had developed for him lay the knowledge that returning to the Planelands was more important to him than her life. Kaimaradan was weeping within him.

"Do you not want me to go?" he asked stiffly, torn between what he wanted and what he wanted more.

"*I do want you to go; there is nothing for me in these wastes. Everyone I loved is gone. I want to see you succeed.*"

Her sobbing was eerily human, but it was difficult to imagine what her demon physiology was doing. Breowakoe's frowned. He supposed there were some things about the Spoil, about herself, and even about him that she preferred to die without sharing.

"Dunstan. I am sorry, but the things you want to know will not help you to rescue Mr. Doggy or in your return to the Planelands. The story of Breowakoe is poison and is best forgotten. When you leave this place, I want you never to look back. I want you to forget that name. I want you to forget this place and love your life."

She now spoke with such passionate intensity that Breowakoe hung on her every word. Perhaps she was right. Perhaps it was best that he not know. He felt uncomfortable to see her so vulnerable and tried to quell the feeling. He was beginning to appreciate all she had done for him - so much more than his own mother had ever done. And she would give her own life to help him get home.

"Ok. Thank you, Kai," he said vacuously.

The centipede trembled within him for another while, nuzzling her head against his sternum as he drifted off to sleep.

-

"The last King of Katharnia, King Breowakoe, was a very weak man who was uninterested in ruling." Mrs. Barrister said.

-

Breowakoe awoke in a frenzy; the heat of the sun was boiling his blood. What was that just now? Another dream? He had not slept since the night he received the capsule of essence. Did he have more to remember from the time he lived? It was hot, and the pull of his friend against his skin was uncomfortable. He took off into the sky, too impatient to walk, rocketing into the downstream.

Breowakoe was lost in thought. 'Breowakoe' had been the last King of Katharnia... THE Katharnia? That king had been a weak man uninterested in ruling... wasn't he the reason their civilization fell apart? No wonder his name was so hated by the likes of Tiricora and Stynia - but who were they? Was Kaimaradan the last queen of *that* ancient civilization? She did say she was thousands of years old. Breowakoe wrestled with this knowledge, wondering if he could really have spent all this time in the company of an ancient people.

Kai's brain activity seemed idle; she was still sleeping or in a deep trance, certainly not paying attention to him or his thoughts.

"Whoa..." The aspect of control had come online overnight. Breowakoe noticed that he could achieve the same upward force with a tenth of the thripsis, and his top speed was 10x faster. The rock walls were a blur and he blew past a strange rock and clay formation, nearly buried by sand off toward the starboard wall.

"*WAIT, GO BACK!*"

Kaimaradan was alert now, and called out to him. Breowakoe realized that this rock formation must have been the Arid Necropolis. He did a U-turn in the air and backtracked at a more reasonable speed. Whizzing by it, he noticed that the Necropolis was a lot larger than he had expected it to be.

"*I have not seen these structures in a thousand years,*" Kaimaradan said nostalgically.

Sensing more deeply, Breowakoe could see that the necropolis had a labyrinthian system of underground tunnels not unlike the dwelling of the Piccaros. He started to land, gently, at a perforated clay spire sprouting from the sand.

"Further upstream," Kaimaradan directed him.

Breowakoe picked back up and followed her instructions, now landing at a spot where two clay spires flanked what looked like an above-ground clay oven with a larger opening. His feet made contact with the ground and Kaimaradan was already scurrying out of the wound in his abdomen. He could feel that she was harbouring a deep, aching sadness being here. He didn't feel the need to ask where she was going and knew he wasn't to follow her. It was part of a grieving process for her, no doubt, and he wanted to show her the respect of his patience. He watched on as the last of her legs disappeared into the clay oven, and into the tunnels.

"Always tunnels with these demons," he thought to himself. The Blonak lived under tar sands and the centipedes, flies, and goblins had their tunnels. He supposed it made sense. It ought to be much cooler underground, especially this close to Verivoluae.

Breowakoe squinted, gazing over to the sun. It actually appeared closer this far downstream, although that didn't make sense. He had been told the Spoil was a never-ending tunnel where Verivoluae always lay on the horizon. He wondered what would happen if he flew directly into it, with all the aspects, channeling with everything he had. Would he be able to reach it? Destroy it? And what would happen next? Would the Spoil be forever in darkness? Would it cease to exist? Somehow Breowakoe felt that Verivoluae was not "defeatable" - at least, not by the same means that every other aspect was.

"Probably not worth a try," he chuckled to himself.

A wave of sadness hit as he suddenly remembered that he was only days away from killing Kai. He thought about how to do it… "quick and painless," he repeated to himself. Kai *was* the closest thing he'd had to a caring mother, but she had lived a long life, she had had her revenge, and shortly she would have no remaining business here. Mr. Doggy, on the other hand, must not be left in the hands of that monster on the surface. Breowakoe clenched his jaw as he remembered Mr. Doggy's owner kicking him against the side of the house. He felt heartsick, and worried for the little gaffer. A sense of urgency came over him as he realized how close he was to doing some good in the world above.

Becoming impatient, Breowakoe turned his attention to what Kaimaradan was up to underground. The subterranean chambers in the section they had landed above had a different layout to the rest of the city. While most of the city was more reminiscent of the winding hive of Grobut architecture, this section had symmetry. Perhaps it was the throne room or the royal quarters. He found that he had lost sense of

Kaimaradan's position and broadened his search to find her again.

She was in a small room behind what Breowakoe assumed to be the throne room. The room was a semi-sphere, or dome. In diameter, it was about the length of Kaimaradan herself. She was stopped there, half in the opening, leaning over something - it was another Satrian.

Breowakoe was shocked. Was she not the last Satrian, after all? He wondered if there had somehow been a survivor living there all this time. But the centipede Kai was leaning over wasn't moving, or breathing - in fact, it was hollow, the carapace of a Satrian long dead. Kai was vomiting something over its body and into its shell. It was amazing how many different mixtures she was able to create inside her body.

Breowakoe suspected that this may have been one of the ways Satrians had communicated with one another, or perhaps it was a way to honour the dead, but to whom did this vacant carapace belong? He speculated wildly for a moment, but decided he would not ask her. He was fine with never knowing. In fact, he shouldn't be eavesdropping. One last broad sweep of the tunnels revealed millions of Satrian husks littered throughout the massive hive.

"This really is a Necropolis," he thought to himself as a pang of sadness took hold of him. Imagining all these creatures, like his friend, dying at the hands of the Piccaros. What sort of lives had they lived when this Kingdom did?

After another few moments, Kaimaradan had turned and was making her way back up through the tunnels. Breowakoe took a seat on the sand so it would be easier for her to climb aboard. She came barrelling out of the tunnels, across the sand, and into the pocket of skin without a care for his suffering; but now with the aspect of apathy he felt only a little pressure.

"*Sorry. Thank you for stopping there, Breowakoe.*"

"Of course," he replied, sincerely. "Is there anything else you wanted to do?"

"*No, we can go to the Silo Blades if you wish.*"

She sounded anxious to get out of there.

"Wasn't there some favour you were going to ask me for?"

"*No, not anymore. You have done plenty for me, Breowakoe. More than you know.*"

She sounded resolute. One last lingering fleck of childish weakness in him wished she would talk him out of it.

"Ok, well if you think of something just let me know."

Breo took to the skies once again and flew even deeper downstream.

Six Macabre Wires -18

Passing a lake of clay on the port side of the Spoil, Breowakoe could feel that although its surface had cracked, there was still moisture underneath. Even flying at close to top speed, he couldn't get past the seemingly endless tar sands.

"Wow," he thought to himself and slowed down, becoming anxious that he would miss the Silo Blades or fly straight into them.

Verivoluae's light burned more intensely this deep in the Spoil. It seemed more present in the barrel of rock that surrounded them, perhaps it was hovering in a tangible place rather than existing in the infinite distance, after all. The first tar sands began to thin, and finally they petered out to nothing but more sand.

Breowakoe slowed even more, scanning the horizon for the glimmer of the blades. But when some time had passed, he began to doubt Kaimaradan's tale.

"Could they have been destroyed?" he asked.

"*Impossible.*" Kaimaradan left it at that. He trusted her confidence and smothered his impatience to glide relentlessly into the sun.

Trying not to think about how long it was taking, he

focused on the sheer joy of flying at this speed; and when at last he let go of the desire to reach his destination, he saw it: a strange, linear glint on the horizon that looked like suspect lines on an abstract painting.

To Breowakoe's surprise, the blades were about halfway to the port wall from the middle. He had expected them to be symmetrical with the outlay of the Spoil. Kaimaradan was silent as Breowakoe sailed over to them. They were so haunting a sight – so simple and yet so incredibly unnatural - that they looked out of place. Perfectly clean, the six sword blades were just as she had described them: they formed a pentagon with the sixth blade running down the middle. Breowakoe circumnavigated them and flew up to the ceiling to examine the hole where the blades met the rock. He couldn't see very far in, but the central blade appeared to continue through the hole while the other five blades appeared to stop at the lip of the opening. The blades were too narrowly spaced to fit his torso between them with Kaimaradan under his skin, but it seemed that he would be able to fit if he were alone.

"Do you think I could just fly up there?" Breowakoe asked rhetorically. He tried to reach between the blades to feel the interior of the ceiling passage.

Breowakoe stubbed his fingers - there was some sort of force field between the outer blades that was invisible to the eye. He paused, alarmed, and tried to crack a blade with the aspect of power. Indeed, they were very clearly a derivative of Spoil rock - utterly immovable. He gazed in the direction of Verivoluae, enormous this close to the blades and seeming to become even larger as he descended about midway from ceiling to floor. Finally, from the sand one metre below the blades, Verivoluae appeared as it had at the ceiling.

"*Interesting,*" Kaimaradan whispered in his mind.

"What?"

"*Did you feel that heat? It would seem that if you can make it past the halfway point the journey will get easier for you.*"

"Oh... I guess you're right."

Breowakoe was lost in thought. The sand was burning his feet and Verivoluae crisping his skin – and yet he stalled. In the back of his mind, he had hoped for a solution that didn't involve killing Kaimaradan. There simply wasn't one.

"All right, Kai. This is it," he said coldly, burying his emotion.

"*...Just like that?*"

Breowakoe could feel that she was trembling. She was afraid to die.

"Breo... do you not... Do you not remember me, at all?"

He could feel her close to tears.

"Kai... I thought you didn't want me to remember that life..."

"I had wondered if fate would have you remember on your own."

"You thought I would remember you as a human, you mean?"

"Well, yes."

"And what would that change, Kai? I need to get back to the Planelands. My only friend is being held prisoner up there by a killer."

"I know. It is stupid... I just wish you could have seen how I looked when I was human... I wanted you to remember how beautiful I was." Kaimaradan laughed nervously through her tears.

Breowakoe sighed, deciding to give her more. He placed a hand over her head, sandwiching her under his skin between his hand and heart. "As I was sleeping, I remembered learning about the last King of Katharnia, Breowakoe, in school... and I now think you were his queen." Kaimaradan's heart fluttered. "I am not him, and I don't remember being him, but in a strange way I have thought you were beautiful for a little while now, as far as centipedes go. You have a certain... aesthetic that I appreciate."

It was the truth, but he felt uneasy admitting it to her. He appreciated the sleek and agile nature of the beast within his chest, her efficiency as a weapon, and the deadly looking colouration on her back. A bizarre feeling was flooding from her mind and accidentally slipped into his; it was as though she felt ashamed at just how much she wanted to hear what he was saying.

"Breowakoe... you think that I am beautiful?" Kai muttered sheepishly.

He laughed out loud as she displayed a level of vulnerability that he was unaccustomed to.

"Yes, I do…" he said with an honest smile. He allowed another brief moment to pass. "Ok, it's time," he said, semi-impatiently.

"Ok..." Kai sniffled.

Slowly, she began making her way out of the hole, dawdling excessively.

"Please don't make this any harder for me," Breowakoe pleaded, as he looked up at the opening at the top of the Silo Blades. He felt that he could hear Mr. Doggy barking and was anxious to return to his side.

"Ok, that's enough."

Breowakoe grasped her midsection, which was bulging out from under his skin, ready to tear her right out of his body.

"*No, wait - please. Just one favour!*" Kaimaradan panicked.

"Go ahead?" Breowakoe tried his best to be patient and honour the agreement they had.

"*Breowakoe, originally I was going to ask you to bring an end to the Spoil, to delete this reality from existence. So many suffer unnecessarily under it, but now – but now I just want to tell you to follow your instincts. Do as much good as you can in the Planelands.*"

He could feel the human in her as she spoke.

"*Whatever happens and whatever choices you make, I will always lo -*"

"Thank you, Kai. I will always cherish our friendship." He cut her off.

"*No, wait!*" A disturbed feeling filled the air,

Kaimaradan had activated the aspect of cruelty. She sheared the muscle over his chest and injected something into his heart. Breowakoe could feel it traveling straight up into his brain, making him light-headed, dizzy. A strange feeling entered his mind and disappeared - corpusapien.

"What are you doing!?" Breowakoe roared as he reached toward her outline. He dug his fingers under his own skin, pushing them between Kaimaradan's legs as blood bubbled and squelched out of the wounds. With a forceful motion he tore her out of his body, flaying his entire torso in the process with the sound of a wet tarp ripping. Kaimaradan's powerful legs scraped and clacked at his ribs, trying to hold on, but she could not.

He cast her to the ground. Now unable to hear his thoughts, she twisted to right herself. She lifted her head and upper body to look up at him with her beady eyes. She was trembling, but brave.

Breowakoe's blood was pooling in the sand, so he used the aspect of control to hold what remained tight within his skinless torso. Breowakoe smiled, thinking back to the torment Kai had put him through when they first met. In a way, he appreciated that suffering as it had forced him to grow up, to contend with the world, to become strong enough to achieve his dreams. She deserved the best death he could provide her.

Breowakoe lifted his foot to show Kaimaradan how he meant to kill her and she got the message, placing her head snugly under it even as she trembled. A wave of empathy overtook him and his throat started to close. He knew what she had been about to say - before he yanked her out, that is. He knew that her message was for 'Breowakoe' rather than for Dunstan - but he thought it might mean something to her to hear 'Breowakoe' say it back.

"Whatever happens, Kai, and whatever choices I make. I will always -"

Breowakoe stomped on Kaimaradan's head with every bit of force and precision all his aspects allowed - crushing it instantly. Sand exploded in every direction, hitting the walls and the ceiling and even hissing as it seemed to fly into Verivoluae itself. Unexpected tears streamed down his face as he finished his sentence. The great tornado lifted him high into the sky. The great horn sounded twice, rattling into his bones at such close range, and the skin on his torso healed. Gone were the scars and stretch marks of Kai's dwelling. The sun pulsed blue and a part of Breowakoe lamented the fact that he would never again have the pride of the centipede's mark showing from under his skin.

As he descended, and the tornado began setting him back on the ground, the image of a beautiful woman appeared on the other side of the air column. She smiled at him as she flew past in her spectral, flowing dress. She cradled something in her arms but Breowakoe couldn't make out what it was. The ghostly woman approached Verivoluae and a crater appeared in its plasma to accept her. She disappeared into the star. Breowakoe shivered in silence, his left hand prickled and somehow he knew he had caused whatever this was. After returning to the sand, he decided that he must have been hallucinating.

Kaimaradan's body was gone. Perhaps it had been obliterated in the blast, perhaps some of the sand in the air had buried it shallowly somewhere.

Breowakoe swallowed his stew of feelings and now in her absence set his sights on the Silo Blades. He positioned himself directly under them and confirmed his suspicion that there was no force-field below or within the column.

With all aspects but creation flowing through him, Breowakoe felt absolutely heavy with power. But that feeling dissipated almost instantly as he lifted himself into the blades. Grasping two of the outer blades in his hands and allowing the central blade to penetrate down the length of his torso, puncturing his right lung and skewering his intestines, he climbed. It was as though the aspect of apathy had disappeared, and even worse. In all his agonized existence, he had not felt such pain. He paused to absorb the shock he felt but understood intuitively how this place worked. He knew he would need the central blade to impale him, and he knew there would be no reward without exquisite suffering.

Impaling himself, Breowakoe continued to climb the blades, sometimes finding the grit to climb faster and other times just desperately trying not to slide down. His stamina was crippled, as well, it seemed. Verivoluae burned more intensely than ever, and his skin was periodically catching fire. He could not channel thripsis; he just had to try his best to smother the flames with his hands. To avoid burning out, Breowakoe now climbed more slowly. As hot as the sun was, he found that he did not keep burning if he kept moving. Finally, after hours, he made it over the midline hump and his progression was easier as he climbed the remaining five kilometres to the Spoil's roof.

Ten kilometres into the sky he climbed, fueled by guilt, urgency, and to keep a promise to himself. As Breowakoe finally crossed from open air to Spoil rock, and Verivoluae's light could no longer scorch him, he breathed a sigh of relief.

Now between planes, the climb continued: through what felt like endless kilometres of a single, central sword that he could no longer see. The light of the Spoil below had faded to nothing and dirt began to appear, suspended in the space of the narrow column as in a snow-globe but frozen in time. Progressively more dirt clouded the tunnel the higher he went; at first, he was able to push it aside but eventually he was digging upwards. He could no longer feel the blade; the pain in his torso seemed simply to fade away, but he could not pinpoint the exact moment it had gone.

Suddenly, Breowakoe found it difficult to breathe. He was being smothered in dirt. He started to panic but then measured himself and, curiously, found that he was able to channel thripsis. But that wasn't right - he should be getting close to the Planelands. Was he heading back to the Spoil, somehow?

Although anxious, he could hear something above him, the soft murmuring of a white noise and another rolling sound.

He channeled everything he had straight upwards. His total power output felt like only a fraction of what he had wielded just hours ago in the Spoil, but it was enough to tear away the dirt between him and the sky. The shock of cold for the first time in well over a decade broke over his skin as a welcome rain washed the rot and cinder from him. He gasped as the mud that he had launched upwards now rained down upon him in satisfying plops, and a flash of lightning streaked over the clouds. As he reached the surface of the world he had long ago left, Dunstan planted his hands in the slop to hoist himself out of his grave.

The Great Eclipse - 19

At last, Dunstan lived again; then, a 9-year-old boy with nothing, now a 20-year-old man, the King of Hell. He was born into a fresh, unfamiliar wilderness, a field of mud with some dismal, grey-green trees in the mid-distance. He hadn't realized how much he had missed the cold and the colour green, or just how raw and beautiful this murky land smelled. He could not understand how he had once believed it to be a hellscape. It was teeming with so many neutral souls and honest objects. His first steps onto the land of his birth echoed like drumbeats as his soul lifted in joy. A smile broke across Dunstan's face as he felt the mud slush between his toes. He ran through it, jumped and dove into a puddle and rolled around as Mr. Doggy had done in his backyard, those many years ago. Even now, as a grown man, he couldn't help giggling to himself. Dunstan channeled his thripsis downwards as he had learned to do in the Spoil and found that even here, with reduced thriptic potential, he was still able to fly, albeit more slowly.

"Why is there thripsis in the Planelands? Why am I still able to do this here?" The haunting question pushed him into his head as he ascended.

In the distance, Dunstan spotted a large manor surrounded by a stone wall. The stone was carved beautifully – much more attractive than Spoil rock. Thinking someone there could direct him to the Shallaway, he made off toward it.

-

It was just another Thursday afternoon at the country club for Edgar Mullen. He was retired now at the age of 63, able to maintain the life of decadence he had built, sitting on the board of Harrison Brothers Mining Company. Married thrice, but now freshly out of a third divorce, he sat at the end of the club's dining hall across from Jay Notte, an old friend from his university fraternity. Edgar stared out across the mud flats, chewing lazily on a stringy piece of roast beef, growing rapidly dissatisfied.

"Waitress!" he snapped, whirling around lazily while making eye contact with no one.

Jay, reading a newspaper, didn't care for anything but to sip on his Earl Grey and grumble to himself. Edgar resumed his distant stare out the window. "Aytres!" he yelled even more lazily over his shoulder, drawing a few irritated eyes to himself.

A young brunette came over hesitantly, and without turning to look at her, Edgar continued.

"My beef is chewy; make me another one!" He lifted the plate toward her.

"Sir, I don't work here. Please keep your voice down; this is my grandmother's 70th birthday and we are trying to enjoy our meal, thank you."

Edgar turned to her with a half-confused look of disgust. "Piss-off, bitch... Go get me the waitress," he growled at the woman who was already walking back to her table. His eyes followed her over his fat shoulder to where an elderly woman with pursed lips was glaring daggers back at him. "What's up your twat? Old whore," he chuckled to himself, his loose lips hanging open in a little smirk as he looked back toward Jay for approval. "Old whore," he snorted once again as Jay, completely oblivious to anything besides the newspaper, grumbled something incomprehensible in reply.

The bustling chatter in the dining room was suddenly silenced, and Edgar picked up on the change.

"Oh boy, am I in trouble?" he joked, turning around while lifting an eyebrow.

To his surprise, every head in the room was turned away from him; following their gaze to the end of the hall, he laid eyes upon a young man wearing nothing but a few tattered rags that might once have been his clothes. The man was covered in the residue of a watery mud and had a miner's physique - a good layer of gamey muscle with next-to-no body fat. This is what Edgar's underlings had looked like all his life, so he wasn't intimidated like the others in the room.

"Can anyone tell me where the Shallaway is?"

The air felt thicker, somehow, as the young man spoke. His voice was full of resolve. None dared speak; this event and this young man were too alien to them. Staff approached the young man to try to usher him out of the room and out of the club, but he paid no attention to them.

"Please, sir, you cannot be in here dressed like that," one of the club staff was heard saying while another was on the phone, no doubt contacting the authorities.

"I just want to know where the Shallaway is; tell me that and I will be on my way."

For whatever reason, the club staff would not honour this request. None of this mattered to Edgar Mullen, though. He saw an opportunity to have a little fun. He had fired dozens of guys like this in his lifetime and he took pleasure in seeing them break down in front of him. He rose to his feet and crossed the room, weaving his heavy body between the circular tables. He approached the young stranger, who stood half a head taller than he, eyeing him expectantly.

"You had better not be one of my boys..." Edgar scowled.

"Sorry?" the stranger squinted.

"You should be. Who do you work for?"

 The young man sighed, becoming impatient. "How do I
-"

"- What's your name, boy?" Edgar interrupted forcefully.

"Dunstan."

"Dunstan...?" Edgar queried, gesturing for more as though he were speaking to an idiot.

"Dunstan Briar," he realized aloud, the words escaping his mouth in a tone of quiet revelation.

"Briar... No way. Are you Mark Briar's son? That piece of shit?" Edgar went on in the background as Dunstan excitedly recalled that that was indeed his father's first name. He hadn't heard it in so long but to hear it now suggested he was on the right trail. Who was this ugly, fat man? Dunstan racked his brain and remembered that the day he was killed, his father had mentioned something about being fired by an 'Edgar.'

"Sir, we've contacted the authorities; if you don't leave right now, you'll be dealing with them," a club staffer shouted over Dunstan's shoulder as he snapped out of his daze to grin at the fat man still yelling and yacking in his face.

"Edgar?" he asked.

"So, you *are* one of mine, but not much longer, you fucking peasant -"

Dunstan grabbed the top of Edgar Mullen's head in a vice grip, and reality began to bend in the room and through Edgar's mind. As he had seen Kaimaradan do previously with the aspect of cruelty, Dunstan made Edgar see terrible things before him, conjuring hallucinations of some of the things he had seen in the Spoil and the Squalor.

Edgar went quiet and then made musical, guttural noises as he choked on his saliva, wetting and soiling himself, staring off into space. As the oppressive energy spilled into the room people began screaming; they didn't know why, but they could feel it twisting their little bodies into something else, crushing them. Even Jay at the back of the room now felt uncomfortable and ran out with the rest of the crowd, past the scene unfolding between the two men.

"Now, Edgar. Where is the Shallaway?"

"I-it's west of here!" he choked out.

"Not good enough, Edgar - which way is west?" Dunstan crooned, stepping up the pain the fat man was feeling and the intensity of his hallucinations.

"That way - that way! Please stop this!" he cried, pointing a finger over Dunstan's left shoulder, out the window behind him, and toward the front door of the club.

"Thank you, Edgar. Isn't it nice that at the end, you finally did something useful?"

Dunstan twisted Edgar's head off his shoulders with a rapid burst of uncontrolled thripsis and then bowled it out the far window into the mud flats. In the distance, it could be seen skipping several times before skidding into a roll. It hadn't come off cleanly and a bloody string of throat sinew hung in the smashed, far window, ornamenting a table holding a glass-covered roast beef sandwich.

Horrified club staff reached for rifles and handguns and shot at Dunstan, but even five times less powerful in this dimension, his thripsis when channeled blew away the bullets.

Many of the staff closest to him boiled alive instantly - eyes exploding from their heads - while cinders ignited the dining hall in blue flame. Dunstan flew through the roof, back into the sweet kiss of the rain.

He searched with a feeling of longing, drifting westward across the sky. The rain stopped and the clouds began to thin. A few golden rays of afternoon sun shone through, piercing his eyes. It was a rare occurrence in the Shallaway to encounter these breaks in the cloud, but he could recall a few such times from childhood.

This light felt so weightless, so unlike the deep light of Verivoluae. Strangely, that deep light did not feel so far away. Breowakoe still felt conscious of everything that was happening in the Spoil in real time, or... Dunstan, that is. For a moment he was unsure of who he was. Verivoluae's light was bleeding up into the world, shining off its people and things and reflecting their locations back into his soul. Even now, the energy of the Spoil was all around him; it always had been, but as a child he had been unattuned to the sensation of thripsis. He could feel that he was moving in the correct direction. He could sense a plot of wood and stone and mud that matched his memory of the old corner house. On his right, he saw many rolling hills and, beneath them, the mines where his father had worked. He had no way of knowing that this was his father's mine - he just felt it to be true.

The Shallaway had seemed so large when it was all he knew of the world but was something he would hardly have noticed in the Spoil. How many hundreds of little towns of little huts had he passed by without a second glance downstream of Goliah? It scared Dunstan to realize how easily he could destroy the town of his birth, and everything he remembered being precious to him.

His parent's house sat in shadow and his heart skipped a beat when he saw it below, but now was not the time for a visit or a reunion. He didn't even know if his parents still lived there, if they were still together or if they were even still alive. Dunstan's heart ached as he flew past it, but he could not encumber his mind with that now. He had a more important task to focus on: using the aspect of destruction he searched for Mr. Doggy's presence to the west of his parents' house. That was the direction Mr. Doggy had come from when they had played together in their youth.

And then he sensed him - his friend was still alive! Five houses down from his parents' house in the backyard of a little shack, chained to a post, Dunstan found his friend. He feared this mission might end in futility but was also terrified at the thought that he might actually do some good in the world - that his actions might count for something. He needed to kill Mr. Doggy's owner before being recognized to prevent the spiteful harm that might befall his friend. But where was the bastard?

Dunstan scanned the property for a sign of Mr. Doggy's owner and detected the presence of a man inside the back shed, seven metres from where Mr. Doggy warmed himself - bathing in the few rays of sun that poked through the clouds. Dunstan was close enough now that he could see his only childhood friend from the sky. His heart pounded even harder as he gently landed on the roof of the wicked man's dwelling. Dunstan was expecting a fight like no other - this man was the nemesis who had killed him once before. Unsure if the man could detect thripsis but not wanting to take any chances, he suppressed his thriptic presence as well as he could while glaring down at the shed. This would be a surprise attack. Mr. Doggy was currently out of view, but they would be reunited soon.

The doors of the shed did not move even as dusk was falling. Tapping into the aspect of destruction, Dunstan investigated the shed once more. Sure enough the man was still in there, his head tilted back as he sat in a small, wooden chair. His legs were sprawled apart and a rubber band was tied tight around his bicep. His right arm bent towards the left, and he was dispensing some liquid into the vein at the pit of his elbow. Dunstan was not sure what this behaviour was, perhaps it was some stimulant the wicked man used to ready himself for battle.

Dunstan crept closer to the edge of the roof, wanting to be ready for anything. A loose piece of untethered sheet metal slid from the roof into the home below and crashed to the ground. Dunstan was breathless as Mr. Doggy started barking, turning to look up at him. The man started yelling in the shed.

"What the fuck is going on out there?"

Dunstan gritted his teeth, sucking in air. The shed door burst open and the man emerged with a shotgun in hand. He was definitely the right guy - cargo pants and a dirty tank top. He looked as though he had aged thirty years in the eleven since he had murdered a nine-year-old boy.

"Clearly, he was never caught," Dunstan realized, grinding his teeth harder.

Unaware that he had dilated time, Dunstan moved so fast

he seemed to teleport to the mud yard where the man stood. They were of an even height now, so the fight must be fair. A thin blade of air sliced both the wicked man's hands clean off, allowing the shotgun to fall safely to the ground where it would not be able to harm Mr. Doggy. A blast of concentrated thripsis to his gut had the man doubled over, puking blood. The weak bastard looked up into the face of his executioner, screaming out of shock before pain had time to come.

In a full rage, without intention, Dunstan allowed the deep light of the Spoil to bloom through him. With all aspects in unison and conducted by the sun, Breowakoe opened a portal below Mr. Doggy's owner and the man fell to the streets of Goliah. His confused screams drew the attention of every Nethriel cretin around him as the portal closed behind.

Dunstan dropped to his knees to catch his breath in wonder. Was that really it? The man he had deified as some dark god was really that weak? The man who had murdered him when he was powerless, was himself powerless? Dunstan gasped as he remembered his dear childhood friend, the soul for whom so many others had been sacrificed. He turned in elation only to see Mr. Doggy growling at him.

"Hey, it's ok, boy! It's me!"

Dunstan walked towards Mr. Doggy with arms outstretched. The pup had clearly aged and had reached the later phase of his life - but his lovable mounds of matted brown fur looked so inviting. Mr. Doggy's growling became whimpering until Dunstan was within three metres of him, at which point the dog collapsed onto his side; he was breathing heavily, unable even to whimper. Dunstan gasped and backed away. Slowly, Mr. Doggy recuperated and was able to stand up again but looked confused and disoriented. Gradually, he came to his senses and upon detecting Dunstan, became aggressive once more – growling, nipping at the air, and barking.

"Could it be that my thriptic presence is too great for his body to sustain, even when I am suppressing it?"

Through incremental experimentation Dunstan slowly came to the realization that the energy of hell, conducted through his body, was crushing the poor animal whenever the two came close to one another. Furthermore, he was unrecognizable to his childhood friend, by smell, sound, and sight.

With control, a thin blade of air freed the animal of his collar and chain, allowing him to roam the yard freely. But Mr. Doggy used this freedom to go to the shed where his cruel owner had sat just moments ago. He sniffed at the ground where the portal to the Spoil had opened, and he whimpered. He howled for the loss of his abusive companion.

Tears streamed down Dunstan's face as a familiar feeling of hopelessness crept back. The dog he had risked everything for - traded everything for - loved the hateful man who had murdered Dunstan. In order to return to Mr. Doggy's side, he had become a being not compatible with the frail animal's existence. He had become something greater and more terrible than was physiologically tolerable by the thing he loved most.

Kaimaradan was gone. She had died for nothing. How many more beautiful, warm nights in the Spoil could he have shared with her, had he not traded her away?

Dunstan retreated to a nearby rooftop, weeping at the unfairness of the world and feeling sorry for himself; his friend howled below at the loss of Dunstan's murderer. But after an hour, Mr. Doggy's behaviour changed. He paced back and forth from the shed to the back porch before making his way past the side of the house to the front. Dunstan stopped crying to follow Mr. Doggy from the shadows. A mother with two young daughters was walking past the house. Mr. Doggy whimpered as he approached the trio; Dunstan felt concern for his safety, heart pounding as he readied himself to jump in.

"Aww look, Mommy, a dog!" the older of the little girls swooned.

"Doggy!" the younger chimed in as they rushed to shower him with love and affection.

Mr. Doggy's whimpering transformed into happy panting and a wagging tail as they played with his ears and rub-a-dubbed his wriggling torso.

"Ok, girls, come along! Daddy's waiting for us!" their mother called from up the way.

The girls began to follow and Mr. Doggy ran after them, whimpering again.

"Bye Doggy!" the younger girl squealed, obeying her mother.

The older daughter turned and reached a hand down for Mr. Doggy's moist little snout to brush up against. "Where's your master? Go find your master!" the little girl encouraged the recently orphaned dog.

Mr. Doggy only whimpered.

"Mom, I think something might have happened to his owner!" the girl called up to her mother, who sighed at the tedium of it all.

She approached the door of the shanty and knocked, peering in the one small window to see only darkness. "Hello!?" the mother called in. Of course, there was no response - and now she tried around the back of the house. Excuse me, is this your dog?" she called into the darkness from which there was no response. At last, she tried the shed, but peering into the darkened window she realized there was no helping it. "Ok..." she said, turning to her daughters with another sigh. "We should take him with us until we find his owner."

"We can keep him!?" the older daughter confirmed, trying to repress premature excitement.

"- Until we find his owner, yes," their mother reiterated responsibly.

"Y-A-A-Y-Y-Y!" The little girls dropped to their knees in the mud to hug their elderly new companion. Dunstan, still creeping from the rooftops, was at a loss for words as the quadruple now made their way off joyfully down the street and out of sight. He was stupefied by the resilience of Mr. Doggy; even this old he did not give up on himself. His childhood friend had now taught him what it is to grieve - and move on. It had been fun, but their time had long since come to an end.

The only way forward was forward.

The rain was starting up again and Dunstan dropped to the ground to walk east down the ashen street, still harbouring a low feeling but having unearthed a whisper of insight that his story was not over. He felt relieved that Mr. Doggy had found a good home.

The sun had gone down and disappeared, which Dunstan was unaccustomed to, and he shivered. He came to the side yard of his parents' house with heaviness in his heart, fearing they had died. At the back gate he carefully lifted the latch, trying to make as little noise as possible. It appeared dark inside and was a lot quieter than he remembered his parents being.

Dunstan could feel his heartbeat in his fingertips and pressed them to his parents' bedroom windowsill, leaning in to see, standing barefoot in the muddy lot. The curtains were closed but there was a crack between them. He didn't breathe and allowed his brain to make sense of what his eyes were seeing.

His parents sat on the side of their bed, side-by-side, looking at something in a picture frame. Their cheeks were wet. Dunstan's father had his arm around his mother whose hand was placed on his chest. They were smiling. He almost couldn't believe his eyes. Never as a child had he seen them affectionate toward one another. They should have been a decade older but somehow they still looked the same age. There was a calm in his father's brow that he had never seen and an unfamiliar, soft kindness in his mother's lips. Dunstan's heart fluttered as he considered entering the house, surprising them with a reunion after all these years. He stepped up to the back door and placed a hand on its handle, then hesitated. "Would they recognize me?" he wondered.

A series of scenarios played out in his mind where the terrified couple attacked him, thinking him some monster of a strange man that had entered their home. He could visualize the fear in his mother's eyes and his father's despair when no weapon would work. Dunstan took his hand off the knob and went back to the window. His father was placing a framed photo of 6-year-old Dunstan back on the nightstand before crawling into bed behind his mother in an endearing cuddle. Dunstan's heart skipped a beat.

"My death must have brought them closer together."

The waterworks started up again and Dunstan beamed. He had thought everyone here in the world of the living, everyone he loved – Mr. Doggy, his parents – needed him. He had felt so desperate to get back, to give them his love, but they were all doing fine without him. He was so relieved they were happy without him while he had been gone. Dunstan's eyes flicked from the bed where his parents were falling asleep to the bookshelf on its far side. A face in a picture frame caught his eye.

Dunstan's blood prickled. He had seen her before... but where? Who was that old woman whose portrait hung over his sleeping parents, and why did her image fill him with such dread? She had long, grey, curly hair and a glazed look in her eyes that must have been cataracts.

It was the old hag who had drugged him in Goliah when he first fell into the Spoil. Why did his parents have a framed picture of the hag from Goliah? Dunstan was again pressed for breath; he backed away from the window and the realization came to him. "*Is she my grandmother?*" Dunstan didn't try to suppress his feeling of horror; he had never met her when last he lived, but in death she had singled him out. *She* had named him Breowakoe before his memories returned; why had she identified her own grandson as the last King of Katharnia? It made no sense.

Dunstan walked back out through the gate and into the street; he felt on edge, almost expecting his grandmother to be watching him from behind a lamp post or rooftop. He paused and searched for the old woman using the aspect of destruction. Sure enough, the deep light shone upon her below - still in her shack in Goliah - but that wasn't all. A weaker energy resonated with the call of the deep light, and it was refracting from the Planelands. Dunstan's eyes widened as he gazed to the North-East, to the direction of an elevated hill of dirt many kilometres outside the Shallaway, past the mud field where he had spawned to live again.

He took off into the night air and in half an hour landed to see a beautiful grassy knoll interspersed with well groomed trees. It wasn't raining here. There were strange stones scattered over the hill and with the aspect of destruction he identified that corpses lay under each. A strange light appeared from the sky, and Dunstan whirled around to gaze up at the moon as it broke out from behind the wall of cloud, bathing the field in grey-green. He had forgotten about the moon. He blinked looking into its craters, which were difficult to see in the moon's brightness. Its effect on the Planelands, however - its pale hue on the trees and graves was beautiful and calming.

Dunstan reached toward his chest to feel for the outline of Kaimaradan – and his heart ached, freshly realizing that she was gone. He shunned the sadness. He would do right by her and destroy the Spoil, but he needed to get to the bottom of this, first.

In the moonlight he could make out the inscription on the stone before him: "Here lie Frederick (3465 -) and Mary-Jane Briar (3468 - 3541)." He recognized his own surname, and the name "Mary-Jane Briar" escaped his lips once more. Sure enough, the body below him resonated with the hag sitting in her hut in the Spoil.

Dunstan pointed a finger to the ground and lifted himself into the air. The thripsis, twisted into a cone vortex, drilled into the earth, peeling the dirt away and exposing a rotten, wooden coffin. He brought himself back to the earth. Standing in the hole he dragged the coffin up to the surface. Looking around to be certain no one was watching him, he then proceeded to open the decayed box. Inside was a short skeleton with a crooked spine, a thin film of ashy beige skin adorning it. He didn't know why he had expected it to look like the woman in hell. Dunstan placed his hand on the ribcage of the remains and a cacophony of knowledge flooded into his mind but in the next moment disappeared before it could be processed.

"What? Corpusapien?" Dunstan muttered under his breath.

Unconcerned with what was possible and what he thought he knew, Dunstan acted on a feeling in the recesses of his mind: he closed his eyes and focused on the sensation of breathing - not the air, but the deep light of Verivoluae itself. He drew it up through the Spoil and into himself. The energy had whetted his aspects; he could feel them in some higher place within himself, charged and ready. He exhaled and inhaled again, this time capturing the essence of the hag as she sat in her hut below. He filled his lungs with her. He leaned to press his mouth against the skeleton's face and breathed her damned soul back into her lifeless corpse.

As the exhale expired, flesh erupted into being over her body; her face took shape into the ripe tissue of her old form, appearing as she had at the moment of death. Muscles and organs exploded out of nothing like the form-fitting unfold of a flotation device just after reaching the critical threshold of air. Blood raged through the contained rivers of arteries and veins and the layer of grey skin coating her bones ripened into a wrinkled pink. Grey hair grew out into the ugly long fibers that had populated her head in the Spoil. Thripsis shot into her lungs and heart, steadying them as another jolt awakened her brain.

Dunstan pulled away from the reanimated corpse as the old woman gasped, sitting up awake with a look of terror upon her face. She coughed uncontrollably, shaking tremendously and looking around, trying to make sense of what was going on.

Dunstan sucked all the grass of the yard together into a robe that wove itself into being in his hands so he could wrap it around the woman to clothe her. He crouched down to peer into her widened eyes, level with her face. "We need to talk," he said resolutely.

Mary-Jane's pupils dilated as she reared back to get a better look at him. "Lord Breowakoe!" she gasped. "I am not worthy to be called back." She bowed as best she could while seated.

"My name is Dunstan; I'm your grandson… I think you are aware of that. You are not alive. You are reanimated." Dunstan explained impatiently. "None of the damage that killed you has been repaired. You are being held in this body by my thripsis."

"Y-yes... Of course. I didn't mean to offend." She looked at him quizzically, afraid for one last moment, then her gaze hardened, she was examining him. "Are you sure that you are *still* my grandson?" she asked, coldly.

It was the same look that Tiricora and Chief Stynia both had given him at the end. They were never comfortable with the fact that he was Dunstan, all so certain that he was someone they had known in the distant past.

"You were the first person to call me Breowakoe when I entered the Spoil. Why? Why did you invite me into your hut, and why did you drug me?" Dunstan snarled, ignoring her question.

Mary-Jane sighed, looking down, avoiding his gaze. "You really are Dunstan," she started, looking disappointed. "Very well, then. Breowakoe was the last King of Katharnia, the ancient civilization that was erased 2000 years ago."

"I know that already," Dunstan snapped. "Every school child is taught the story of the Katharnians and that they discovered the Spoil and the Squalor."

"Not exactly, child. The Katharnians created the Spoil - and the Squalor was only ever an artifact of it."

"What do you mean, an artifact?"

"Something that wasn't intended to exist when the Spoil was created; well... to be frank, the entire Spoil is an artifact. It was never supposed to exist – at least, not as it does. Near-realities were forbidden in the creation of a new dreaming, but the Spoil was likely created during the moment of collapse itself."

This wasn't making any sense. The old woman's words were beginning to slur, her fingers twitched, there was a glazed look in her eye. Dunstan became quietly livid as a million new terms were introduced to him with no explanation.

"What are you talking about? Tell me everything you know from the beginning! Enough of these riddles!" He half-yelled into her face.

"Sorry. I didn't mean to frustrate you, Dunstan. I was a scholar of sorts, and these notions to me are... exhilarating." The old woman seemed unphased.

Her gaze shifted over to his face. Moonlight, pooling in her reanimated eyes reflected the chaos of her mind. She continued.

"The Katharnians were a civilization far more advanced than we are in the Planelands today. They had technology that we will not understand for centuries to come. The Planelands still lives through a dark age caused by the fall of the Katharnia and the failures of Breowakoe."

A warm wind blew, sending rippling waves through the combed lawn and into the silent darkness beyond the cast iron boundary of the graveyard.

"The most powerful of these Katharnian technologies was called an incubus - a device that can create a new reality using an energy source many times more powerful than the sun. However, that energy exists only in that new reality. It's a paradox: the energy used to create the reality exists only in that reality. Well, under normal circumstances, that is… The fact that you are able to use your thripsis here is a symptom of how dangerously conceived the Spoil reality was."

Now it felt like they were getting somewhere. Dunstan was glued to her every word.

"Not everyone in Katharnian society had access to an incubus. They were considered extremely dangerous in the wrong hands and their use was reserved for royalty. They weren't used for leisure, either; the Katharnians had a strong belief in monarchy. Sulomar, the first King of Katharnia, was seen as a god and the Kings and Queens who followed him were the descendants of god. They thought that it was right that a monarch should live on forever. As a monarch came to the end of their natural life span, the Katharnians placed them inside the central chamber of an incubus where their bodies were preserved alongside those closest to them. Yes, you understood correctly. When the King was freshly dead, or near to it, they would immediately round up those closest to him and all their lives in the Planelands came to an end. The King then had the right to determine the course of 'the dreaming' - the nature of the reality that he and his loved ones would spawn into as their 'afterlife' played out. The projection of the monarch's mind onto the nude reality determined what became of it. After the King and his companions were preserved and the course of the dreaming was set, the incubus would be permanently sealed."

"Wait, so do these incubuses exist in the Planelands?" Dunstan wondered.

"Correct. When I was young, only one incubus had been discovered, not far from where we are now. It was impossible to see into and was utterly impregnable with the technology at our disposal. In my late twenties, a second incubus was discovered. I was granted access to it because my father was a member of the Forgotten Dreamers Society, an elite order dedicated to the study of the ancient Katharnians. One of my colleagues was a physicist who had developed a method for detecting incubian energies, what those in the Spoil call "thripsis." Frederick was his name – he later became your grandfather. He and I studied both known incubuses and found that the incubian energy in the air was least polarized nearer to the second incubus."

Mary-Jane could see the look of impatience on Dunstan's face.

"The short version is that we believed that this second incubus was the one responsible for creating the Spoil. The existence of the Spoil was considered a historical fact, but the idea that it was created by this impenetrable box underground in the Miren woods was controversial. Two more incubuses were discovered before I passed away, but even after forty years of waiting, our technology couldn't come close to cracking one open."

Dunstan retreated into his head. "If we were to open the one that you think created the Spoil, are you saying that inside we would find the body of the real Breowakoe preserved for over 2000 years?"

"That is correct."

"HEY, WHO'S THERE!?" a man's voice called out behind Dunstan who could see that a flashlight was pointed at the back of his head. "YOU BETTER GET- OH, NO... DID YOU DESECRATE A GRAVE!?" The man sounded panicked.

Dunstan rose to his feet. "If you want to live, turn around, walk away, and never look back," he said coldly, enthralled with what he was learning and furious to be pulled away from it.

The man was clever enough to do as he was bid, and turned to enter the mausoleum. Dunstan read the inscription carved into its stone top: "The Forgotten Dreamers Society Cemetery," he turned back toward his grandmother who had also risen to her feet.

"I want you to take me to the second incubus," Dunstan told her.

A smile cracked along her old face. "I hoped you would suggest that!" she cackled excitedly.

Dunstan swept her off her feet and carefully ascended into the night air. "Which direction?" he asked.

His grandmother looked around, trying to get her bearings, and pointed to the north-east. Dunstan set off in that direction, sailing through the calm night with his reanimated companion. Again, he was reminded of those warm desert nights with Kai, in hindsight some of the happiest moments in his memory. "If there are three other incubuses, are there not also three other Spoils?" Dunstan asked.

"No. This is what I was starting to explain to you about near vs far realities. It was forbidden in Katharnia to project a new dreaming on space so close to the Planelands because of the dangers posed if the new reality were to intersect with the old. I believe that Breowakoe created the Spoil just as his civilization was collapsing around him. Otherwise, the Katharnians attending his incubus would not have allowed such a horrible near reality to spawn. But there is no danger in dreaming a far reality. There are likely hundreds of incubuses hidden in the earth - hundreds of dreamings playing out right now that we will never know about, interact with, or be able to detect, because they are far-realities. They run perfectly parallel to this 'mother reality.'"

What's also peculiar about the Spoil that I would never have known before going there is that there are not one, but two points of intersection between the Spoil and the Planelands: what was formerly the Squalor, and the Silo

Blades. This warped reality would have been unheard of in Katharnian society, which tells me that Breowakoe wanted to anchor the Spoil to the Planelands. I believe he wanted his descendants to experience the Spoil, to suffer for eternity. Also, the fact that the Silo Blades were positioned so close to his ego, Verivoluae, suggests to me that he wanted to continue to have influence in the Planelands, long after his death. He was so distraught by the collapse of his kingdom that he wanted the power of the incubus to bleed dangerously into the world."

Dunstan frowned, realizing that this petty malevolence was the source of his own power.

"Dunstan, with all aspects but creation, you possess half of his entire consciousness. At this point you are as much Breowakoe as is Verivoluae itself."

Dunstan felt a sensation of dread in his gut as he contemplated this. They had reached the precipice of a vast forest that looked lush and beautiful even in the haze of dark. He dropped to the ground and let go of Mary-Jane.

"What are you doing? We have many more kilometres to go!" she exclaimed, confused.

"Grandma. Why did I spawn into the Squalor, already

with the aspect of destruction?" He glared at her. He could see the confident look on her face quickly dissolving into a look of guilt and fear. "Why, when I touched your corpse, did I suddenly know how to call a soul from the Spoil?" A deep anger was building inside Dunstan as his grandmother played nervously with her hands.

"I suppose you've heard of Katharnian artifacts holding corpusapien, or 'body-knowledge' within them, knowledge apprehended by the body upon touching the artefact or someone else who has touched it. Some of the lesser of these artefacts made their way into Katharnian museums, but The Forgotten Dreamers Society has a private collection of more powerful items. There is an artefact in this library we referred to as the 'mare' - a toy horse that we believe Breowakoe played with as a child. When touched, it grants the skill to summon back to the Planelands the consciousness of a soul within a dreaming. I thought that if I could summon the consciousness of King Breowakoe, maybe I could convince him to put an end to the madness."

She stared into his eyes with her own look of madness. She believed her actions were justified.

"Frederick built a device that could store incubian

energy and... well, when you were an infant I did come to see you once, while your father was at work. Your mother never liked me - for good reason - but she trusted me enough to leave me alone with you and, well... I dropped you into the device and tried to summon King Breowakoe's consciousness into your feeble, developing young mind. Your mother came into the room and looked horrified. I thought she was going to kill me, and I never saw you again. I thought the device had not worked - but I simply hadn't realized Breowakoe's consciousness was so fragmented. I thought I had not succeeded until, to my surprise, sixteen years after my own death I saw you on the street of Goliah. I could hardly contain myself. I thought that surely within the Spoil Breowakoe's consciousness would awaken in your mind. I slipped hallucinogens into your tea and encouraged you to destroy the sun as you stumbled out onto the street, but unfortunately your constitution handled the drugs inelegantly -"

"That's enough." Dunstan cut her off. He didn't feel attached to her, which made it hard to feel betrayed, not to mention that without the aspect of destruction he would still now be writhing and melting in the Squalor. "Let's just go," Dunstan said as he picked her up again, and they flew off silently into the night once more.

-

"This is the place."

The sullen tone of Mary-Jane Briar drew Dunstan out of autopilot and he descended between the treetops into the thick of the woods. The darkness swallowed them in the last few moments before reaching the ground. He placed his grandmother gently on the ground and lit a bright blue flame from the tip of his left thumb.

"Put that light out!" Mary-Jane yelled in a hoarse whisper.

Dunstan did as she asked, confused.

"The excavation site is guarded at all times by the military, these days. We have to sneak in."

Dunstan followed her lead through the black forest until they happened upon a large crater, complete with white tarp tents, surrounded by barbed wire and floodlights. There were armed guards in two towers within the compound, one near to them on the south-east corner of the site and one in the north-west.

"How are we supposed to sneak in here?" Dunstan stared at what presented a seemingly impossible task.

"I don't know. With the aspect of control and cruelty perhaps you can make us invisible?" His grandmother really didn't have much of a plan, after all.

"Yes, well... maybe, but then we still have to fly over the fence and everything... You know what? Just wait here. Get behind a tree," Dunstan told her, rising to his feet.

He jumped high into the air over the excavation site, amassing thripsis and holding it tightly to his form. No one saw him as he plummeted almost instantaneously into the middle of the compound. None of the researchers, soldiers or guards had time to react before they disintegrated in the explosion. The tarps and labs were blown away; the towers and fences were launched in scattered directions throughout the forest. All that remained were burning shrubs stretched and nearly blown out of the dirt. As the dust fell, Dunstan noticed an odd, chrome, diamond-shaped chrysalis with windows that glowed a haunting green and pulsed; he quickly reasoned that this must have been the incubus.

"You should not have done that, Dunstan." The old woman's voice gained in amplitude as she walked up on him.

"Many of those were likely good people. They simply share our curiosity for ancient technology."

Dunstan might once have felt guilty, but he had already killed so many innocent people in the Spoil.

"- Those people will all end up in the Spoil, now…" Mary-Jane continued her scolding.

"Well, they won't be there for long…" Dunstan muttered, as they both approached the incubus.

"It's been so long, and its allure is still so powerful," Mary-Jane said. "I wonder how it will respond to you. They were designed to never be opened, once sealed, but I would think if there were an exception to that rule it would be you."

The high-pitched rattle of cicadas started up in the humid trees once more, and Dunstan looked over at the incubus. It was different from every other object he had ever encountered, and he could not sense past its outer walls. He approached this beast of technology to place his hand against one of the pulsing, green panels. Feeling nothing at first, he tried feeding thripsis into it. The machine hummed awake and seemed to conduct and absorb the thripsis. The light pulsed faster.

"There is something to this, but I don't understand it. I'm

going to try overloading the outer hull of the incubus with thripsis and see what happens, but I can feel that it might take a while."

Mary-Jane looked over at him with a wild look in her eye. Many moments of silence passed as Dunstan's channeling became autopilot and his mind wandered.

"Grandma?"

"What is it?"

"Do we know exactly how Katharnia collapsed?"

It was a topic he had been avoiding. He knew it was a story familiar to many aspects he had killed in the Spoil, real people who had known the Spoil's creator while he lived. Dunstan had seen the immense pain on their faces as they thought of it - but he felt ready. He wanted to know.

"Ah, yes. The historical record preserved that tale quite well. A funny thing happens to a society when it enjoys wealth and prosperity for long enough, not knowing hardships. Its people became weak – and few were as weak as King Breowakoe. At an early age it is said he was spoiled, groomed to be King. He was a mild-mannered boy, however, and did not flaunt power over others. In adolescence he stewed in quiet arrogance, believing himself to be special because that's what he had been told by the kowtowers of the court and because his mother was the Queen, Drafari. But being Queen, she had been too busy to raise him, and before she could impart discipline and the knowledge of how to rule, she died unexpectedly, leaving the young man to figure it out for himself.

He never did and instead relied on his advisors for counsel. His chief advisors, Tiricora and her husband Beratu, had adored Breowakoe's mother and tried their best to advise her honestly, but were not chosen by the Queen to join her in her dreaming. Breowakoe had grown up thinking of them as an auntie and uncle but did not take their counsel seriously. He respected the King's guard, Globramora – but Globramora had no sense for politics. Instead, Breowakoe placed his trust in his scientific advisor, Stynia. Stynia's job was to oversee the development of new technology. He was an ambitious man and he was deeply self-interested."

Dunstan listened intently as the Spoil unfolded within this story.

"Later, in adolescence, Breowakoe started to take an interest in girls, and Tiricora found him a match. While many of the young ladies at court wanted the status of being Queen, Tiricora chose Kaimaradan, sensing in her a genuine affection for Breowakoe. Although he was a goofy kid and he did not take his responsibility seriously, Kaimaradan found delight in his pleasant demeanor, and early in their courtship it is said that she fell in love with the young King."

"In his twenties, ten years after his rule began, Breowakoe seemed to lose all enthusiasm. Violent factions had emerged as many regions of the country were plunged into poverty due to negligence in policy-making and law enforcement. Tiricora begged Breowakoe to allow her to step in and get matters under control, but Breowakoe took offense at the suggestion, thinking she wanted his power. Tiricora petitioned pregnant Kaimaradan to bend the King's ear but Breowakoe had started to disconnect from his wife and could not be swayed by her either.

During this time, a group emerged from the chaos of the civil unrest. They called themselves the 'Arm of Katharnia.' Claiming that they wished to restore Katharnia to its 'former glory,' they were really little more than a bloodthirsty mob. Katharnia's military was still more than enough to deal with the Arm, but Breowakoe would not deploy them, fearing that it would only exacerbate the unrest that so strained his soul. One by one, his advisors abandoned the court; they could see that there was no appeasing the Arm of Katharnia. In lazy apathy, Breowakoe allowed what remained of his government to fall apart."

The green light on the hull of the incubus was pulsing rapidly now. Dunstan knew he didn't have much further to go.

"Stynia, hoping to seize the Kingdom for himself in the chaos of a coup, outfitted the Arm of Katharnia with a top-secret bioweapon he called 'Gloom.' It was a gas that rapidly mutated people into monstrous creatures. The gas was to be deployed throughout the Kingdom to further destabilize the cowering King. Instead, the very next day, the Arm deployed the gas in the court, turning Globramora, pregnant Kaimaradan, Breowakoe, and Stynia himself into monstrous creatures. It is said that Kaimaradan miscarried their abomination of a baby in the presence of the King. The creature survived for 10 seconds, thrashing on the ground, burning an image of hopelessness into the King's eyes and taunting him with the inevitable.

Beyond that legend, no one knows. But I suspect that in that moment - in that overwhelming feeling of impotence as the mutant King and his counsel were ushered into the incubus by the King's guard. As innocents screamed, as his child died, as all the beauty he loved was defiled: all that was in Breowakoe's heart was self loathing, and in his dreaming he created the Spoil to punish himself for his own mistakes, forever."

The light on the incubus glowed solid green, and the chrome structure's front opened like a flower petal to reveal a short hallway leading to a chamber of vats. Dunstan moved into the chamber as the stale air flooded out. There was no noise in his head, his heart would not beat, and his diaphragm would not move. He walked past a symphony of electrical panels with flashing and beeping buttons and lights to the center of the room where a vat was planted to the floor. He peered inside upon the lifeless body of a man covered in boils. Atop him was a giant centipede, but it didn't look like Kaimaradan; it was much wider and brown like the one he had seen in the dream after inhaling the capsule of essence. In the man's hand was a clump of gore that looked familiar, still covered in placenta, the legs of a baby and the upper body of a bird. It was Kaimaradan's miscarriage, the bone child.

Dunstan fainted. His body seized violently and his mouth foamed. He bit at his tongue and his head smashed into the chrome casing of the pod as blood filled his mouth and spilled out onto the floor. He lost perception of the world around him as the exorbitant deluge of Breowakoe's memories coursed through a mind that by comparison was new to trauma. Dunstan fought to retain dominion over his own thoughts, but it was futile. The older intellect wrinkled his brain thirtyfold and made itself at home, pushing Dunstan and the twisted, bitter-sweet memories of his short life into the far recesses of consciousness. And just like that, the boy who fought so hard for another chance to live, to join with his childhood friend, to seek the approval of his parents, was gone.

Breowakoe's deep consciousness batted open the eyelashes of his new body. He burned shut the wound in his mouth and sat with his back against the wall. Mary-Jane rushed over to him, trying to get a sense of what had happened, trying to provide remedy.

"It's ok. Thank you, Mary-Jane." Breowakoe raised a hand. Mary-Jane stepped back, noticing the change behind his eyes.

"Lord Breowakoe?" she asked.

"Yes," he said, sullenly.

Breowakoe replayed the words he had just heard Dunstan's grandmother speak. Every one of them was true.

Every tear that had to be shed over his failure was long gone, however, and all that remained was a numb sadness.

"Thank you, Dunstan," Breowakoe said aloud. "Thank you so much. You were brave in the Spoil, and you were clever up here. As a boy, you were much more noble than I was when I lived, and I consider it to be the greatest honour of my journey to have shared your body, and your thoughts. I promise you this Dunstan, I will do right by your principles. I will put a stop to this madness."

Breowakoe rose to his feet and gazed down upon his original body, the mutant remains of the love of his life, and the child that never was. Mary-Jane watched silently as Breowakoe paced to each of the vats around the room, containing the bodies of Tiricora, Beratu, the mutant Stynia, Globramora, and another woman.

"Fascinating," said the old woman, and continued to muse: "These must be the counsel members, but who is she?" Mary-Jane smudged the glass of the vats as she peered in, nosily.

Breowakoe ignored her query, but turned towards her. "Thank you for helping Dunstan, Mary-Jane."

"Of cour -" Mary-Jane started exuberantly as Breowakoe

undid her reanimation. Her flesh imploded just as easily as it appeared, and her soul departed as her skeleton collapsed into a heap.

"Thank you, everyone, for guiding me. I'm sorry that it took so long to hear you. I'm sorry for what I put you through while you lived, and after you died."

Breowakoe returned once more to the center of the room. A tear caressed his cheek and he placed his hand on the glass. "Kaimaradan, my love. Thank you for showing me the way to my true self. I will always be deeply grateful to you. I regret what happened when we lived, and I hate that I put you through such literal hell. I remember the woman you were. I remember how beautiful you were." Breowakoe smiled through tears. "Thank you for loving me, for believing in me, and for trusting me even as I repeatedly let you down. I must release the past. I will keep hostages no more."

Breowakoe turned to leave the incubus, but hesitated, and turned back one more time. "Kai, where Dunstan couldn't, please know that I do... I will always love you."

In a fury, Breowakoe turned and opened a portal to the Spoil. He jumped down, plowing through the dirt, impaling himself on the Silo Blades - sliding down to the beginning, the far downstream.

Creation - 20

Breowakoe stood on the sand and faced Verivoluae's fury. Its flames licked at his skin and its heat sang through his body. He could only smile, staring into the face of the indignant sun, his own ferocious ego. A prick in his leg snuck up on him.

"*Dunstan?*" a high-pitched female voice said. Breowakoe's heart skipped a beat as he looked down and saw a Satrian, but this centipede had no stripes and a feeling of immense disappointment overtook him. Why was there another Satrian? Had they not all become extinct?

"*Dunstan, if you hear me now it is because you came close enough to my body in the incubus of the Planelands that your thrae stimulated my brain. Although I am brain dead, the memories recorded in my preserved body may be replayed through the remains of my terminal in the Spoil. I am Fairglow, the sister of Kaimaradan.*"

Breowakoe was in awe; he recognized her voice from millennia ago and sure enough, what was before him was the reanimated husk of a Satrian - it had no flesh. Breowakoe sifted back through Dunstan's memories and recalled seeing Kaimaradan tampering with her corpse while on her own in the

Arid Necropolis.

"*This reanimation serves one purpose. I will tell you how to bring about the end of the Spoil, as I foresaw in my vision.*"

"Kaimaradan, you were too clever, my love," Breowakoe couldn't help but laugh. "Thank you Fairglow, but I am Breowakoe. I know what to do."

"*Oh. Breowakoe. Never mind, then - for you I simply have a message from Kaimaradan.*"

Breowakoe's heart fluttered. She had left him a note through the reanimated corpse of her sister's demon avatar.

"*Trust yourself, as in death I have come to trust you, and do not punish yourself for your failures: recognize them, learn from them, but move on. You are not the worst in yourself, and I so regret that at one time that was how I saw you. Forgive yourself, as in death I have come to forgive you. You are nothing like that great burning mass of insecurity and self-loathing that hangs in the sky. This part of yourself, the person you are now could have done anything, and now, can do anything. You can rebuild the world from nothing into something beautiful again. And even if you remember me too late - if you lose sight of what is important, just remember to always, always move forward no matter what, and I promise you that your intuition will lead you to happiness as long as you have the courage to follow it."*

Breowakoe was lost for words.

"P.S. If you still feel guilty, remember the couple's shack."

He burst out laughing through his tears as Fairglow collapsed into a lifeless form, her purpose fulfilled.

"Yeah, I don't know if a few hours of torture makes up for what I put you through, but thanks, Kai. Thank you," Breowakoe sighed, and looked on to the burning ball centered perfectly between the walls, ceiling, and floor of the Spoil.

Everyone he had loved in Katharnia was now brain dead in their vats. It was time to put a stop to this hell. For a moment he felt guilty for Dunstan's grandmother, and for the girl from the Grobut brothel, now living in Thelise. There were good people here managing somehow to live half-decent lives, but this dreaming was never meant for all of humanity. Their time to live had been in the Planelands; death should have seen them dissolve into the void. Those in the Planelands now - Mr. Doggy's new family, and Dunstan's parents - did not deserve an eternity in this place. They deserved the comfort and solace of oblivion.

Breowakoe glared up at Verivoluae. He ascended to the median of the Spoil to meet the full fury of the sun, thripsis erupting from his feet.

"*Breowakoe.*" he bellowed in his mind. The walls of the Spoil rattled as he called out to the other fragment of his consciousness.

Verivoluae glowed a deep crimson and a blast of a horn that had never been heard before sounded, rupturing the air. Breowakoe raised his arms and released all his thripsis from all his aspects, which now, in the Spoil at full power, rivalled the brilliance of the sun.

"*Thank you, Verivoluae, for creating this hell. For having me suffer my failures so justly! In observing the horrors of this place for so long, you have more than atoned for betraying your people, for betraying Kaimaradan. But those who you wronged are now at rest, and you must rest as well.*"

The fury of Verivoluae increased and it became engorged as if threatening to swallow the man before it.

"*I forgive you for the mistakes you made when you were afraid and didn't know better.*"

Breowakoe strained against the might of his ego as it burned through a supernova. His skin melted off his muscle as he fought his self hatred with a smile.

"*I love you.*" He grinned.

Verivoluae released a relentless, dying horn that attempted to drown out the voice of its deep self, but through action, the deep self had become the core of the man.

"*Come home.*"

Verivoluae expanded boundlessly, merging with Breowakoe to fill the infinite tunnel, engulf the Spoil, and implode to nothing.

The End

Maps

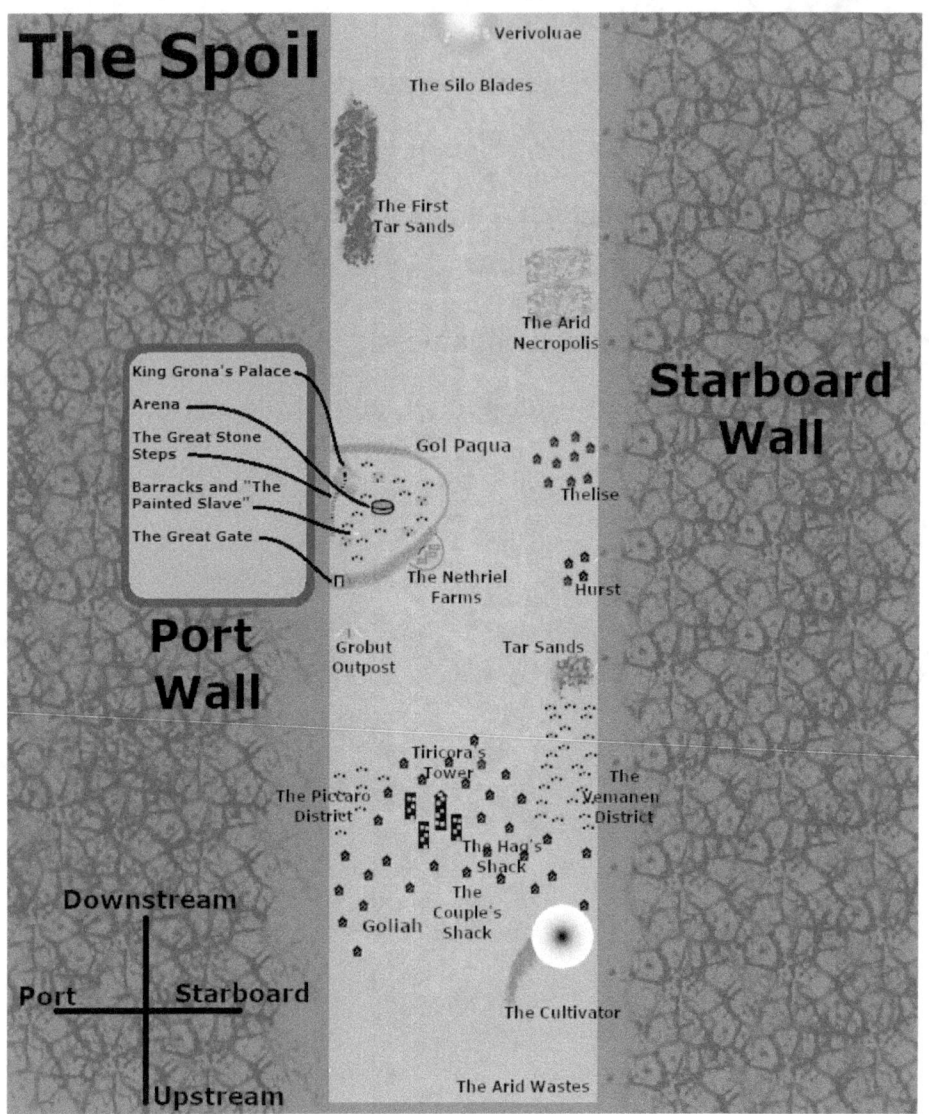

Cosmology
(These dimentions are only accessible when specific conditions are met)
The Planelands
The Squalor
The Silo Blades
The Spoil
Optic Nerve of the Cultivator

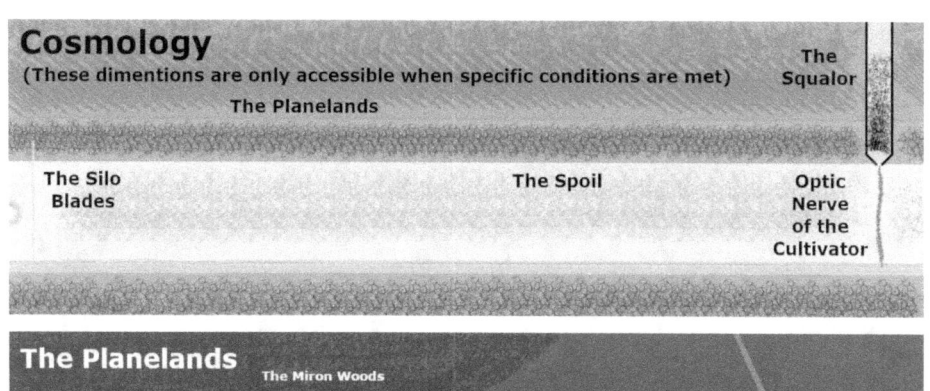

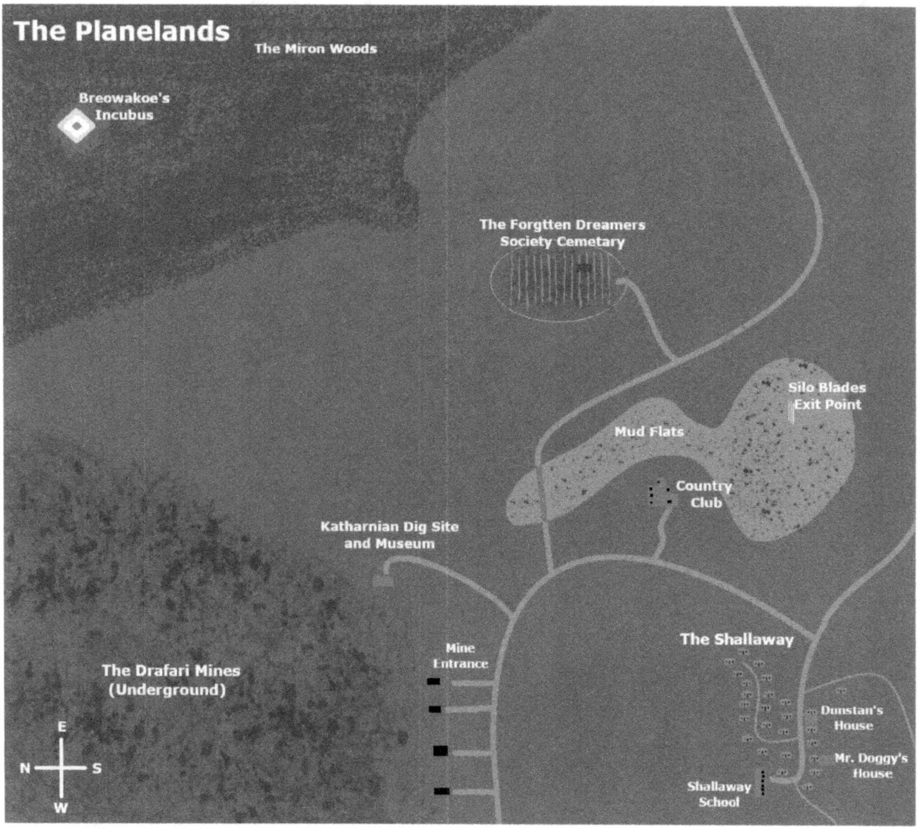

The Planelands
The Miron Woods
Breowakoe's Incubus
The Forgtten Dreamers Society Cemetary
Silo Blades Exit Point
Mud Flats
Country Club
Katharnian Dig Site and Museum
The Shallaway
Mine Entrance
The Drafari Mines (Underground)
Dunstan's House
Mr. Doggy's House
Shallaway School
E
N
S
W

www.ingramcontent.com/pod-product-compliance
Lightning Source LLC
Chambersburg PA
CBHW070620260626
47161CB00007B/2512